When We Were Strangers

Also by Alex Richards

Accidental

WHEN We WeRe STRANGeRS

ALEX RICHARDS

BLOOMSBURY

NEW YORK LONDON OXFORD NEW DELHI SYDNEY

BLOOMSBURY YA
Bloomsbury Publishing Inc., part of Bloomsbury Publishing Plc
1385 Broadway, New York, NY 10018

BLOOMSBURY and the Diana logo are trademarks of Bloomsbury Publishing Plc

First published in the United States of America in July 2021
by Bloomsbury YA

Bloomsbury books may be purchased for business or promotional use. For information on bulk purchases
please contact Macmillan Corporate and Premium Sales Department at specialmarkets@macmillan.com

Library of Congress Cataloging-in-Publication Data
Names: Richards, Alex, author.
Title: When we were strangers / by Alex Richards.
Description: New York : Bloomsbury Children's Books, 2021.
Summary: Seventeen-year-old Evie, devastated by her father's death and the knowledge that he had
planned to leave their family for another woman pregnant with his child, finds a way forward
through a prestigious photography class and handsome classmate Declan.
Identifiers: LCCN 2020044416 (print) | LCCN 2020044417 (e-book)
ISBN 978-1-5476-0364-0 (hardcover) • ISBN 978-1-5476-0365-7 (e-book)
Subjects: CYAC: Grief—Fiction. | Mothers and daughters—Fiction. | Photography—Fiction.
Classification: LCC PZ7.R3783 Whe 2021 (print) | LCC PZ7.R3783 (e-book) | DDC [Fic]—dc23
LC record available at https://lccn.loc.gov/2020044416
LC e-book record available at https://lccn.loc.gov/2020044417

Book design by John Candell
Typeset by Westchester Publishing Services
Printed and bound in the U.S.A. by Berryville Graphics Inc., Berryville, Virginia
2 4 6 8 10 9 7 5 3 1

All papers used by Bloomsbury Publishing Plc are natural, recyclable products made from wood
grown in well-managed forests. The manufacturing processes conform to the environmental
regulations of the country of origin.

To find out more about our authors and books visit www.bloomsbury.com and sign up for our newsletters.

For Harvey, my ninja in training

When We Were Strangers

CHAPTER 1

The house aches with silence.

All I can do is stand there until I remember to lock the front door behind me, dropping my keys on the console table and inching through the darkness. Numbly, I climb the stairs, fingers tickling plaster walls to remind me that I still have nerve endings. That I can still *feel*.

Mom stayed behind at the hospital. She needed to deal with insurance and morgue and cremation stuff. Things you wish could be put off but can't. While she handled it, she insisted that I come home. To rest, to shower, to get the hospital stench off my skin. Maybe I'll burn my clothes too, but when I walk past my parents' bedroom door, I completely lose track of all purpose.

A thousand seconds tick by.

Because I guess this is it. This is what the rest of my life is going to be, walking into a house with no wisecracking, slipper-wearing, grunge rock–loving dad. *No. Dad.* But their bedroom is still full of his smell, his things, and right now I need to be close to what's left of him. I push the door open and tiptoe across the carpet and into my parents' bed. Which is weird, maybe? Hiding under their covers at seventeen? I curl up on a dead man's pillow anyway. The memory foam still smells of him. Still remembers him. Cedar and sunblock. It spins my heart into a long, thin thread.

For a while I lie here, sobs avalanching off me in the darkness. Crying's never been my thing, and now I remember why. It's brutal to convulse like this, ache like this, all while I'm trying to catalog the past fifteen hours. The fact that *I woke up with a dad.* Said goodbye to him from behind the Pop-Tart between my teeth. Drove to school thinking about how it was T-minus five days till summer vacation. Physics, calculus. My English teacher doling out summer reading syllabi. Right around seventh period, *that* is when a pain so sharp and vicious crept up my father's left arm. Blue eyes bulging while his chest cramped. Keeling over. An unexpected heart attack called in by a terrified receptionist.

Mom was in hysterics when I got to the hospital, dousing me in our new misery like a bucket of water. Together we sat in the waiting room for three hours. Hands intertwined, forming a closeness we hadn't had for years. We didn't talk or move or breathe. But in the end, it was the end. Just like on TV, the way weary surgeons slink into the waiting room to deliver bad news, the doctor's eyes apologizing before their lips. Because not even miracle hands could save him.

My tears soak clean through Dad's pillow.

I shudder and stretch, feet banging against something hard and unexpected at the foot of the bed. When I sit up, my head throbs, dehydration tugging at my temples. The lights are still off but my eyes have adjusted, aided by a waning moon through the skylight. Dad's suitcase, that's what I kicked. Which is weird because he didn't say anything about a trip, although his accounting firm would occasionally send him to regional conferences.

I force myself off the bed, reaching for the lamp on Dad's nightstand, *click-click-clicking* the switch till light stings my eyes and the room feels real. I want to cry all over again but I force a swallow, hauling the suitcase toward me. I've barely unzipped it when I spot an even bigger suitcase on the floor. And then a garment bag and a box by the door.

Hold on, *what*?

With skinny breath and weak fingers, I reach for Dad's dresser, sliding open the drawers, one by one. Empty, empty, empty. My eyes ping-pong around the room. His bathrobe missing from the hook behind the door; no bird-watching books or laundry pile or mounds of electronics. The room wobbles as I soak in its lopsidedness. Mom's late-for-work clutter, rumpled clothes and coffee mugs and stacks of half-read novels. The only traces left are of her, nothing of him. I choke on my own spit when it hits me.

Holy shit—was my dad moving *out*?

I'm still gasping, rubbing swollen eyes, trying to steady my breath while my brain tornadoes inside my head. Because, I know you're not supposed to jump to conclusions, especially when you're in the throes of grief or whatever . . . but give me a break. He packed *everything. My dad was leaving us.* There is no other explanation.

And I'm finding out now. Like *this.*

I start to pace around the room, sorting more than a day's worth of memories. The evolution of their silence, occasional fights. Mom whisper-shouting behind closed doors about another woman's perfume on his clothes. I mean, there was a time I thought *divorce* . . . but it kept not happening. As if a scab formed over their discontent. Which—okay, fine—I rallied around. With half the kids in Santa Fe bouncing from mom's to dad's and back again, I'll admit to *wanting* them to work through it. Parents don't always stay married but *mine* were supposed to. At least, that's what I wanted. Maybe it's what Mom wanted too, and now she's devastated and filling out paperwork at the hospital, crying into a nurse's arms, thinking she just lost the love of her life, but . . .

I cringe when it hits me.

She doesn't know.

My poor, wrecked mother must have no idea. There's no way. We can't stand each other sometimes, but she wouldn't *intentionally* send me home from the hospital alone to find *this.*

Jesus, my brain is on fire. Like, what could have pushed him over the edge? Why *now*? And why did he leave his bags? Was he planning to break the news over dinner? *These are excellent enchiladas, Rita. By the way, I'm leaving you.* And then what—divorce? The thought of it shouldn't crush me, but I can't have the ground pulled out from under me. Not after today.

Neither can she.

Pretty soon Mom will be home. She will walk through the front door as I did, exhausted as I was, and stumble up the stairs with the intention of wrapping herself in her dead husband's sweaters in order to feel him all over her and smell his cedar scent, only . . .

Silent sobs bend me in half and break my insides. It's bleak as hell, imagining her finding out this way. As much as I literally can*not* stand her naggy, criticizing bullshit, no one deserves *this*. And, sorry for the realness but, like, what would this truth do to *our* relationship? Like, if she were to not only be grieving but also reeling from this development? I mean . . .

She can't find out. I can't let her.

My brain's not in charge anymore when I walk back over to Dad's suitcase, silently sliding the zipper so the house won't hear what I am about to do.

A stockpile of socks and rolled-up boxer briefs on the left. T-shirts, neatly folded by Mom, stacked perfectly on the right. I run my fingers over the well-worn Pearl Jam shirt on top—the shirt I used to give him shit for because what's-his-name has such a goat voice when he sings, and who listens to grunge anyway? To which Dad would roll his eyes and start singing "Alive" to taunt me.

Alive. Kind of ironic, but I don't stop to think about it,

instead scooping the stack of shirts into my arms and walking over to the dresser drawers I left open.

Now comes the real challenge: remembering what goes where. Was it T-shirts on top? Or, no. T-shirts were in the third drawer; underwear on top. And, no, I am not gross or creepy for knowing that. Or, I mean, maybe I am, but I remember it from way back—from when I'd spend sick days under their covers, surrounded by books and soup and Kleenex, watching Mom sigh as she puttered around the house doing everyone's grunt work rather than going to her office. Groaning as she dumped the laundry basket at the foot of the bed, huffing while she separated, folded, and distributed each item. Underwear in the top drawer, then socks, T-shirts, sweaters, jeans. That's right. The other suitcase must have the sweaters and jeans, so I zip up the first empty case when I'm done and switch to the next, gentle as I return each garment to its rightful home, careful not to cry too hard or leave stains.

Evie, what are you doing?

What the fuck are you doing?

You can't do this. It's not right.

But I *can* do it. *Am* doing it. Driven by a force beyond my control that will not stop until everything. Is. Just. Right.

When I put the suitcases back in the hallway closet, a warm curl of relief settles inside me. Next, I'll unpack the garment bag, then the box he left by the door. Books will return to their shelves, gadgets back in their docking stations. Two-piece suits will once again burden the closet rod. Their bedroom will no longer be dizzy and lopsided. It will be whole again. Theirs, again.

I take one last look around the room—the masterpiece I've curated—then finally do what I came home for. I walk into the bathroom and turn on the shower, unpacking Dad's toiletry kit while I wait for the water to heat up. Then I strip down to nothing, tossing my clothes into the wastebasket like I said I would, even though I'm wearing the only jeans that make me look remotely slim. Because, like, what are skinny jeans when your dad just died and you had to unpack his bags because you don't want your mom knowing he was about to walk out on you both?

Exactly.

In the shower, my hospital stink turns hibiscus; salty cheeks surrender to Neutrogena foam.

Any minute now, my devastated mother will walk into the wreckage, standing there silently, afraid to turn on the lights. Forgetting our usual frustration, she and I will curl up together on her too-big bed. We'll weep and mourn and curse, and our hearts will be broken. But at least hers won't be destroyed. That, I have made sure of.

CHAPTER 2

You'll never eat so good as you do after the death of a loved one.

Casseroles. Baked goods. Frigging crudité platters.

The last of about twenty grieving guests finally stumbles out of our bereavement cave—aka Dad's funeral reception, aka home—and I unleash my flesh from a pair of control top pantyhose, exhaling for the first time in hours, maybe even days. A wave of Dad-less-ness bobs up my throat, tugging at my chest. I choke it down, navigating through a sea of disinfectant because those who did not bring salad brought sponges and all-purpose cleaner. Our house gleams like a Clorox ad. Which is weird, after the way it morphed into a maze of used tissues and junk mail over the past week. Tonight, it looks like a home again, even if it doesn't feel like one.

I drop-kick my balled-up tights toward the laundry room, following the smell of bleach and despair into the kitchen. The white tile floor is almost reflective. I poke my head through the swinging door where Mom is hunched over the dining table, eyes lost in a glass of Chardonnay. Juana Lujan—aka our only remaining guest, aka my best friend—stands at the counter, quietly unpacking containers from our favorite Mexican joint. As if we need more food. Apparently, not even besties are impervious to the lure of edible condolences.

"Evie, good timing." Juana drops a cylindrical mound of tinfoil at the empty spot across from Mom and pats the chair. "Take a seat, babe. My mom ordered all this stuff from Baja—*before* she saw the truckload of food people brought over today. Anyway, it's your favorite. If you're hungry."

"Better have extra cheese," I mutter, forcing a smile.

Juana forces a laugh.

Mom forces an inhale.

Force is the only thing driving us at this point.

Before anyone's taken a bite, our giant calico, Lips, jumps up on the table and makes herself the centerpiece. The name is short for Ellipsoid, some geometric math term Dad chose after we brought her home from the shelter. It seemed cool enough at the time, until Dad started drilling calculus into me in ninth grade, insisting that my future depended on it. Except, look where math got him: an overworked CPA, dead of a heart attack before forty. Thanks but no thanks.

So, yeah. I call her Lips, for short.

"Mrs. P, how about a soft taco—just a little one?" Juana,

way more polite than I'm used to, rests a Styrofoam container on the table in front of Mom. "You were so busy being a hostess, I didn't see you eat all day."

Mom looks down at the dainty row of bean-filled tacos and blinks. She's been on pretty much a liquid diet for the past week. Coffee till noon, wine till bedtime. Today's no different; it just happens to be the day she buried her husband. Her smile masks a wince. "Looks delicious, Juana. I'll have some in a bit," she says, nudging Lips back onto the floor.

"You sure?"

Her eyes settle more comfortably back onto her wineglass.

Steam clings to my face as I unwrap the foil on my carne adovada burrito. The moisture absorbs some of my gloom, coating the numb and broken haze that ferried us to the cemetery and back home to a crowd of mourners. It's a relief to see our house empty again.

Maybe to set an example, I dunk a tortilla chip into the guacamole and crunch extra loudly. "Thanks, JJ. This is way better than that crap-ass lasagna Mrs. Conrad tried to stuff down my throat earlier."

My eyes flit over to Mom. To see if crap-ass (or dissing our elderly neighbor) is going to elicit the usual scolding. Her brown eyes are corroded though, lips in a gravitational pull toward her heart. Honestly, I don't even think she's listening.

"Or those fish cakes. With the raisins?" Juana shudders. "I don't know who brought 'em, but—nope."

The kitchen goes quiet with the subtle stench of ammonia and Hatch green chiles.

"So . . . how was the rest of school?" I ask, even though I already know because Juana texted me hourly. Four days' worth of Chavez Academy micro-debriefs. Exams were already over when IT *happened*, and nobody cares that I skipped a few days of bullshit classes. I mean, they care. They all care. Our house is suffocating in declarations of sympathy and healing; voice mails from the school guidance counselor offering, well, guidance.

Juana flashes me a funny look and my eyes practically invert, desperate to make conversation. "Any newsworthy pranks?" I ask pointedly. "Farm animals let loose on the quad?"

She takes the bait and cackles. "Oh my God, can you imagine? If a herd of goats rampaged the final assembly? God, I would seriously *die* laughing."

The room goes ice-cold. Juana tries to swallow her words, but it's too late. Death puns blare like sirens lately. Whether Mom is *dying* for a glass of wine or I'm scared to *death* of answering yet another pity phone call. Now the idea of high school high jinx is about as funny as the heart attack that took the life of Victor Elias Parker.

But I swallow. Offer a small smile. "So, not even any TPing of lockers, huh? How disappointing."

"People still do that sort of thing?" Mom says, a sort of

vacancy replacing her usual hint of judgment. "Rearranging furniture and TPing? It sounds so old-fashioned."

In a daze, she rises from the table with her suddenly empty wineglass and takes it to the refill station—aka the makeshift funeral bar, aka our kitchen island. She's still wearing a soft black blouse, but we clearly had the same idea in the bottoms department. Her pencil skirt has been replaced with Juicy sweats, various hues of which she's been wearing since the dental office gave her bereavement leave. Today's are a sunburn pink that bring out the Hershey's Kiss color of her hair. She refills her glass and looks at the clock. It's almost 7 p.m., almost time to crawl into bed and erase another day.

"There's a party tonight." Juana breaks the silence, her voice on eggshells. "Up at the ski basin? Pilar and Oola are throwing it but all the seniors are going. Which means *us*, now." She taps my shoulder with the back of her fork after licking it clean. Gross. "So, party? Que viva? You in?"

"I'm not really in a partying mood."

"Yeah, but . . ." She drifts off, swallowing her plea.

Which almost pains me. The old Juana wouldn't back down so easily. She'd roll her eyes and swear and tell me to get out of my funk because we are *going* to that party and she is *not* taking no for an answer, and then she'd look for a slutty top in my abundantly non-slutty closet because I have enough cleavage as it is without actively advertising more of it. But that was before. This is now. This is mourning.

"At least think about it." She tucks her long, black hair behind her ears and scrapes the last forkful of pinto beans into her mouth.

I force a lopsided smile, my eyes drifting back to Mom as she lights a cigarette. Smoke creates a wicked spell around her. She flicks a bit of ash into a chipped saucer because we don't actually have a real ashtray because she hasn't really been a smoker since before I was born. The Marlboro thing is a post-death transgression, and apparently she no longer cares about giving her only child secondhand lung cancer.

But I get it—I'd probably bum one if I liked the taste. Anything to help navigate this Everest of grief I can't stop climbing. Both of us scrambling against the tide, unsure how to process our insurmountable loss. But, like, in such wildly different ways. We're both devastated, but I'm not used to seeing someone so organized lose her shit so aimlessly. It's hard to look at her without thinking about the part I played in it. My suitcase wizardry. Juana knows—I had to tell *someone*—but leaving Mom in the dark has only added thorns to my guilt. I keep playing it back in my mind. Picturing myself in their bedroom, mind spinning, heart cracking, convincing myself that what I was doing was for the best. With Dad dead, *I* chose to be her knight in shining armor. But was it gallant, what I did? Would the honorable thing have been to lay out the full deck? If she knew he was leaving, maybe foresight could have balanced out her heartache.

Or, I don't know. At least I'd have someone else to commiserate with.

"What's up, chickenbutt?" Juana raises one eyebrow comically high. "You look all kinds of Sam Winchester right now."

A grin escapes before I can stop it. We've binge-watched *Supernatural* since seventh grade. Not just once, but over and over and over again. Yes, because they're hot. Yes, because it's scary and sometimes cringingly dated. But also because we are basically seventeen-year-old girl versions of their smoldering, snarky-ass selves.

Juana—aka Dean, aka my steadfast protector—cups her hands around mine. "Want to talk about it?"

"Not really."

"Then come to this party."

The look I give her pretty much says it all. She laughs, pulling a cardigan over her matronly black dress. Bet she can't wait to go home and change into a midriff top and short shorts.

She stands up, walking over to side-hug Mom. "Bye, Mrs. Parker. Love you."

Mom tries to smile. "Thanks, sweetie. I love you too. And thank your parents for coming today—and for the tacos."

"Sure thing."

We link arms and walk to the front door, leaning so hard against each other that we'd topple over if one of us moved. It ends in a hug, my body curling into hers.

"Promise you won't sit in the kitchen all night, watching your mom cry?"

"But it's so fun." I let my palms drag heavily down my face, tugging at my lower eyelids till I'm sure I look *gorgeous*. "You think I did the right thing, right? Unpacking my dad's stuff?"

A groan drains from her lips. "Dude, I don't know. Why? Are you having second thoughts?"

"No?" I scrunch my nose.

"Aw, honey. Just, like, don't forget that you were acting out of love."

Love . . . self-preservation—potato, potahto.

"Your mom is lucky to have you."

Before I can respond with something glib, the landline rings. "I should get that."

"Yeah, okay. Call me later."

As soon as the front door shuts, the phone stops ringing. I lean against the wall. Give myself a minute to let my second thoughts play out. Wondering what this funeral would have been like if I'd left Dad's things as is. Who I was really trying to protect by covering it up . . .

I walk slowly toward the kitchen, pausing in the hallway to gauge the tone of her voice.

"Thanks, Sharon. I thought so too."

Ah, Sharon. One of the other dental hygienists—aka Mom's very own cavity. I pause a little longer, listening to them talk.

"No, you're right." Mom sighs. "At least it's over . . . God, no, we've got leftovers for weeks. Don't trouble yourself . . . Right, I will."

She's quiet for a minute, going "mm-hmm" and "I know" a lot. I almost slink off to my bedroom because this eavesdropping is way too boring but, in an instant, her voice seems to grow fangs.

"Are you kidding? I wouldn't let that bitch anywhere near this house."

Wait. What bitch? Who the hell are they talking about?

All the blood drains from my face, pooling in the pit of my stomach.

"No, it's fine. I'm not. Well, I'm *trying* not to."

I hold my breath, waiting for something—*anything else*—about "that bitch."

"I'm exhausted. It was hard to have everyone from Victor's office milling around the house today, but at least *she* didn't come . . . Fucking Bree . . . You're right. I know, I know . . . But fuck her."

Bree.

My heart stops.

Was *she* the perfume lingering on Dad's clothes? I turn her name over like a coin. A worthless word said in parenthesis. But my brain is a meat hook, digging in, gorging on each letter. One syllable, smooth and destructive.

My hands form fists at my sides.

"Thinking with his dick," Mom mutters. "What else?"

She laughs till it crashes into a sob. I can't take the sound of it, pebbles plonking into a well, one by one. I try to tiptoe past but Mom clears her throat, quickly wiping her eyes.

"Oop! Hey, Sharon, I better go, Evie's here ... Yeah, of course. See you—yes, see you then."

I stand frozen in the doorway. "Everything okay?"

"Yeah, honey, yeah. That was Sharon."

"And?" I press. "What did she say? You look upset."

My jaw tightens, sour and sick. I'm playing chicken with my mother's grief, I can feel it. I should have kept my mouth shut. But. My hangnail heart. I can't stop picking at it.

"Nothing," she says quickly. "Just what a beautiful service it was. How much she liked the crab cakes. At least someone did, right?"

She manages a laugh and sits back down beside her cold, congealed tacos and a full glass of wine. I wait a beat. Hoping for another scrap of "Fucking Bree." Something to feed my curiosity. For once, wishing that she'd turn the conversation on me—ask me if I knew things were bad between them. One push and I'd tell her everything ...

The refrigerator groans in the silence.

And that's it, I guess. Whatever she and Sharon were talking about, she's not going to tell me. I sit across from her, and she squeezes my shoulder, her fingers running the length of my cheap funeral dress.

"You must be exhausted, baby. Can I get you anything?"

I shake my head, and her smile turns melancholy. She reaches for her pack of cigarettes. I'm about to slink off to the living room to binge-watch something random when Mom clamps her fingers on my arm to stop me.

"Evie, I was thinking."

"What is it?"

"Earlier today, Sharon mentioned her sister's farm, in El Paso? It's apparently beautiful. Less than five hours' drive from Santa Fe. We were thinking maybe you'd like to spend some time out there this summer."

"What?" At first, I only blink. "Hold on. You want me to move to *Texas*? And live on a *farm*?"

Mom rolls her eyes. "Stop being so dramatic. Of course not. It would only be until things die down."

She pauses when she says it, because, well, you know.

"I meant, until things go back to normal."

"I'm not going."

"Please think about it, Evie."

"I'm. *Not*. Going."

"I *knew* you wouldn't give this idea a chance," she snaps. "You can be so stubborn."

Her forehead crinkles. I cross my arms. I swear to God we both shiver, secretly expecting Dad to waltz into the room. For him to pat the air with gentle palms, melting our feud with a butter-soft grin. *Ladies, ladies, why so tense?* We'd laugh, give in, move on. Now, though? She thinks I'm stubborn, but it's no wonder where I get it from. Neither one of us will be the first to back down. I miss him so much that I almost do. Desperate to keep the peace in his honor—today, of all days. Mom won't. She's too dazed. Too busy thinking of herself. Bloated from too much alcohol and not enough sleep. It takes all my power to focus on her eyes and not the bags beneath them.

"I really *don't* want to go to El Paso."

Mom groans. "Texas could be good for you right now. School's out, and I think you could use a change of scenery. Daddy's death is still so fresh. Don't you think working on a farm could be fun? Remember how much you used to love sheep?"

I squint at her idea of a pep talk. "Look, if you're kicking me out—"

"That's not what I said! Jesus, I'm sorry for thinking you *might* want a fresh start." She grumbles under her breath, and her nostrils flare. "But of course you don't. *Earth to Mom.* Well then, Evelyn, what *do* you plan to do?"

"Why do I have to *do* anything? Why can't I just be depressed like a normal person, without *farming*?"

"Because it's not healthy."

"Who says I have to be healthy?" I shout, silently adding, *You're not.*

Maybe it's harsh, but isn't it true? I kick my chair back and stomp toward the living room, flopping onto the couch and pulling a neatly folded plaid blanket onto my lap.

Mom pads after me. "You're about to be a senior, Evie.

You're supposed to be thinking about college. You have no direction—think about what Daddy would say if he were here. He'd be hounding you. All I'm asking is that you pick *something* that interests you."

"Like sheep?"

Mom sighs, but she's fighting a grin, I can tell. "Oh, forget the damn sheep."

"Thank you."

"You're welcome." She sits at the edge of the sofa and squeezes my toes. "Do you want to talk about it?"

If she means my summer plans, pass. If she means dad's heart attack, hard pass. If she means the on-the-side girlfriend she thinks I don't know about? ROCK-HARDEST PASS OF ALL TIME.

I shake my head, pulling the blanket up over my whole face where Mom can't see me cringe, picturing Dad kissing some girl from his office. And, like, who even was she? This "Bree." I squeeze my eyes shut, scanning hallways and cubicles, mentally stopping in the copy room where the edgy, brunette paralegal hangs out. The break room, with the grumpy HR ladies. Back to the lobby and their bubbly blond receptionist. *Thank you for calling Cisneros and Associates, CPAs. This is Bree, how may I help you?* My insides jolt.

Bubbly.

Blond.

Bree.

"I know you're hurting," Mom says softly. "I miss him too."

"Mm-hmm," I mutter from beneath my plaid asylum.

She keeps talking, but I'm too busy thinking about Bree. Did I ever utter more than two words to her? Did she know I was Mr. Parker's kid? *This is Bree, how may I help you?* Welp, you could *not* bone my dad, for starters.

"Evie?" Mom rattles my knee. "Are you even listening to me?"

I pull the blanket down to my nose. "What."

"I *said*, I need to know what you're going to do now that school's over. I'm not saying you have to work at the firm—now that Dad's gone, they'll understand if you renege on the internship. But you need a *plan*. What are you going to do? You can't loll around with Juana all summer. You've got to have focus! A way to properly channel your emotions."

Part of me is relieved to hear she's not forcing me to be a bullshit intern at Dad's accounting firm this summer. I mean, it was going to suck anyway, but, my God, filing documents in the taupe cubicle where my father literally collapsed? Passing *Bree the receptionist* every morning?! Shudder. Now my head's spinning, though. Because, yeah. Mom's annoying for calling me out, but WTF *am* I going to do this summer? Surely I can't have *another Supernatural* marathon . . . Can I?

"I'll figure something out."

"But *what*?"

"Some-thing," I enunciate and go back under the blanket.

"Great." She groans into the air. "I ask one *simple* question, and she vanishes."

"God, Mom. I'm under a frigging blanket."

That's not what she meant. I know it, she knows I know it. If Dad were here, he'd start tickling the arches of my feet. Singing my name in a theatrically menacing baritone. Giving me no choice but to crack up while Mom stomped into the kitchen to cool off.

Instead she sighs. I can't see her, but I picture her rubbing tired eyes with meaty palms. I let out a loud, depleted yawn. If only narcolepsy could be my superpower.

"Fine, have it your way." Mom huffs, and I feel the cushions lift as she rises to her feet. On her way back toward the kitchen, I hear, "Please, God, don't let her get into drugs."

Right. Because *she's* the poster child for sobriety.

Ten seconds later the familiar *pop!* of the corkscrew echoes through our immaculate home. Next, I'll be getting an earful of Billy Joel on the kitchen speaker. I don't know why she's so worried about me when "You're My Home" is her most-streamed song on Spotify.

Sitting here alone fans the flames of my emptiness. Makes it painfully clear that Mom and I are as distant as ever. Instead of Dad's death bringing us closer together, she's still the spinach in my teeth. I'm bird poop on her windshield. It sucks, realizing how intrinsically he was our glue. More than that, he and I were buds. Cookie dough connoisseurs, gurus of Monopoly. Mom doesn't get it. She just . . . doesn't.

I roll onto my side. Before I can help it, I'm crushed by the memory of my father, his image burned into every fold of my brain. Brown hair combed, gray suit loose around his torso. Did I tell him I loved him the day he died, or barely blurt a goodbye on my way out the door? Was I in his thoughts as his heart gave out?

Did I do the right thing, keeping a secret he never asked me to keep?

Right on cue, Billy Joel contaminates the silence, shattering my trance. He croons while I fester in this crypt, bombarded by mementos. Framed photos everywhere. Dad's favorite slippers, his collection of binoculars and old maps. Boxes of muesli that Mom and I won't eat but can't bring ourselves to throw away.

All of that fades away when I retreat to my bedroom. In here, I am recalibrated by Beanie Boos and bookshelves crammed with YA and fantasy. White walls covered in selfies; favorite memories of Juana and me that I've tweaked, perfected, framed. My Glade plug-in smells of Hawaii as I sigh stale hurt into the air. Part of me wants to call Juana, but—even more than my best friend's sympathy—I need sleep. Since before dawn, this bullshit day has chipped away at me, shredding me down into nothing.

Fatigue hits like a citywide blackout, thick and hollow as I crawl into bed. Covers up to my chin, heavy on my toes. Tired as I am, I can't take the silence, so I press shuffle on the SUPERNATURALLY SAD PLAYLIST that Juana and I made after the soul-crushing season twelve finale. For some reason, it's the one playlist I've been able to stomach, and I'm instantly comforted by Adele on piano. My breath slows, an inhale blooming into a yawn.

By the time "Someone Like You" fades into "Smother," I am gone . . . dreaming melted crayon dreams of a world where my father never left us and is still holding me tight.

Chapter 3

Morning, cutie. You up?

    I roll out from under the covers to grab my phone off the bedside table, waiting for another text. Juana never sends *just one text.* My tongue's dry, rolling over my teeth while I wait; stubborn fingers combing through curly, bedhead knots. *Am I up?* I scoff. Honestly. Considering it's the first week of summer vacation, I *should* be halfway through my Netflix queue and sleeping till noon. But I am neither of these things. Despite exhaustion reaching all the way to my bones and back, I've been bright-eyed and bleakly staring at the wooden beams on my ceiling since like 6 a.m. My phone buzzes again. And then again. And again.

That party last night. OMG.
You should have seen Gabe P

impersonate Mr. Alto.
FUCKING EPIC.

Oh, and the cheerleaders
were selling wine coolers
for 5 bucks each to pay for
some bullshit cheerleading
competition. 😫

But seriously tho. How are
you? Did you end up getting
some sleep? I was gonna
come by after but ur lights
were already off.

I wait another few seconds. Like, *are you done yet?* But she is, so I answer, using as few characters as possible to explain the cold, cruel fact that my dad was having an affair. Seeing those words in a perky text bubble turns my heart gray.

I'm still waiting for a reply when my phone rings, Juana screeching, "Wait, *what?*" into my ear because this shit is too messed up for emojis. "An affair? I mean, I guess it's not a *total* surprise. You already figured out he was leaving. But, Jesus. What a slime ball. I mean—crap. Sorry, I shouldn't have said that. Sorry, Ev."

I clench my jaw. "It's okay."

"What's her name?"

"Does it matter?"

"No, but I like knowing people's names when I hex them."

"Well, in that case, Mom called her Bree."

Juana snickers. "Your dad was doing it with fancy cheese?!"

Her laughter unravels, but I hesitate. *Fancy cheese*. It's a bad joke. Literally terrible . . . yet it somehow laces my brain with déjà vu. Hovering over mental archives, I navigate all the way back to seventh grade, to the first big pep rally at my new school. Juana and I were twelve-year-olds, lowly and insecure. I remember how the cheerleaders danced and clapped and kicked their way onto the stage, aglow in teal and pompoms. Big boobs, bigger grins. The prettiest, blondest one took the mic. *How y'all doing out there? I said, HOW Y'ALL DOING!? All right! That's more like it, Chavez Academy! I'm your cheer captain, Bree! Now, let's make some NOISE for the basketball team!* JJ's shoulder brushed against mine as she winced. *God,* I remember her saying, *can you imagine being named after a wedge of cheese?* Same lazy joke, nearly five years earlier. I'd ridicule Juana for recycling bad material, but there's a mudslide happening in my heart. Something sick and sinister.

"Ev?" She bird-whistles a few times into the phone. "You still there?"

"I'm here. But hold on for a second."

My breath weakens as I cross the clothes-strewn carpet toward my bookshelf, in search of a maroon spine with chunky festive lettering. I know it's here somewhere, some-where, somewh—aha: my seventh-grade yearbook. I'm almost afraid to crack it open, but I do, poring over glossy pages, one by one. I get to the senior portraits section and nausea tickles my ribs.

I put the phone back up to my ear. "Hey, do you remember seventh grade?"

"Seventh *grade*? Dude, *what* are you talking about?"

No wonder she's lagging, juggling a hangover along with my epiphany, but I can't explain it, not till I know for sure. My fingers struggle to keep up with my brain, tripping through pages. Past the Ds, Es, Fs. And then, there it is. A fucking atom bomb explodes in my head when I find her. She's younger, obviously. Fresher-faced and beaming. But it's her. It's so completely *her*. The phone slips from my fingers as I hold the yearbook up to the light.

"Evie?" Juana's voice echoes from the floor. "What was that sound? You're freaking me out—should I come over?"

Bree. Clarice. Hewitt.
Marshmallow teeth and
blueberry gumball eyes.

"It's her," I murmur. I grab the phone, grab my guts and my heart and my shock up off the floor. "Juana, it's *her*. She went to Chavez."

"Who did?"

"Fucking Bree!" I snap. It's not her fault, but my heart is

clobbering my chest, words tumbling out of me. "My dad's girlfriend—mistress—whatever. It's Bree mother-effing Hewitt. She was *there*. At our *school*. When *we* were."

Juana gasps. "Oh, no *way*. Are you shitting me? What grade? What does she look like? Are you sure it's her? Do you think your dad knows—or, I mean, knew?"

Questions barrel out of her with machine-gun force, but I can't keep up. Can't take Bree's face like this, smiling up at me. Shark teeth and poison lips. I slam the yearbook shut with a vengeance and slap it onto the floor. "God, Juana, I don't know! She was a senior when we were seventh graders—it's not like we braided each other's hair at sleepovers. And I barely saw her at Dad's office. It seriously never occurred to me."

"Right." She pauses for a hefty exhale. "Wow. I am literally mindblown. I'm so sorry, babe. Are you in total shock?"

"I'm—God, my hands are, like, shaking right now."

"I bet."

I squeeze my forehead, thinking about the Loss of a Loved One pamphlets Mom has been using as coasters for the past week. I wonder if they make one with a "barely legal mistresses" section.

"Do you think my mom knew he was robbing the cradle?" Juana makes a gagging sound.

"Holy shit. Do you think my dad was moving in with *her*?"

"I don't know," Juana says. "Try not to think about it."

But it's too late. My mind's already there, conjuring up this perfect clapboard house with its white picket fence; Bree right beside it, waving like a 1950s housewife.

"You're thinking about it, aren't you."

"No."

"Then what are you thinking about?"

"Um." I look down at the Beatles T-shirt I stole from Dad in ninth grade. "Apples."

"Right. Apples. Look, give me a couple hours to wash last night's party off my skinny ass, and I'll come over."

"A couple of *hours*? Jesus, how dirty *are* you?"

"It was a fun party!" she shrieks. "Melanie was there. We had a *lot* of *fun*, if you know what I mean."

"I can guess." I try to mask my sigh but, like, *Melanie*. Ugh. It's hard to get jazzed over the girl who broke Juana's heart last Christmas and has been jerking her around ever since. Apparently things are very much on again, and all I can do is swallow my judgment as Juana rehashes some of last night's fonder Melanie moments.

"Sounds very . . . yogic," I manage.

"Right?" She chuckles. "But don't worry, I'm still coming over. See you around one."

Maybe I should tell her she doesn't have to. That I'll muddle through on my own, like a big girl. But. Screw that. JJ's my lifeline right now, and I would drown in her support if she'd let me. The call ends and loneliness creeps back around my ribs. I'm left with no choice but to picture Bree, flirting with Dad in the conference room. Bringing him coffee, rubbing his shoulders when he worked late, filing his *documents*. Fucking Bree.

I get the urge to hurl but am restrained by Lips, in all her silky calico glory, as she jumps onto the desk to head-butt my waist. Before I can nuzzle her, she dives back onto the floor, meowing to be fed. I follow her toward the kitchen but pause at the cloud of family photos in the stairwell. Pictures I never used to look at and now can't get enough of. There's Dad holding a giant trout on our last family trip to Arizona. Hugging fourth-grade-me-in-a-tutu (before I got hips and boobs). Childhood photos of Dad and his brother Luke, back when Luke made time for family photos. And, my God, the hideously dated wedding portraits. If only lace-clad Mom and cummerbund-sporting Dad knew what the future held. Dad's mistress was probably still in diapers. How sick is that?

I turn away and flare my nostrils, determined not to cry. The only thing that hasn't changed since those pathetic wedding pics is how in love Mom is with Dad. Still. And she *knew* he was cheating! I mean, seriously, Mom—what the fuck. My blood boils, wondering how she could have loved him *that* much. So much that a secret girlfriend didn't make her run screaming to a divorce lawyer. I seriously do *not* understand adults.

In the kitchen, I wince at the sight of our dining table. A dozen snotty tissues, the saucer overflowing with cigarette butts, an empty Chardonnay bottle. Mom must've stayed up late letting Billy Joel remind her that "Only the Good Die Young."

"C'mere, girl." I pour some dry food into a metal dish, then make a bowl of Cheerios for myself and stare out the window. A deceit of devilish boys across the street catches my attention, howling with laughter as they fire slingshots at an innocent jackrabbit. One of 'em gets shot in the nuts and howls for a whole different reason.

I snicker. "Take that, asshole."

A *deceit of devils.* I used that phrase without really thinking about it, but it dawns on me now: another one of Dad's birding gems. The correct usage is a deceit of lapwings.

An exaltation of larks.

A murder of crows.

A bleakness of Evelyns.

The boys get called back into their house, and I exhale, eyes dull and latching onto the dried-out piñon trees bordering our dusty dirt road. Much as I hate to admit it, Mom was right. I'm going to go out of my mind with boredom this summer if I don't find something to do. Because, yeah, I love *Supernatural,* but a marathon honestly sounds a bit death-y for my current mood, and working my way through every limited-edition Pringles flavor won't qualify as productive. I'm lucky I don't *need* a job, but I do need purpose. Build a bike, write a novel—something to show colleges I'm still in the game. That I'm not paralyzed by the fact that a third of my family won't be joining us this summer. We won't drive to Arizona for two weeks at Lake Havasu. No mandatory math tutoring sessions or Dad's enthusiasm for old Marx Brothers films. He was nerdy but loveable. Easy to have a thousand inside jokes with. Mom doesn't laugh like he did. Or, I don't know, maybe I never tried making her.

A melancholy of Evelyns.

Saggy exhaustion sputters out of me. Counting the seconds till Juana comes to save me. Till we can have an *Avengers* marathon and eat so many Skittles, our tongues shrivel. I dump my bowl in the sink and wander aimlessly into the living room.

"Morning, sweetie," Mom says. She's wearing yesterday's sunburnt sweats and sipping coffee. "You sleep alright?"

"Fine, I guess?"

But I'm nearly in tears now, seeing her curled up on Dad's favorite chair, a worn-out leather recliner. Taking ownership, stealing its scent. If Dad were here, *he'd* be there, reading the *New Mexican* or eyes glued to a baseball game. *Pull up a chair, Evie-Bear, the Mets are on fire! This is our year, I can feel it.* It was almost never their year, but Dad never lost hope.

I wonder if Mom's thinking the same thing, biting down on her quivering lip.

I swallow. "What are you up to?"

"Gearing up for more paperwork." She pulls her messy brown curls into a velvet scrunchy. I can tell she wants to say more, but she forces a weary smile. "Grown-up stuff. Nothing you need to worry about. I'm starting back up at work tomorrow. So, last day off. Maybe we could watch a movie later? Or . . ."

Her voice hitches, wobbly and precarious before trailing off.

The lump in my throat's too big to respond, so I nod, debating whether or not to hug her when the doorbell rings. Oh, right—Juana, Skittles, *Avengers*.

I offer Mom an apologetic shrug and head to the door . . . except, it most definitely is *not* Juana on the other side. There's a man standing on our Welcome mat, holding a small duffel bag and a bouquet of black carnations. And I have to blink a few times before I realize that it's my uncle frigging *Luke* of all people. How long has it been? Two years, maybe? He's still lanky and freckled and wildly bearded. If he shaved and got glasses, he'd look exactly like Dad. Which creeps me the fuck out.

"Uncle Luke?" I ask. The name sounds foreign on my tongue. Part of me wants to smile, high-five like the old days, but the bouquet in his hand is unavoidable. "The funeral was yesterday."

"Wow. Evie. Look at you," Luke says. Even his voice is like Dad's. Bright and animated as a pogo stick. He awkwardly air-hugs me, which I didn't know could feel so stifling. "I tried to come earlier, but I was on location—barely thought I'd make it at all."

FYI, he doesn't mean he's been on a movie set or touring

with Taylor Swift. Nothing so glamorous. Luke is a scientist. "On location" probably means scooping seagull poop into petri dishes on an Alaskan oil rig to uncover migration patterns.

"Right," I say. Because, I mean, WTF? He missed his own brother's *funeral*. Maybe they weren't close, but it's still insulting as hell. And now, here he is, showing up more than a week after the worst day of my life. Past when Mom needed her brother-in-law; when I could have used another shoulder to cry on. And he's simply standing on our doorstep, holding a bouquet of my dead dad's favorite flowers dyed black.

I'm about to give him shit for it when I hear Mom gasp.

"Rita." His eyebrows pinch together. "It's good to see you."

I steel myself for her massive hissy about shirked family duties, but Mom practically catapults herself into Uncle Luke's arms. "Lukey! I hardly recognized you—you're so skinny! Don't they feed you up there in Alaska?"

"No more baby fat, huh?" He laughs until he remembers why he's here. "God, I can't believe he's really gone."

"I know, sweetie. I know."

My cheeks flush at the way their arms intertwine. His brown hair and wide shoulders, her ponytail and gentle giggle. They look like *them*, only not, and the nostalgic flutter slays me.

I clear my throat and pinch the doorknob. "Are you coming in, or what?"

"Evelyn Parker," Mom scolds. Her side-eye bores into me as she ushers Luke into the house. "The flowers are beautiful. I'll find a vase."

Uncle Luke hoists his duffel bag over his shoulder and ambles into the living room, straight for Dad's recliner. Jeez, like, *make yourself at home, why don't you?* But I'm suddenly remembering that's Luke—awkward one minute, oblivious the next. Kinda like my dad that way.

"Coffee?" Mom yells on her way to the kitchen.

Luke hesitates before yelling back. "Herbal tea? Only if it's not too much trouble."

"No, sweetie. Of course not."

Kitchen cupboards clunk at random as Mom hunts high and low for some ancient box of dusty mint leaves. This household is 100 percent caffeinated, but Mom would never admit the imposition. I swear, she would slaughter a cow and make steaks if her baby brother-in-law asked her to (which he won't, because I'm pretty sure he's vegan).

"So." Luke leans forward, scooting closer to where I'm flopped down on the couch. "How are you doing, Evie-Bear?"

It throws me off a little, the way he uses Dad's nickname for me. But I let it slide, clear my throat, offer up an aloof eye roll. Because, I mean, how the hell does he THINK I'm doing? Exactly.

"I can't believe any of this. I mean—my *big brother.*" He strokes the width of his jaw, shaking his head. "Vic used to buy me Hot Wheels with his allowance. We weren't always there for each other, but it doesn't seem fair. I know it's not the same as losing your dad, though. I've been there too."

My bottom lip wobbles, and I suck it tight against my teeth.

Luke accepts my silence with a broken smile. "What are you going to do now? With your summer, I mean. Rita said you usually intern at Vic's firm over summer break?"

"Is that why you're here?" I spit, heat pulsing off my glare. "You came all the way from Alaska to gang up on me with Mom? God, I can't be*lieve* her."

"No, no, no, no, no." Uncle Luke doth protest a little too much, IMO. He waits a beat and bites his lip. "We've been emailing, that's all. To be honest, she sounds iffy about the internship—you being cooped up at your dad's office all summer. I think she's worried."

My heart suddenly jolts. It never even occurred to me. Like, why Mom was so gung ho about me bailing on the internship. Of *course* she wouldn't want me working side by side with that skank. The thought of it gives me chills, frustrated and relieved that she wants to protect me, even if she won't say why.

"Evie?" Luke's fingers dance in front of my face. "You okay?"

"What? I'm fine. Just, like, trying to process the exciting prospect of being your lab assistant—that's what this is about, right? You want me to clean Bunsen burners all summer? Because I can tell you right now, that is *never* going to happen."

"God, no! Hah. I swear, I am not here to foist my love of

ornithology on you. But I did have an idea that I wanted to run by you. Preferably while your mom is in the kitchen looking for a teabag that probably doesn't exist."

Okay, touché. That earns him a smirk.

"So, I know your summer plans are kind of . . . up in the air, and I hate to throw this on you so fast, but it's a bit time sensitive. An old girlfriend of mine is a great photographer. Maybe you've heard of her, Georgina Denton?"

"Nope."

"Well, you'd like her work." He ignores my indifference, chewing a ragged thumbnail as he talks. "She does every-thing. Street photography, portraits, fashion. You know that black-and-white photographer what's-his-name? Larry Fink? And cinematic, moody stuff too. Like that filmmaker, Jenny Gage? Plus, some kind of ethereal landscape shots."

Luke seems to have zero clue what he's talking about, which makes two of us. "And what exactly do ethereal landscapes have to do with my summer plans?"

"Just hear me out. Georgy is here in Santa Fe for the sum-mer, teaching a class at the New Mexico Photography Institute. It starts next week, and it sounds really, really cool. The class is called the Art of Storytelling." He pauses, gets no response, and goes on. "I told her my niece could use a challenge, and she's willing to put you into the class. The photography institute isn't easy to get into—it'd be a favor to me."

"Photography? I don't even have a camera."

"Ah!" His joy ripples through our dreary living room. "It so happens I've got a sweet DSLR I'd be happy to loan you. Great digital camera. Tons of clarity and depth. I was just using it in the wetlands."

He starts rifling through his duffle bag, a dog digging up bones. I let the ink of his words bleed onto my brain. I mean, a photography class? Not counting Instagram, when have I ever taken a picture? What about bike building or the novel I was going to write? And yet . . . *photography.* The word sizzles on my skin. Would the world look safer from behind a lens? One degree farther from my heartache . . .

My imagination is starting to go all bold and Hefe-filtered when Mom scoots into the living room with a tray of tea and Newman-O's. She's changed into jeans and brushed her hair. I'd almost call her normal, but there's this glint in her eye. One hundred percent Hallmark Christmas movie as she doles out stale chamomile and cookies. She obviously knows what Luke and I were talking about. Obviously orchestrated the whole frigging thing.

"Oh, Lukey, you're a sight for sore eyes." Mom swats my legs off the coffee table and sits beside me. Her smile is genuine, but I can't help noticing fresh concealer beneath her eyes. She wants to fool Uncle Luke into thinking she's okay. I wonder if he's oblivious enough to fall for it. "What are you two talking about? Did I miss anything?"

Ugh. The *hope* in her voice. It's almost enough to make me

say no on the spot. Really rub in the fact that she's not the boss of me. God, I sound like I'm five sometimes.

"Nothing," I mutter. "Just, like, catching up and stuff."

Luke nods, his disappointment shifting into a smile. "I'm so sorry I missed the funeral, Rita. I've been in the absolute middle of nowhere. Had to pull some major strings to get away at all. How are you holding up?"

Mom takes a shaky breath. You can almost feel the dull jab of her words before she says them. "It's been tough. I mean, it all happened so quickly. He was fine—I went to work, he went to work. And then . . . he was gone. I really thought we had forever."

My heart jerks in a thousand directions. *Forever,* packed into two suitcases, on its way to a newer model. I shudder, and Mom squeezes my hand, reading me all wrong, not knowing the guilt I've got sandwiched between layers of pain. Maybe she's a fool for thinking they had forever, but it's my fault she isn't any wiser.

"I'm so sorry for both of you."

"Aw, Lukey." Mom reaches across the coffee table to rough up his hair. "We're so happy to see you. Let's see, last we spoke you were dating a Michelle?"

He laughs. "God, has it been that long?"

"No more Michelle?"

He shakes his head, and they both laugh.

"Well." Mom puts her arm around me. "We'd love to hear about your latest adventures in Alaska. Wouldn't we, Evie?"

"Bring it on," I mutter through Newman-O's.

As if on cue, sun streams through the skylight as Uncle Luke obliges, whipping up some jolly tale of life in America's icebox. I tune out his voice pretty quickly, eyes focusing on the living room window, imagining how the warm midday light would look through a wide-angle lens.

Frigging Luke. Planting frigging ideas in my frigging head.

———

An hour later, JJ's in my passenger seat, drumming the dashboard to our SUPERNATURALLY SASSY PLAYLIST as we drive aimlessly down the Old Taos Highway. Listening to her sing, feeling the desert sun on my skin, it's like I'm me again. I mean, Dad's still gone. The fact that he was cheating with a cheerleader still burns; Mom's still a wreck. But she's got Luke now. Maybe that'll help at least get her off my back for a while.

"Have you ever heard of someone called Georgina Denton?"

Juana turns the volume down. "Who? Oh, shit, was your dad having *two* affairs?"

"No! God." I shudder. "She's, like, a photographer or something."

"Oh. But, still no." She grabs her phone, distractedly mumbling Lizzo lyrics while she types. "Voilà. Georgina Denton. A trail-blazing artist named one of the twenty-five most talented photographers of her time. At age thirty, she's already shown her work at—blah blah blah, a bunch of museums and galleries. She's had photo shoots with—blah blah blah, a bunch of famous people. And she's received a dozen awards and fellowships."

"Cue the parade."

"Look at her—she's gorgeous." Juana angles the phone for me to see. Like *that's* going to help make up my mind. "So, what's the deal? Why do we care about hot photographers?"

"I guess my uncle Luke knows her? She's teaching a photography class at the institute this summer, and he thinks I should sign up."

"Aaand you don't want to." She shakes her head. "God, you can be difficult sometimes."

"What!" I giggle, not really asking so much as whining. "I don't know anything about photography. Besides, I was thinking maybe I could come work with you this summer."

"You want to work at Casa Buena?" Her incredulity blares. "Wait, let me rephrase. You think selling home accessories, dealing with cranky tourists all summer—dealing with *my parents as your bosses* all summer—sounds appealing? Not that I wouldn't love the company, but let's be real: my mom is a tyrant. I mean, a tyrant with impeccable taste. But, still."

"A *well-dressed,* impeccably tasteful tyrant," I add. "Yeah, I guess being Debbie's employee might suck. My God, did you hear her yesterday? After the funeral? Eyeing my mom's frumpy black top, offering to take her shopping?"

"OMG—seriously?" Juana groans, smacking her palm over

her eyes. "Not that I'm surprised. My mom would take Hitler shopping if it meant a trip to the mall."

"Are you calling my mom *Hitler*?! You raging bitch!"

Juana sticks her head out the window, cackling into the breeze. I pump the gas a little, exhilarated and grateful that our old repartee hasn't been entirely swallowed by my gloom.

Her hair is windswept and stormy when she pulls back in through the window, brown eyes narrowing on me. "You're going to accept Luke's offer though, right? The photography class?"

I purse my lips. "It's not that simple."

She opens her mouth but then stops, an exhale slithering out of her. Even with my eyes on the road, I can see her fingers flexing around nothing. It's that walking on eggshells thing again—treating me like I'm a grenade she doesn't want the responsibility of detonating.

"Whatever you're trying to say, just say it." I squirm in my seat at a red light, talking over JJ's silence. "This isn't *only* about some photography class. My mom went behind my back to set the whole thing up. Like, she actively thinks I'm going to become a junkie if I don't do something productive with my summer. Why does she have to be in control of *every*thing I do?"

"So you're punishing her."

"What?"

Juana wags her head. "You've been offered this amazing

opportunity. To study with a world-renowned artist. And you're going to miss out on it to spite your mom. Jesus, Evelyn. Check your fucking privilege."

Oh.

My body turns to stone, cheeks roasting.

"Look. I love you, Evie. You're my bestest friend. But think about how you're acting right now. Do you know many people would kill for the opportunity to take a fancy photography class? It's being handed right to you. I know you're grieving but, come on. It's okay to admit that you want to be depressed all summer and sleep off your grief. Or, I don't know, maybe you actively *loathe* photography or you've secretly applied to fucking pole dancing school. I don't know. Just . . ."

Her words end in a puff of frustration, and the car goes quiet. And slow. So slow that the truck behind me lays on its horn and swerves past. I'm numb from Juana's tone though, gripping the wheel, eyes stinging and glued to the road. Trying to blink back some of my . . . my what? Shock? Humiliation? Guilt? So much for my walking on eggshells theory—Juana's crushing chickadees in combat boots. She's also right, the reality of which flattens me.

"Don't get all quiet."

"I'm not," I sulk.

"Yeah, you are." She reaches under my driving arm, pinching my armpit. "You know I love you. But try not to let your constant urge to butt heads with Rita stop you from a cool-ass opportunity. Isn't she suffering enough? Punishing herself already, thinking the heart attack was her fault? Like, if she'd only fed your dad avocado toast instead of bacon all those years, he'd still be alive. Even though, *damn*, she makes some delicious bacon, all crispy on the edges. How does she do that?"

I giggle at her salt-cured peace offering. "You're right," I mumble. "Not about the bacon—I mean, it's delicious, and it crisps up because she cooks it in the oven rather than on the stove—but for calling me out. I'm an entitled dick."

"You're not." She tugs my hair. "You're sweet—well, ish. You're mostly a snarky bitch. And smart and talented and brave. But you're also going through the hardest thing ever right now. It's okay to wallow and be selfish. And it's also super-*duper* okay to tell Cisneros and Associates you will not be their bitch all summer. Sayonara to *that* job. Besides, I have a psychic inkling that you'd make an awesome photographer. You're all kinds of angsty to begin with—imagine how good you'd be, working through your grief and suffering like some kind of two-eyebrowed Frida Kahlo."

"I do have great eyebrows."

Juana snorts. "And, look. If you twist my arm, I'll be your model. All summer, free of charge."

Before I can respond, she starts posing in the most extra way. Zhuzhing her hair, arching her back, throwing me thick lips and a bugged-out smize. I'm laughing so hard, I almost swerve onto the shoulder. We drive a little farther, giggling, snorting, ending up at our favorite gelato place, the one with cute wicker tables.

"There's another party tonight," Juana says, licking stracciatella off her chin. "Dejah's house on Apodaca Hill. Should be epic."

"*EPIC*," I repeat with devil horns and a death metal growl. Juana laughs, and I don't tell her how un-epic everything in my life feels right now. How I'm afraid I'll feel un-epic forever. Instead, I say, "Thanks, but I'll pass. Don't let me stop you, though. I mean, the keg's not going to drink itself."

"You got that right."

Her phone buzzes, a giggle bursting out as she sees a text from Melanie. I bite into my chocolate-dipped cone and wait. Downtown Santa Fe twinkles in the distance. It's going to be a long-ass summer if Juana and Melanie are back together, flouncing around from party to party while all I'm doing is moping. Mom and I will grieve in parallel. We'll binge on geriatric British crime dramas and do jigsaw puzzles when we're not bickering. Knowing the whole time that I could have been doing something cool. Juana's right. It's a great opportunity, and I'd be a snobby dick to pass it up. Urgency whips through me as I reach for my phone.

> Were you serious about that
> photography class?

I click Send, hoping Uncle Luke's number hasn't changed since the last time I texted him, probably a year ago. I chew my lip, heart click-clacking, bones aching.

Dead serious! he writes back a minute later. And never mind his un-fucking-believably appropriate word usage. You want to do it?

> Okay sure.
>
> I mean, yes. Please.

Great!!! I'll text Georgy right now!

Minutes pass, and an unfamiliar buzz starts to warm my limbs.

Hang tight. She's double-checking there's still room in the class.

Hey I'm waiting for Rita (she's in Whole Foods). Can I tell her?!

Ugh. My eyes backflip in their sockets, because *UGH!* But, yeah, fine. Mom's going to be thrilled that I gave in to her pestering and found something better to do than Dad's internship.

                              Sure. I guess.
Great!!

GUESS WHAAAAAAAT!!!!!
Georgy says it's a go!!!

She's going to email me the
registration packet! The class
starts next Monday. She says
she can't wait to meet you!!!!!!

I'm so distracted by Luke's obsession with abundant excla-
mation points that I almost switch over to Instagram without
replying. But I don't want to look like a dick, considering he's
lending me his fancy camera and paying for the whole thing,
so I type out a quick thanks and then finish my gelato, deep in
thought.

One week. To figure out how to use a complicated Nikon.
And then spend the whole rest of my summer with complete
strangers.

Cool cool cool cool cool.

CHAPTER 4

Georgina Denton reminds me of the long-tailed widowbird I used to see in Dad's bird-watching books as a kid. Her eyes are like cocoa nibs dipped in amber; her hair, a rippling sheet of black satin. When I walk into the classroom on Monday, she flashes me the warmest cashmere smile. Similar to the widowbird, she seems to soar toward me, with arms full of dragon tattoos and a firm yet delicate handshake.

"You must be Evelyn."

"Evie, yeah. What's up?" *What's up?* God, I'm such a natural with adults.

"Luke said his niece looked like a young Zooey Deschanel," she comments. I wait for a "more like Zooey's chubby cousin!" joke, but it never comes. "He was right! It's great to meet you. I'm Georgina, but, please, call me Georgy."

I nod, scanning the room awkwardly. "I'm the first one here?"

"Yes, but that's actually better. I was hoping I'd have a chance to chat with you privately." She twirls her hair into a bun, spearing it with a wooden chopstick. "Luke told me about your dad. I'm *so* sorry. How awful. I lost mine when I was young too. He had cancer, so it's not the same, but I get it. Losing a parent is never ever easy."

"Thanks," I say quietly. Maybe I'm horrible, but it actually does make me feel .01 percent better. Like it *is* possible to grow up and heal, despite the emptiness still choking me. "You're not going to, like, tell the class though, right?"

"God, no! I may be secretly addicted to gossip, but I'm no snitch." She pauses and bites her lower lip. "You won't tell anyone I love TMZ, right?"

I shake my head. "Pinky swear," I say. Because I am *five*.

"Since you're early, give me a hand with these packets? There should be ten copies, one for each student. Divvy them among the chairs and sofas, I guess."

Dutifully, I take the handouts and wander around the room, dropping stapled photocopies on each poofy, Southwestern-upholstered chair and leather sofa. The first page is full of technical terms I've never heard, followed by pages and pages of articles on lighting and composition and this, like, super comprehensive-looking photo checklist. The whole thing leaves me kind of frozen.

"You okay?"

"Huh?" I stare up at Georgy who's looking back at me, one

eyebrow arching up. "No, yeah. I'm fine. I sort of thought we'd be sitting at desks or at least around a table. This place is like a hotel."

"A bit much, eh? The institute likes to exude an intimate vibe. Give 'em their money's worth."

How fah-bulus, I think, but I keep my mouth shut. Luke graciously (guiltily?) paid my tuition, and I don't want Georgy thinking I'm ungrateful. With the last photocopy, I commandeer a loveseat, forgetting my nerves as this giraffe-tall redhead struts in, her dusty-rose cowboy boots clanking against the brick floor. She dumps a denim blazer and matching purse on a chair near me and waves with both hands.

"Hey, y'all. I'm Suze!" She does a little shoulder shimmy on the "ooz" part, a sticky-sweet twang coating her words. "I can't tell y'all how excited I am to be here."

Georgy's grin brightens to match. "Hi, Suze, welcome to class. I'm starting to remember your application."

"I'll bet!" Suze plonks down on the leather chair beside me and pulls a notebook and a fancy Canon out of her bag, then proceeds to reel off her life story, despite not being asked. "I'm a proud mama of two girls and a recently-declared *they*. All three of 'em off at college, so I finally got some time to myself! Photography is my passion. My late husband always said I had a gift." Again, her shoulders perform their signature *cha-cha-cha*. "But I'm about a million times older'n you—what's your name, darlin'?"

"Me?" My eyes pop wide. "Um, Evie."

"Aren't you cute as a bug."

And I'm not sure if I'm supposed to compare her cuteness to an insect too? But I'm saved by the door as it swings open, distracted by a skinny South Asian man in a beret who quietly takes the corner seat, followed by this leather-clad twosome, already midconversation.

"You're missing the point!" the woman argues.

Her words seem to poke the air like mosquitoes as her stocky male counterpart swats them away. He saunters in yawning, groaning, shielding disinterest behind giant Ray-Bans. They're both dark-haired and hipster, cradling cappuccinos in their pale hands.

"*The Birds* is probably Hitchcock's most macabre masterpiece," she says in a thick (German, maybe?) accent. "It is a profound exploration of female sexuality and our antagonizing relationship with nature."

"Jesus, Ada." The guy flops onto a sofa and laughs. "Did you wiki that before you said it?"

Ouch. What a dick.

Suze's mouth drops open too, and we share a millisecond-long gasp before pretending not to eavesdrop. This poor Ada chick, though. She turns beet red and almost slaps her boyfriend/brother/mortal enemy across the face before diving back into her tirade, which I like her for, instantly.

"They've been at it for half an hour," someone whispers beside me.

My head swivels, a zip of adrenaline whooshing through me, thrown off by a strikingly beautiful boy beside me. Never-mind the fact that he could have chosen half a dozen other seats in the room but decided to sit here. Beside *me*.

"I was behind them in line at the canteen," he whispers again, nodding across the room. "First, I thought maybe she's a film professor at NYU, but now I'm thinking avian rights activist."

I swallow a smirk and reach down for my bag, pulling a notebook and an orange juice into my lap. My seatmate goes back to watching the couple argue, and I let myself subtly dissect his stealth-eavesdropper cuteness. Because I'm surprised. Not that he's cute, because it's not up for debate, but that he's making my stomach flip. In the past seventeen days, I've felt so rough and hollow—my stewing-in-gloom thing—that crushing is literally last on my list. So I savor this shiver; let it wash over me. See what I'm missing before the emptiness swallows me whole again.

Fair skin

lean limbs

eyes dark and

peeking through

Marvel-hero bangs.

I'm not his type. Barely cute enough to play his sidekick. And yet, here he goes again, talking to me.

"Can you believe this jerk?"

I giggle. Damn, I need to pull it together. "Right?" I whisper. "Like a real-life Gaston."

"Who?"

"You know, from *Beauty and The Beast*? Eats a million eggs? Likes to expectorate?"

His nose scrunches blankly as he laughs. Not *at* me, but with his whole heart and a soft curl to his lips. My ego can't help but climb a few notches, despite the feel of his narrow hips bumping against my wider ones on our tiny sofa.

Across the room, Ada—aka the avian rights activist, aka the female half of this bickering duo—pauses. Like she's realizing for the first time that the rest of us are here. In particular, that me and whoever-this-is beside me are maybe, probably laughing at her.

"Sorry," she says, revealing gap teeth in her smile. "I'm Ada Fitz. And my husband, Ed. I didn't mean to be so loud. Our house rental is stocked with old Hitchcock DVDs, and we decided to have an impromptu festival this summer. As you can see, *The Birds* is already up for debate."

Ed, with a scratchy, burlap voice I already *loathe*, jumps in to inform us that Hitchcock's earlier mysteries *Shadow of a Doubt* and *Strangers on a Train* are superior films. Georgy's favorite is one called *Dial M for Murder*. My seatmate's big into *Rear Window*. Everyone's all kinds of amped, batting around film terms like SAT words. My insides are clenched, locking down, clinging to the word "birds." Because—it's ridiculous, but—*birds*. Suddenly there's this aching, throbbing, palpitating wrench inside me. Razor-sharp thoughts of my father. We never had a

bird in the house because Dad thought they deserved their natural habitat (plus, Lips would have terrorized 'em), but my dad
loved birds. Like, in the nerdiest possible way. You've never
seen anyone so freaking amped over a toothless, beak-jawed,
feathery friend. He loved birds like most guys love football. It
makes my heart scald and shake, thinking about all that one-
of-a-kind-ness being gone.

"What about you?" Georgy asks. I have to look up to realize
she's talking to me. "Do you have a favorite Hitchcock film,
Evie?"

My face reddens. I mean, when did this become a frigging
film society meeting? I look around and blink, my insides still
throbbing. Mystery guy leans toward me and discreetly doodles something on the edge of my notebook. When he's done, I
realize it's . . . a noose. *What the actual fuck?*

"Okay . . . Hitchcock," I stammer, yanking my notebook
away. Two old men scurry in, arms linked as they nestle down
on the last remaining loveseat. I'm distracted by the huge
grins on their wrinkly faces, but I force myself to focus. "Um.
What's the black-and-white one where the lady gets stabbed
in the shower?"

"*Psycho*," they all say. Like, all of them. Even the gay couple
who missed the entire conversation.

"Right, *Psycho*." I manage a curt smile, pale skin on fire as I
start chugging OJ like I'm hypoglycemic.

"Solid choice," mystery guy murmurs.

His voice is low and close and only for me. I nearly blush, but then I remember the noose etched onto my notebook. A freaking *noose*. So, I dismiss this rare, bubbly, flirtatious feeling, and focus on Georgy as the last few students straggle in.

After a quick headcount, she widens her arms. "Welcome to the New Mexico Photography Institute—NMPI for short. I'm Georgy, and this is the Art of Storytelling. I'll be the angel and the devil on your shoulders for the next ten weeks. My job is to urge you to see the beauty in the everyday and to help you take the risks that make truly captivating photographs."

Instantly Georgy has each of us feeling like warm bowls of chicken soup, ready to be stirred and seasoned and poured down the gullets of our own imagination. She forces us to do the painful intro bit, and in addition to boisterous, Texan Suze and the hipster Fitzes who run a PR firm in Malibu, we learn that the beret-wearing guy is actually a French *professeur* called Henri, on sabbatical from his Parisian *école*.

I'm immediately in love with Peter and Sten, the elderly gay couple who came in with arms linked. They're adorably silver-haired and dressed for a safari. They finish each other's sentences too.

"We're Santa Fe locals," says Sten. "And NMPI regulars," Peter finishes.

Then there's mommy blogger Beth, with a personality that seems as stiff as her blond bouffant. She's renting a ranch in Tesuque for the summer with her tycoon husband, four sons, and not one but *two* au pairs. Which I try not to roll my eyes at, but Violet clearly does. She's also a blogger, but closer to midtwenties and a bazillion times cooler. Like, it shocks *no one* to hear that she's an influencer, with her flawless, dewy brown skin and lots of boho jewelry. I'm not really sure why she's here, if she's already famous-ish? But I guess there's always more to learn.

Panic rolls through me when she stops talking, afraid I'll have to go next, but then Mystery Boy leans forward, dipping his head as he smiles. "Hey, guys, I'm Declan Maeda from Brooklyn. I'm building up my photography portfolio for NYU in the fall, crashing with my grandparents for the summer. Really excited to be here."

Not gonna lie, the word Brooklyn has this kind of neon effect on me. I've never met anyone from New York before. But whatever. So what if his shoulders slope like gentle, rolling hills and his Adam's apple juts out like a diamond, or that he probably spends his free time riding the subway to concerts and indie bookstores and coffee shops. Like I said, whatever.

The room goes quiet, and I feel Declan nudge my knee with his. "You're up."

"Oh, right." I nod, swallowing spit like rubber cement. "I'm Evie Parker. Sounds like a superhero name, but I'm just a regular seventeen-year-old. I am completely *not* a photographer, and I am sure this is going to be a humiliating summer. Also, I'm a Virgo. And I like cheese."

I'm not a superhero and like cheese. Honestly. HONESTLY.

"Thanks for the intros, everyone." Georgy smiles and then claps her hands with a bang. "Now, let's get started! For those who don't know, Santa Fe is called the 'city different.' Galleries. Green chile culture. Spanish pueblo architecture. Sunsets to *die* for. I swear, I could shoot in front of those stunning orange, mud-brick adobe buildings all day. But, what I'd like to see *you* all work toward, is finding a balance. It's easy to go overboard and photograph *every* turquoise jewelry stall on the Plaza, but I want you to create subtleties. Photograph one freckle rather than the entire face. The flick of a wrist, the folds of a skirt."

All around the room, everyone's furiously jotting down notes. I don't want to feel left out so I write:

Freckle good, face bad.

"I see that you've all brought your Fujis and your Rebel Ts, but we're going to start off with the cameras most of us carry around every day. The ones on our iPhones. Everyone here's got a smartphone, right?"

Heads bob, although Suze and her million-dollar Canon look forlorn.

"Here's the deal: we're going to break the ice with a photo showdown. You'll split into pairs, and then I want you to take advantage of the weightlessness and ease of your cameras. Shoot up high, up close, from the hip, from the ground. I want to see landscapes, portraits, action shots. Get creative with your filters and cropping. This is a 'getting to know you' exercise—don't overthink it."

Again, everyone nods, but my heart's starting to thud, dizzily wounded, wondering again if I should regret what I've gotten myself into, because I didn't think photography was going to sound so technical. *Why did I think it THAT?!* What am I even doing here? The rest of these people have real purpose. Actual #PhotographyGoals. I'm a fake. I should be watching TV right now. Sleeping. Moping.

I snap back to attention when I hear my name called.

"Evie and Declan. Violet and Suze, Henri and Ada . . ."

Ada coughs at the idea of being separated from her jackass husband, but I'm borderline distraught. Declan? Putting aside the fact that his cologne is all kinds of lost-in-the-woods, and he's got an adorably skinny little nose, what about the noose? The NOOSE! The thought of it drenches my palms and rocks my brain. Declan grins dimples at me and it's not just my palms anymore; now my heart is skipping beats.

"Remember to look for broad light sources and shadows," Georgy adds, ushering us out of the room. "We'll circle back in an hour for critique."

I cling to my messenger bag and pretend Declan's not inches away as we head outside. Walk fast, act tall, exude thinness—in case he's looking at me from behind. But he's easily six feet tall, so Declan and his ostrich legs have caught up to me within seconds. We get to the parking lot, and it's cluttered with Beamers and Jags and SUVs because *that's* the kind of clientele they're used to at NMPI. The staff must have died laughing when I rolled up in my five-year-old Subaru. Before I can berate myself over "died laughing," Declan clears his throat.

"Where to?"

"Oh, um . . ." Our eyes meet and I'm momentarily silenced by a cluster of freckles on his right cheek. "I don't know."

"I've spent a bunch of vacations here, but you're the local, so . . ."

"So, what? That makes me a fucking tour guide?"

"Apparently not." He chuckles. "Guess I'll ask Ed if we can tag along with him and—"

"Okay, okay!" I roll my eyes, curbing a grin. "Follow me."

Even though, yeah, I'm the local, I feel suddenly lost and desperate to impress. I squint in the harsh sunlight and notice Peter, the British half of the gay couple. He's paired up with stuffy Beth, the two of them weaving through a path of spiky yucca shrubs toward a wooden bench. It's a cute spot but too obvious. I'm guessing everyone else beelined for the manicured rose garden out back. NMPI shares its grounds with a nunnery or a monastery or whatever, and those holy types have some seriously green-ass thumbs.

"You like living in Santa Fe?" Declan asks as we walk down the sidewalk.

"Are you kidding?"

"Um, not that I know of?"

I shrug. "It's pretty boring."

He shrugs too. "Pretty *pretty* though, at least. Besides, not-boring is overrated." He kicks a stone, coaxing it along the path with us. "Take it from a New Yorker. It is possible to be too un-bored."

That statement barely even makes sense. I inhale for a long, confused sigh, but all I get is another whiff of his serene woodchip-ness, mixed with something like crayons? I weirdly love the smell of crayons, the chalky waxiness of them. But it's making me sweat again, so I pop some Trident and let cinnamon overpower my olfactory nerves. Much better.

Neither of us says anything for a few minutes. I'm not entirely sure where I'm going, but Dad used to bring me down around here for bird-watching. What is it with the goddamn birds today? It sounds so dorky, and it was, but Dad loved birding, and I loved exploring with him. As a kid, at least. Then I turned thirteen. Too cool for his gray jays and his spotted towhees. Walking along this path now, it's almost like I can hear his voice.

Wait! he'd whisper. *You hear that, Evie?*

I would stand so still. Mouth wide, ears open. *Is it a bird whistle?*

More of a squawk. That's a western scrub. And he always had a second pair of binoculars to hand over. *Take a look. Aren't they beautiful, Evie-Bear? Blue the color of your bedroom walls. Some people confuse the western scrub for your common blue jay, but they're not the same. Scrubs forage in pairs; they like to be part of a family.*

Just like us!

God, I can still hear the Pollyanna glint of my voice. *A family.* Yeah, right.

"Hey, are you okay?" Declan asks.

"What?" I snap. "Yeah. Why?"

"You started walking so slow. I wasn't sure if . . ."

"I'm fine," I say quickly, voice trembling.

Only an idiot would believe me, and I guess he's not one, because it looks like he's about to pry. Rather than let him, I make an impromptu right and start skidding down into the arroyo, tripping as I reach the dry stream bed.

"Whoa!" Declan peers down at me, one eyebrow hiking up like some kind of high-seas scallywag. His Adidas don't budge. "Where are you going?"

"Scared?" I giggle, instantly regreting my flirty tone. Or, just, like, surprised by it. The sun stings my eyes as I glance up. "There are some cool trails down here that might make decent backdrops . . . unless Mr. Brooklyn can't handle off-roading."

Challenge: accepted. Declan grins and skids down the hill, colliding with me when he picks up speed at the bottom. He mumbles a husky apology into my hair.

"It's fine. I'm steep—*it's* steep," I manage. "I should have warned you."

I step back, and he straightens up, stepping into the clearing. "What are these, pine trees?"

"Piñons."

"They smell nice."

"I guess," I say, because it's one of those things you never think about—that the trees you've smelled a thousand times have a distinctly sweet, nutty scent. But they do.

The arroyo is wide and dry thanks to a perpetual drought, but it allows for a crystal-clear echo of kids at a nearby day camp. I sneak a peek at Declan, and his eyes are already on mine, studying me.

"Now what?" I say, panic in my voice, waiting for a whistle or a gun blast or *something* to happen.

"Now, we shoot." Declan grins as he makes the first move, grabbing an iPhone from his back pocket. Within seconds, he's snapping close-ups of bristly, green piñon branches; lying on his stomach to capture the salmon-colored sand. "Go for it," he says gently, looking up at me from the ground.

"I don't . . . I can't—"

But I do. I can.

I fish my phone out of my pocket and raise it up and out over the arroyo, clicking a few pictures of fading jet contrails crossing paths overhead. Is that what a real photographer would do? A real photographer would get the jet streams in focus or at least make them look better than tiny white blobs. But the more I snap, the more I start to have fun with it, which feels like mission accomplished, as far as I'm concerned. Declan's following his own pursuit, giving me space. I loosen up a little, shooting some graffiti on the side of a boulder, squatting down to photograph the soft spikes of a prickly pear cactus and rolling onto my back to snap the clouds. Anything, everything. There is no wrong answer.

Pretty soon, Georgy's checklist is all checked off, except for the portraits. My stomach lurches. No way am I going to be the one to ask first. Declan's way too busy shooting the dried-up wood of a cholla cactus, and I refuse to look eager. Instead, I lean against an old fence post and start texting Juana. She's working at Casa Buena today and could probably use a distraction as badly as I could.

"Portraits?" Declan asks, leaning beside me. "Whenever you're done texting."

A burst of heat tickles my neck. "I'm done."

He laces his fingers behind his head and looks from side to side. Armpit hair usually creeps me out, but the little tuft I can see poking out of his Virginia Is for Lovers T-shirt is oddly not puke-inducing. Almost the opposite.

"How about here?" He rattles the beat-up coyote fence. "You should see how the light is shining through your hair right now."

He angles his phone at my face, and I automatically stiffen, rolling my eyes. Maybe even *extra* rolling them so he knows for sure how *not* into this I am.

"Damn, that expression!" He laughs but doesn't stop shooting. "All kinds of tough. Lonely too, though. This is gonna look incredible in black and white."

"Excuse me?" I push myself off the fence. "Lonely?!"

WHEN WE WERE STRANGERS 65

"Wait, don't be mad." He reaches for my wrist. "I only meant you're photogenic."

"Well, that's not how it sounded."

"I'm sorry, I didn't mean anything. I only meant . . ." He pauses, looking at me so closely, I wonder if there are words printed on my freckles. After a second, he shakes his head. "Never mind. Where do you want to shoot me?"

"In the head," I mutter.

Without even hesitating, Declan jams his pointer and middle fingers against his forehead and manages a pretty stellar backward cannonball into the thick, packed sand. After some brief and gratuitous writhing and a pained yowl—fake? hopefully?—his eyes flop shut, head lolling to one side. I raise my phone, snapping a wide angle of Declan Maeda, shot dead in a New Mexico wasteland.

"Wait!" I shout, running up a little closer. "Don't move, dead boy." I kneel down beside him and take another picture, catching the curve of his jaw and the way his skin glistens gold against the sand.

"Can I get up now?" he asks, lips clenched and eyes shut.

I tell him yes, and he props up on one elbow, brushing sand from his jeans.

"Get what you needed?"

"Maybe one more," I say, because he's flashing this smoldering grin that I want to capture. And I do, zoomed in with a ray of light streaming into the frame. "Okay, done."

A dust devil whips down the canyon, and Declan and I

quickly shield our eyes before we're blinded. I look back up when it's safe, smiling at the spattering of sand in his thick, black hair. There must be just as much in mine, because he laughs and shakes out one of my curls.

"You're a mess."

"Look who's talking!"

I start to laugh and then—bam—Declan's taking more photos of me.

"Whoa, buddy. Way too close."

"But, it's awesome," he says. "Just a few more?"

I nod, playing chicken with my inhibitions until I can't take it anymore and finally swat his phone away. Declan helps me to my feet with strong hands. "Thanks."

We trudge back up the steep incline and stand on the sidewalk for a minute, both of us swiping through our photos, deleting the garbage until we're left with ten good images to show Georgy. Sweat trickles down the back of my neck. Not from the climb so much as the scorching bone-dry heat. It hasn't rained in months and it doesn't look like it's about to. Trees have turned brown and crispy. Dirt and dead twigs crackle underfoot as we walk. If Dad were here, he'd lecture me on water conservation.

We're halfway back to the institute when Declan clears his throat. He looks sideways at me. "Rope."

"'Scuse me?"

"That picture of the noose I drew in your notebook," he says sheepishly. "At the beginning of class? It was for *Rope*. It's a

Hitchcock film. One of his later ones. I was trying to help you out, but you probably thought I was a serial killer."

"*Oh* . . ." I say, really milking the *o* while the whole thing comes together in my head. "Yeah, no. I had *zero* idea that was supposed to be a movie clue." I pause to squint at him, cocking my chin. "Wait a second, though. You think I would lead a murderer down into an arroyo? *Alone*?"

Now we're both laughing. "Yeah, I guess you wouldn't."

"Not so much."

We get back to class around the same time as everyone else, and Georgy asks us to upload our photos to her cloud. Because, oh God. Right. This is an actual class, and we're actually going to, like, critique one another's work.

Somebody get me a bucket, I really think I might hurl.

Declan offers to go first, and Georgy opens his folder onto the projector. Thumbnails dot the screen; the room goes quiet. She toggles through them—rushed at first, then slowing to stop on a photo of me. She makes it enormous and my round face fills the screen. Hi, yeah, I'm mortified. Too close, frowning, saturating the frame. Although . . . Declan's put a cool filter on it. Black and white, like he said, but with a hazy glow that darkens the edges. It makes the photo look like it was taken in 1920. Like I could be in an old silent movie or something.

"The vignette brings a lot of depth to the photo," Georgy says. "Eerie juxtaposition with her skin tone. And I love the high contrast. Great use of dramatic light and framing."

"The cropping bothers me," says Henri in his melodic (okay, arrogant) French accent.

"You think so?" housewife Beth squeaks.

"*Oui*. It makes me feel, er, claustrophobic."

Everyone squints back at my face on the screen, all giant and stark. Yeah. I guess it is kind of close. But isn't that what Georgy wanted? I'm no expert, but it doesn't bother me. My billboard-sized face does, but not the cropping.

Georgy juts her chin toward Declan. "Care to defend yourself?"

"Yeah, sure." He ruffles his hair. "I see what Henri is saying, but I wanted to eliminate all the exterior crap so it would feel intimate. There was something in Evie's eyes—I didn't want to miss it. Another photographer might have widened the angle, but that's not my style."

"Subjective." Georgy nods contemplatively.

I'm blushing so hard, it's like someone's ironing my cheeks until finally Georgy closes Declan's folder. And I'd be relieved, except then she moves on to—*oh, please, God, NO*—me. I sink lower in my seat, positive that I'm the worst photographer in the room. Maybe even the world. You have to squint to see the contrails in the jet stream photo, and the cactus shots are total crap. I like the ones of Declan looking all cute and dead in the arroyo, but Georgy ignores those in favor of my graffiti picture.

"That one's cool." Violet leans in, combing her fingers

through fuzzy black curls. "I would completely post this and get a million likes. The colors really *pop*, don't you think?"

I cock my head a little because, yeah? I guess they kind of do?

"What does the tag say?" Ada asks. "I can't read the curly letters."

Ed loops his fingers at the screen. "Says, 'Keep It Clean.'"

"'Keep It Clean,' graffitied onto a boulder." Sten, the smaller/younger/frecklier of the gay couple, rolls his eyes. "Don't you *love* the irony."

"And the angle," Georgy adds. "Notice how Evie shot this completely level? She's managed to anchor the franticness."

I have?

Everyone nods, heads angled and chins stroked as Georgy closes my folder.

And that's it. For me, I mean. Sten's next, with lots of colorful wooden doorways and chile ristras. Beth is instructed to try a macro lens if she's going to shoot butterflies. And I find myself getting kind of into it. Agreeing that Ada needs to utilize the rule of thirds, and that Ed's "industrial photographs" of a dumpster could use more context. Violet makes Suze look like Cyndi Lauper in the parking lot, which I love. The way her bright, red hair glows in the sun like a trash fire (in a good way).

"That one's awesome," I say, shocked by the sound of my own voice but not deterred by it. "The colors are so saturated."

"I was thinking that too." Declan nods. "Reminds me of David LaChapelle."

He looks at me like I'm supposed to have any idea who David La-whatever is. I don't, but rather than get flustered about it, I find myself getting preemptively flustered by the sway of his lips as he smiles, the cat shape of his eyes. I tuck my hair behind my ears and stare desperately back at Georgy, who's reminding us how important it is to connect with our subjects this summer.

We move on to Henri's photos after that, but my pulse is still questionable and hard to rein in. Declan leans forward, elbows on knees to get a better look at Henri's clouds, and I stare at the back of his head for a second, noticing little details, wishing I could photograph his narrow shoulders or the small Asian symbol tattooed at the base of his neck. I open my notebook to write down Georgy's advice to "connect with your subject," and the first thing I see is Declan's sketch of a noose.

I can't resist smiling as I turn to a fresh page.

CHAPTER 5

I am exhausted when I get home from day one but clearly not as wiped as Uncle Luke, breathless in short shorts and a soggy MIT T-shirt in the middle of our kitchen. He's standing there doing side bends, fingers on his pulse. As luck would have it, I have a camera hanging from my neck, so I lift it up and take some highly incriminating photographs that I definitely intend to show Georgy at tomorrow's class.

"Yo, Evie!"

"Oof, don't say *yo*." I cringe, reaching for the never-ending bowl of pistachios that's been sitting on the kitchen table since Dad's memorial service. I lean back in a chair, judging Luke's mediocre flexibility, wondering how long he's planning to stick around. It's been nice having him here. Home-cooked meals, science chatter, movie nights. The duffel bag he brought was pretty small, but if it's filled with shorts as offensively tiny as the pair he's got on, he could be here till fall. "I can't believe you dress like that when you run."

"Short shorts offer the least resistance. Runners need freedom!" He grins from behind a bottle of electrolyte water. "Want to join me next time?"

"Unlikely."

"Your loss."

"You stink."

"Fresh as a daisy." He raises one arm to inhale the stench. "So? How was it?"

"The class? It was fine, I guess." But Juana's words ring in my ears, so I add, "Kind of fun, actually. And Georgy seems cool. Thanks for hooking me up."

"She's great, right? I'm meeting her for a drink tonight if you want to join us."

"I spent all day with her—can I pass?"

"Sure, of course. But I'm really glad you decided to do it. Maybe it'll help you get your mind off things." His tone makes us both squirm. I try to ignore it, creating a frowny face out of pistachio shells. "I just mean, this is going to be great. You're a creative soul, Evie. I've always thought so."

"Dad didn't," I blurt out. Shit, where did that come from?

"Come on, of course he did. He wanted you to have every opportunity."

"As long as it was a *math* opportunity."

"Touché." He chuckles. "Y'know, our dad was similar. Always hounding Vic and me to strive for greatness. It was exhausting, but he meant well. Some of us can't help turning into our parents."

I squirm in my seat, jaw tight. We've spent most of the week delicately avoiding too many Dad-versations. I think Luke feels guilty, barely having kept in touch with his own brother. He probably has zero idea what was going on before Dad died. The fact that my parents were arguing behind closed doors; that a bouncy, blond cheerleader had apparently wormed her way in. The reminder bubbles up in me, hot and vivid as it stretches to the surface.

"Did he tell you?" The question splatters against the walls before I can stop it.

"Vic? Did he tell me what?"

Luke seems genuinely curious, which comes as a relief. Mom won't talk to me about Bree, but maybe Dad's brother will. There's only one way to do this though, so I jump up from the table. "I'll be right back. Wait here."

Mom never gets home from work before six, which should give us enough time. I run to my bedroom to get my seventh-grade yearbook off the shelf and then sit beside Luke back at the table, flipping through glossy pages. I find Bree's portrait and thrust the book in his face.

"Do you know who that is?"

He squints down at the picture and back up at me. "Should I?"

"It's the girl my dad was sleeping with."

Electrolyte water spews from Luke's nostrils. "*What*?!"

"Did you know he was cheating on Mom?"

"With a *high schooler*? Vic mentioned . . . I mean, but he never said that she's—"

"*Was*," I clarify. "She graduated four years ago. Now she's the perky-fun-times receptionist at Dad's accounting firm. You seriously swear you didn't know?"

"I swear," he says and lifts a solemn palm. "Vic and I barely ever talked. I knew he and your mom were having trouble, but it's not like he went into detail. And I had no idea they told *you* about it."

"They didn't. I overheard Mom and a friend talking about Bree on the phone. As far as she's concerned, I don't know anything."

"God, Evie."

"That's not even the worst part."

"What do you mean?"

I take a deep breath, banishing the words from my soul. "Dad was going to move out."

"Wait, what?!" Luke gasps. "Rita didn't mention anything about—"

"Mom doesn't know. And you can't tell her." My eyes flit to the doorway. "I only found out that day. She sent me home from the hospital—she was still with the doctor, filling out paperwork. I drove here, and Dad's bags were sitting there on the bed. All his stuff in boxes. So I unpacked everything. I just *did* it. Like I was having an out-of-body experience or something. I honestly don't even know what I was doing. But, I mean, he was already dead, right? What was the point in letting Mom's heart break twice, you know?"

"Jesus."

"Don't be mad." I blink back tears. "She's barely hanging on as it is. Maybe it wasn't the smartest idea, but I was trying to do her a favor. You have to promise me you won't say anything."

He winces, one hand tight around his jaw. "Okay, alright. I won't tell her. But, holy shit, Evie. This is a big secret for a kid to be taking on."

Normally I'd want to deck him for calling me a kid, but right now I don't care. It doesn't even feel untrue. Acid tears well up in my eyes, sizzling at the rims. Torn between incandescent guilt for lying to mom; for having been betrayed by Dad. The sheer bullshit of having been put in this situation at the age of seventeen. Selfishly, though? There's a helium high, getting it off my chest.

"I'm so sorry, Ev. God, what a nightmare. I wish I'd been around more. Maybe I could have talked some sense into him." He pauses, shaking his head. "All I know is he wouldn't have wanted you caught up in the middle. He loves you so much."

Loved. Luke should have said *loved.*

"Thanks," I mumble, but his words can't dilute the cement mixture hardening in my veins. My eyes drift back to the yearbook, burned by the sight of Bree's face. Beautiful and young, fresh and blond. The polar opposite of graying, sagging Mom. I look in the index for her name and then flip to page twenty-eight where Bree is posing almost an island away from the other Key Club members. Middle rung of the cheeramid in the athletics section. On every page, people look normal, hamming it up between classes and on field trips. Good times. All laughs.

Happy people look so fucking obnoxious when you're depressed.

"Luke? Evie? Anyone home?"

The sound of Mom's voice sucks me out of my thoughts and back into the kitchen.

I tuck the yearbook into my lap. "Hey, Mom."

Her eyes land on me. "Evie! I thought you'd be at Juana's." She rests a grocery bag full of wine bottles at her feet, then sighs. "It's awfully quiet in here. Did I miss something?"

"No!" Luke and I yelp. Which doesn't look obvious at *all*.

Mom only nods. "Sweetie, you should see what Juana's up to. I've had *a day*, and I wouldn't want to bore the curl right out of your hair."

"I thought . . ." But I trail off pretty quickly. Because, much as I'm enjoying Luke's company, do I really *need* another evening of weird vegan food and science stories? The nightly ritual of watching Mom hide her pain behind a cloud of nicotine and Chardonnay? Because, I'm sorry, but I don't get why *she's* allowed to drown her sorrows, and meanwhile I'm over here having to be *productive*. Maybe I sound like I'm five, but IT'S NOT FAIR!

I consider diving through the closed window to get to Juana's house, but the yearbook is still in my lap, still burning a hole through my palms. I glare at Luke, and he jolts.

"Let's move this conversation into the living room, huh?" He scoops the bag of wine off the floor and pulls out a bottle of fancy-looking red. "Take a load off, Rita. I'll open this and meet you in there."

Before she goes, Mom comes toward me and plants a kiss on the top of my head. "How are you, honey? Did you like the first photography class?"

"Yeah," I say, but all I can think about is the yearbook in my lap, praying to God she can't see it. "Sorry you had a bad day."

"It's okay, hon. I'm glad you had a good one. That's all that matters."

She kisses my head again, sighing as she turns, sighing again as she kicks hideous Crocs off her notoriously aching feet. As soon as she's in the other room, Billy Joel starts up. Like an obedient dog, he's been waiting for her on the stereo all day.

Relief puffs out of me as I take the yearbook, stuffing it in one of the canvas bags we keep on a hook behind the door. My father's secret weighs a thousand pounds as I hoist it onto my shoulder.

"You swear you're not going to say anything?" I whisper, turning back to Luke.

The corkscrew in his hand stops twisting as he looks up at me. I watch him open his mouth as if he's going to argue, but, I mean, what? Does he think it'd be a *good* idea to come clean with Mom about her dead, cheating husband? Yeah, no. Definitely not. And he must realize it too, because his lips form a grim line as he nods. He turns back to the wine bottle without a word.

I stare at his sloped shoulders for a second too long before heading out of the room. Maybe I was wrong to let Luke in on the secret. Now he knows what his brother did—and what *I* did to hide it. And that helium feeling from earlier? It does what every party balloon inevitably does in the end. It deflates.

CHAPTER 6

I will admit that when Georgy said Friday's class would meet "on location," I was expecting something a little more glam than Bluebell Café, where I spend half my free time anyway because they have the best chocolate biscotti on the planet. The *best*. Today's assignment has all ten of us competing over promotional headshots of this comedian/activist, Nina Gold, who records her podcast in the back. Winner gets photo credit on the promo materials for her next live tour. Which is kind of exciting, not that I'll win.

We're roped off like VIPs, watching Nina toss her wild, gray curls. Hips swaying, posing like she's J. Lo at the Super Bowl and the rest of us are David LaChapelle (whom I finally googled, by the way, and he's wildly talented). I'm about fifteen shots in, messing around with bracketing so I can see how different light exposures look with the subject. Filling the frame, leaving space for movement, but a flash of blond in the distance traps my eye and suddenly only one thing matters.

Bree Hewitt. She's around the far side of Bluebell's L-shaped counter, digging around in her purse. A line of customers sigh on shifted hips behind her while she pulls out keys, concealer, breath mints. No wallet, which I presume is what she's looking for. She's mumbling the whole time, eyes rolling. Eventually she finds a crumpled bill, giggling apologetically as she hands it over. That lemon-zest laugh hits me like a rogue wave. I didn't think I'd remember it, but I do. Didn't think I'd remember *her*, but her yearbook photo has my synapses on overdrive.

A burst of memories shoot through me. The Wonder Woman PEZ dispenser beside Bree's computer. Her welcoming smile. It occurs to me now that her face sometimes paled when she saw me. It didn't register then, but I wonder if she went colorless out of guilt. *This is Bree, how may I help you? Would you like me to seduce your father?* God, gross. My eyes drill holes in her now, willing her to notice me. Daring her to see the hurt in my snarling lips.

"Everything okay?" Georgy asks. She stands right in front of me, blocking my view, arms crossed over a pink boiler jumpsuit. "Having trouble with your camera?"

"What? I'm fine. Just—" I try to peek over her shoulder, around her slim waist. "I thought I saw someone I know. Can I take a quick break?"

"Whatever you need." She flashes a sympathetic smile and moves on to help Sten.

I look back and Bree's finally settled up, shuffling around

the counter with her coffee and her muffin and her Dixie cup of wheatgrass or whatever and . . . and my stomach falls out of my body and splatters onto the wood floor. It doesn't register right away, so I break it down like I'm five years old and doing a *Highlights* magazine puzzle. *Can you spot the difference, Evie?* It's not her smile or her nose. Not those long, lean arms or cheerleader legs. Below her boobs and above her hips, round and planetary and bigger than a football serenading her waist.

Bree is pregnant.

Like, absolutely, 100 percent, mother-effing *pregnant*.

My broken-record brain snaps back to reality, and I quickly slink behind Violet and Declan. They're happily critiquing each other's setting choices, comparing thumbnails. A whole bunch of crap that means nothing in the face of Dad's receptionist girlfriend, five feet away from me and *bulging*. His mistress, *with child*. Because it is *his*, right? It has to be?

Suddenly, I'm tracking everything, taking mental measurements, wondering how far along Bree is and whether there's a non-nasty way to get a DNA sample from the wooden stirrer she just licked and threw in the garbage. Cameras click all around me, technical bird chirps, and I raise Luke's Nikon up to my eye, watching Bree through the viewfinder. I zoom in. Close enough to see the blueberries in her muffin, plump and juicy and dusted with sugar. Her face is still pretty, still warm and inviting, but her cheeks are appleier than I remember.

Now that I'm Nancy Drew, it occurs to me that her hair is

messier too, roots dark brown and clawing through her scalp. Did she stop dying it to protect the baby? Is that the kind of person she thinks she is—kind and self-sacrificing?

Click-click-click.

Come to think of it, she's not in her work clothes either. A gray hoodie and sweatpants have replaced her blouse and slacks. Did she quit when Dad died, unable to bear the sight of his empty corner office? Or maybe they fired her. I hope they fired her—even if I hate that I hope that.

Shock rises farther and farther up my spine with each click of the shutter, turning my pale cheeks pink, making my hands tremble. Like, the fact that I'm standing in a coffee shop.

Taking photographs.

Of my dad's mistress.

Who is pregnant.

PREGNANT.

Bree's finally done adding sugar and spice, and my heart starts racing, pointer finger furious against the shutter. Desperate for proof, afraid it's my last chance. "Afraid" isn't the right word, but I don't know what is. My brain has rugburn, and Bree's standing there smiling, letting some stranger touch her bump.

Click-click-click.

The stranger asks her a question, and the two of them giggle when Bree replies. Fucking *giggle*. Because apparently that's what Bree Hewitt is—hilarious. Funny enough to make my dad happy and whole. *She* did that. Not me, not Mom. *Her*.

It's revolting to imagine my parents with anyone but each other. Picturing Dad, the way he must've been lured into playing house and raising a new baby with this hot mess in spandex and flip-flops. Her toenails aren't even painted.

Click.

The stomach-groping stranger dashes off, and Bree's smile droops. I should look away, but how can I? She's right fricking there in maternity pants. As she heads for the door, she briefly looks toward our roped-off room and all the flash bulbs and music. I hold my breath and sink down, slowly slipping into a coma until Violet taps my shoulder.

"You good?"

I look up. Bree's gone.

"You seem kind of queasy."

I touch the hardened candle wax of my cheeks. I bet I couldn't smile at gunpoint. "I'm fine," I say, forcing a softer jaw. "Something weird happened with my camera, that's all. I think I fixed it."

"Want me to take a look?" Declan asks.

He reaches for it, and I snap back so fast that my elbow bangs against the wall. I wince as my funny bone wails. "I said it's fine. See?"

To prove it, I inch around their suspicion, closer to Nina Gold. Closer to the action, the here and now. I snap a few pictures of her laughing into her microphone. The curve of her wrist. A bounce in her curls. If I take enough pictures, focus hard enough on acing Georgy's assignment, maybe I'll get my heartbeat back and somehow forget the sight of Bree Hewitt's lonely smile. If I put my mind to it, it'll be like that glob of baby growing inside her doesn't even exist.

———

The news bursts out of me at the end of the day as I stand in Juana's doorway, unable to even wait to be ushered into her house, just spewing words like shards of shattered glass.

"Wait, what?" There's laughter coming from the kitchen as Juana steers me out onto the lawn, over near a tree we used to climb as kids. "Are you sure she was pregnant? Maybe it was a burrito baby."

"It was NOT a burrito baby. It was a *baby* baby. Someone touched it."

"What do you mean, *someone touched it?*"

"Like, a stranger," I say, arms flailing wildly. "Like, *Oh, hey, there's a baby in there! Can I feel it kick?*"

"She's far enough along that you can feel it *kick?*"

"No. God, I don't know!" I run my fingers through my hair, squeezing the base of my neck. "All I know is that I am *positive* Bree Hewitt is pregnant, and it is probably my dad's."

"Okay, okay. Let's stay calm." She's quiet for a minute, pinching her lower lip as she thinks. Her phone glows in the evening light as she whips it out, typing PREGNANCY STAGES into the search bar. A bunch of images pop up on the screen, a spattering of illustrated bumps. "Which one did she look like?"

I enlarge one of the charts. Brunette cartoons getting rounder and rounder. Like a row of Rockettes, only not. I point at the closest proximity and shudder. "Six months. Is that possible?"

Juana bites her lip. Under different circumstances, she would probably offer some Dean Winchester-y snark about how babies are made. Instead, she squeezes my shoulders. "What are you going to do?"

"What do you mean?" I mutter. "What are my choices?"

"I meant, what about your mom? Do you think you're going to tell her?"

"I can't," I say, without even thinking. There is no other answer.

"But, she knew he was cheating," Juana says delicately. "She could probably handle this, Ev."

I shake my head. Slowly at first, then faster. Mom won't take the high road and process this information like an adult. She'll dive deeper into her misery and add more bricks to the invisible wall building between us. I don't know if I can handle her being any farther away . . .

"It's my decision. Don't make me feel bad about it."

"Okay." Juana smiles. "Do you want to come and stay for dinner?"

My eyes sting as I look across the street at my house. "I better not."

"No problem." She pulls me into a hug, exhaling hard

enough for the both of us. "I'm so sorry, babe. You don't deserve any of this."

My tears tangle up with her hair. I could stay wrapped in this hug forever, under this tree that used to be Rapunzel's tower or a shipwrecked boat. To be crying over a scraped knee, rather than the fact that my life is in smithereens. I manage a sniffle so epic that it makes my nostrils burn, stopping the tears in their tracks. Can't go home looking a mess or I might raise Mom's suspicions. Or worse . . . maybe she won't even notice.

"I should go," I sigh. "Call me later?"

With the back of my hand, I wipe my cheeks, practicing a fake, friendly smile on Juana. She offers two very somber thumbs-up, good enough to motivate me back across the street. I'm expecting to find Mom caressing a wineglass in the kitchen, but she's standing in the hall when I open the door, stepping into a pair of black pumps.

"You're going out?"

"Oh, hey!" She sees me and smiles, bending to use her thumb as a shoehorn. "I left you a note in the kitchen. Luke's out with Georgy, and I decided I'm going to meet the girls from work. It could be a disaster, and who knows how long I'll make it without crying. But they wanted to help get my mind off things. Sharon convinced me. Do you think it's a terrible idea?"

Her words turn over in my brain as I attempt to metabolize

her straightened hair, her sequined, off-the-shoulder blouse. This dated, young-person top I've only ever seen in pre-Evie photographs. She looks into the entryway mirror to smear cranberry lipstick over her smile, and I picture Bree's pastel gloss. Full, plump lips painted pink; dove-white teeth. Mom's lips are thinner, although her teeth are as good. Better, probably.

"Everything okay, sweetie?" She hesitates, midpucker. "Did you have a good day?"

"Yeah," I say. "It was fine." But I've got that panicky, babysitter's-coming feeling in my gut. Not ready to be left alone in this house with no mom, no dad. "How long are you going to be?" I cringe at the desperation in my voice. "I mean, should I throw a rager while you're out or head to bed?"

Mom snorts. "Ha-ha. I'll be gone for one drink. Maybe two."

As if on cue, she staggers. Does she *need* another drink? Probably not, but I tell myself it's good that she's getting out. Moving on. Being social. That's why I'm not telling her about Dad, right? Or the baby? So that she can get on with her life? That *is* the reason, and yet I feel my pits dampening my shirt as I watch her turn back to the mirror. It kills me that Bree is allowed to traipse through town with coffee and muffins and a baby bumping out of her while Mom wanders through her own life like a shadow. I don't want her to cope like this but what am I supposed to do?

"Oh, honey." She frowns from behind a spritz of French rose perfume. "Don't look at me like that. You think it's too soon, don't you? It *is* soon. God, I don't know what I'm doing. I'm starting to feel so cooped up, and—"

"It's fine. It's weird, I mean? But it's fine. You didn't used to go out."

Her sympathy falters. "What, and now I'm not allowed to?"

"No!" I stammer. "I only meant, I got used to Dad being the one who did happy hour stuff. You always stayed—"

"Home?" she booms. Her exhale knocks into me. There's an argument brewing and all I can think is that if Dad were here, he'd intervene and tell us both to take a step back. Maybe Mom's thinking the same thing, because she leans against the wall, shoulders heavy. "You're right. Daddy always had somewhere to be. He made plans, and I chose to stay home with you. But you're practically a grown-up now. Maybe it's time I . . ."

I search her eyes for the end of her sentence, but she only shakes her head.

Tell her, my gut whispers. Her heart is on her sleeve, and she's maybe even progressing, thinking it's finally Her Time. What if Juana was right, that Mom *can* handle it? But I barely get as far as opening my mouth when her cheeks suddenly sag, eyes dull. A child lost in the park.

"I spent an hour thinking about Daddy's dry cleaning, today. Two of his suits never got picked up."

"Oh—what? Don't they donate that stuff? I mean, if the owner doesn't . . ."

She shrugs. "I don't know."

It's so out of the blue, my heart lurches toward my throat. Cocktail tops and French perfume can't change the fact that she misses him. A man who was about to leave her. Scratch that, the man she *didn't know* had basically left already.

"Look at your face." Mom pauses, brow furrowing. "I didn't mean to fill your head with my morbid thoughts. I'm sorry, sweetie."

"It's fine." I bite my lip, swallowing down the rest of my words.

"Honestly, the strangest thoughts pop into my head lately. I found one of his socks in my underwear drawer, and I put it back in with his things before it even occurred to me that I didn't need to. What am I going to do with all those drawers full of clothes? More for Goodwill, I guess."

I blink, not sure whether to laugh or cry about my sock restocking abilities. The fact that I didn't raise any suspicion. That I'm *that good* at covering someone's lies.

"All I'm trying to get at, is . . . it's okay," she says softly. "Whatever you're feeling. It's normal. You can talk to me about anything. You know that, right?"

My heart hammers in my chest. Talk to her, Evie. *Tell her.* You're both grieving and destroyed. Go through this *together* while she's offering you the chance. Again, I open my mouth to speak.

Words pixelate

on my tongue

until they are

unrecognizable.

Mom's phone buzzes and I jolt. She giggles, sending a quick text. It isn't until she's walked past me and out onto the driveway that I realize we were maybe almost bonding. Now that it's over, I feel even emptier than I already did. Like I should have bottled this moment or drawn it out a little longer.

"There are chicken nuggets in the freezer," she says, blowing me a kiss: "Don't stay up too late."

Then she skitters down the gravel walkway and into this bright-blue Mustang convertible with the top down. Sharon is one of the younger dental hygienists and a major party girl, so I'm sure they'll be out all night. Picturing Mom at a bar— tequila shots and pick-up lines—makes me cringe, but I wonder if it isn't inevitable. Whether or not dad died, he was going to leave her. One way or another, my mom was going to have to move on with her life.

The car speeds off, and I stay standing there, feeling like Mom. Jilted and alone. Wondering how many nights ended like this, for her.

Chapter 7

We're all sitting in our cozy seats, staring at the projector on Monday morning. Me, cringing because it's *my* rushed, blurry photographs of Nina Gold on the screen. Pictures I couldn't put any real effort into because I was too distracted by the real-life presence of *my dad's pregnant girlfriend* in the café. Not that my photos would have been that good anyway. After one week at NMPI, it's not like I've mastered my technique.

Which is probably why Ada says, "They sort of look a bit . . . basic."

Basic. Maybe she's right, but screw Ada and her forthright German-ness, telling me that my images feel rushed and out of focus; spitting my soul onto the ground like a used piece of gum. I swear to God, even my bones blush.

"Point taken, Ada," I say, mostly to shut her up. "I suck."

"You don't suck!" Violet swats her arm across the room at me, almost laughing. "You're so self-deprecating. Personally, I really like the composition and shadows on that one. If it were in focus, I think Nina Gold would absolutely love it—look how fierce she looks. And don't forget about the fact that you were having technical difficulties with your camera, right?"

The technical difficulty of having seen my dad's knocked-up girlfriend. "Oh. Right. That." I nod, flashing her a weak smile.

"Well, I'm sorry about the camera troubles." Georgy exits my folder and crosses her arms. "The pictures you managed to shoot are okay but, to be honest, I think you're capable of pushing yourself a lot further. They lack depth because you didn't connect with the subject. There's no emotional pull. Think about Henri's photos—the way he seemed to turn Nina's movement into a love song."

Heads swivel toward Henri, who nods demurely. I try not to roll my eyes, sulking over the fact that he's a genius and I'm pitiful. Wondering if they'd still be dissing my "emotional involvement" if I showed them the pictures of Bree. Invasive and quiet. Stories in her pale eyes. If I knew anything about photography, I might almost think there was something *there*. But I don't. And I'm probably wrong anyway.

We move on to another photographer, and I forget about Bree for a while. I let myself get into it, adding to the commentary on Ed's artful approach. The way he chose not to shoot Nina's face, instead delineating her clutter. A tangle of cables, metal mic stands reaching out like spider legs. I still think Ed's a dick, but I like his work.

After class, Declan's pulling his messenger bag over an Idaho? No, YOU Da Ho T-shirt when he bumps my elbow. "Hey, you okay? Got kind of pissy there when Ada was giving you shit."

"I didn't get pissy!" I finish packing my camera in its fabric sleeve and then roll my eyes. "Okay, fine. I got pissy. It's not like I thought I was going to win the assignment, I just wanted to fail a little more gracefully."

"I think you're graceful." His bangs drift to the side as he smiles.

"Yeah, right." Flutters squeeze my insides to the point of strangulation, but I shrug them off. "I just want to do better in this class before she prints me a You Lack Vision T-shirt."

"That actually sounds like an awesome shirt." He ducks back when I glare at him. "Besides, she doesn't think you lack vision. She thinks your vision is shittier than Henri's."

A snort of surprise rushes out of me as I glance at Henri, deep in conversation with Ed and Ada, the three of them all frowns and introspection.

"He's a true genius," I mutter. "They broke the mold when they made Henri."

"I wouldn't take it personally. He hates all of us. I even heard him trashing Stieglitz."

I wince uncertainly. "Who?"

"Alfred Stieglitz? Really?"

"Really."

Declan grips his skull all melodramatically. "He was only one of the most brilliant and instrumental photographers in the history of the world. He's probably my favorite photographer ever."

"I thought David LaChapelle was your favorite."

"You remember me talking about LaChapelle?"

My cheeks roast. "I mean, it's a photography class, Declan. I obviously pay attention to those kinds of references."

Nice cover, dork.

Declan tugs at his bag strap, squeezing it tight across his pecs. "Hey, so what else do you do, besides this class?"

I shake my head.

"No?" he smirks. "That's it? You just, like, do *no*?"

"For the love of—" I try to squeeze back a laugh, but it escapes anyway. "Obviously I do other stuff."

"Okay, good. Because otherwise that would have been super weird."

A laugh fizzles out of me, morphing into a groan. Do I really have to tell this strange and beautiful boy that my Dad *died* three weeks ago? That I'm devastated and depressed, and my nights entail awkward dinners with a pushy, simultaneously distant more-than-social drinker with a penchant for Billy Joel? Or I can just be like:

"My life's pretty boring. I watch a lot of TV with my best friend. We have *Supernatural* marathons."

"Demon hunting." Declan nods knowingly. "I knew you

were an old soul. I'm more of a *Stranger Things* guy, but I can respect the classics."

"Muchas gracias."

We're both ready to go, so Declan extends his palm toward the door and the two of us head down the long corridor, past all this weird religious artwork that has nothing to do with NMPI but everything to do with the monastery it's housed in. Lots of weeping priests and ominous cathedrals. Ten out of ten on the nightmare scale.

"Did you hear Georgy talking about happy hour at El Farol on Friday?" Declan asks, squinting into the sun when we push through the doors. "Think you're going to go?"

"What, and watch our photo class get hammered on margaritas while I awkwardly sip Diet Cokes?" I pause to tap my chin. "Lemme think . . . uh, no. How 'bout you?"

"I don't have a fake ID. Even if I do look devilishly mature."

"Yeah, ancient." My eyes flit sideways. "Hey, how come you always wear those T-shirts? With the state mottos?"

"What, these?" He stretches the hem of his shirt, and it conforms to the contours of his chest. "My parents have been giving me state T-shirts for years. I think it started with a City of Angels one from a work trip to California. They travel a lot. I think the T-shirts sorta assuage their parental guilt. But, like, random friends keep adding to the collection. You know how people notice you with something and they instantly assume you collect it? Now it's like, my *thing*."

"Ah," I say, knowingly. "M&Ms."

One of Declan's eyebrows curves like a fish jumping out of the water. "That is honestly not the response I was expecting. But, I like it. M&Ms to you too."

"No!" Warmth bubbles through me as I shake my head. "I mean, M&Ms are *my* thing. One time, a million years ago, as a back-to-school gift, my dad gave me a notebook with M&Ms printed all over it. After that, it was like, *Oh, you know Evie, she's obsessed with M&Ms!* I've got dispensers, pajamas, Christmas lights. So, yeah, it's a thing. I get it."

"I bet the pajamas are really cute."

My face goes up in flames, and Declan coughs into his elbow.

"No, I mean. Sorry," he sputters. "That was so weird and creepy. I honestly meant I bet they're very nice pajamas. Not that pajamas are my *thing*, like the T-shirts. But who doesn't like pajamas? I sleep in my boxers—holy shit, I did *not* just say that."

His cheeks turn cotton-candy pink, and it's actually kind of nice. Not to watch him suffer, but like, to see that I'm not the only person who gets life-alteringly embarrassed from time to time.

"It's okay. Really," I smile. "And you're right. My pajamas are very soft. The M&Ms are ebullient."

He nods impressively. "Ten points for *ebullient*."

I reach for my car keys, and Declan scans the parking lot.

Over in the visitors' section, there's this idling, lime-green Lincoln covered in a generous layer of Santa Fe dust. An old woman with an elegantly smooth, silver helmet of hair starts waving eagerly from the passenger seat when she spots us.

"Fan club?"

"My grandparents." Declan winces as if the words are an unfortunate medical condition.

"They look excited to see you."

"Oh, they are."

"Like, really fucking excited. Are you returning from war?"

He chuckles. "So it would seem."

"I should get going. I don't want to interfere with this long-awaited reunion."

"No, wait." He scrunches his nose. "Do you want to hang with us?"

"What?" My eyes bulge. "Now?"

"Please?" His voice inches up.

"Oh. Um . . ."

Really, though? Is he really *begging* to hang out with me? That's not a thing. At least, it's never been a thing—not with me, not *for* me. But he smiles like it's normal. Well, awkward and nerve-racking, but normal-esque.

"It could be fun," he says. More composed but still eager. "Baba and Jiji play a mean game of pinochle."

"Baba and Jiji? Is that—"

"Japanese. It's what I call them. I'm half-Japanese."

"Oh, okay. I was sort of wondering. I mean, kind of. Not that I was thinking about you. It—thinking about *it*. But, I mean, yeah. I was leaning toward Japanese."

"Bet you can't guess the other half," he says, eyes twinkling, throwing me a life raft, maybe.

"Oh, I suck at guessing." Still, I take a minute to let myself look at him. Those sepia-brown eyes and honey lips. Knowing that I can look at him without it being weird. That this is just, like, for research purposes. The longer I look, the more I notice something else about him. A gingerness to his freckles. "Scottish? Irish?"

"Ah, to be sure!" His Lucky Charms accent is uncanny.

"Thought so." I grin.

"Declan!" His grandmother shouts from the passenger seat and we both jolt. "Over here!"

"Oh God." Declan mutters to himself as he waves back, then points at my elbow. Like, asking permission to touch it. I'm so surprised that I nod, and his arm weaves through mine, skin soft and warm as he guides me over to their car. "Don't worry," he whispers. "This will be painless. I just want them to think I have friends."

We stop by the window and the grandmother leans out, hazel eyes brightening. "Who's this?"

"Baba, this is Evie Parker."

"So nice to meet you," says Baba.

Jiji waves and says something in Japanese.

Declan replies, also in Japanese. Which is incredibly hot.

"Declan showed us the photographs he took of you in class," Baba says. "So beautiful."

"What? Oh." I tuck my hair behind my ears. "I mean. He's the one who took the pictures. Your grandson's a good photographer."

"So modest," she adds, smiling at Jiji. He winks.

Kill me now.

For the tiniest blip of a second, Declan squeezes my arm. Heat courses through me, reassuring me until he takes his hand away. I wobble and go cold again, taking a step back.

"It was nice to meet you, Mr. and Mrs. Maeda. Assuming that's your name. I don't even know."

"It is." Baba chuckles. "And it is a pleasure to meet you too."

Jiji smiles but says nothing.

I turn to Declan, hoping my cheeks aren't as pink as they feel.

The way he smiles at me though, head tilted down, I think, *Yeah, definitely magenta.*

The grandparents are clearly *desperate* to hijack Declan for an evening of pinochle, but we stand on the sidewalk for a second longer, hands in pockets, nerves pulsing under skin. I don't know why, but it's like there's this glimmer of curiosity on his face. I can't figure it out, but I'd like to.

"Hey, do you want to do something this weekend?"

Wait, what? Was that *my* voice?

Declan raises an eyebrow. "Really?"

"I mean, I know you've probably got pinochle, but—"

"I may have overhyped pinochle a tiny bit."

"I thought it sounded too good to be true."

I grin.

He grins.

It's a grin fest.

"That'd be cool," he finally says, then reaches for the car door handle. "So . . . later this week? Friday night?"

"Yeah, I guess. Sure."

"Okay, then. Friday night. But I'll still see you tomorrow in class. Pinhole cameras? Don't forget your oatmeal box."

"Right. Pinholes and oatmeal."

Awkward waving ensues. Declan turns toward the car, and I watch the back door creak as it swings shut behind him. Baba starts fussing over him immediately. Smoothing his hair, handing him a nutritious snack and bottled water as the Lincoln rolls slowly out of the parking lot. I, however, continue to stand there reeling for an extra couple of seconds. Because, yeah. I *actually* asked a cute guy to hang out. With me. And he said *yes*. I kind of can't believe myself right now—this adrenaline-fueled, nothing-to-lose feeling.

If a bolder me is the silver lining to my grief, I guess maybe I'll take it.

CHAPTER 8

The next night, we have Luke's farewell dinner. I guess his duffel bag wasn't filled with short shorts after all. I mean, he's been crashing with us for over two weeks, so it doesn't surprise me that the birds need him back in Alaska. Birds and the Parker brothers—talk about sibling similarities. But more than Luke's love of fowl and his face that's practically Dad's, I'm actually going to miss *him*. Having someone around here to talk to. It's kind of hard to muster a perky grin while a new scar is currently forming over my heart. Even though we're at Tomasita's, which is supposed to be my Happy Place. Best New Mexican restaurant in town; the place my parents would take me whenever I aced a test or Dad got a promotion at work. Back in the good ol' days, when there was shit worth celebrating. I honestly hope I never come here again.

"To Luke," Mom says, raising her sangria.

"To Uncle Luke," I say.

"Yeah, to the uncle I never had." Juana raises her lemonade with a cheesy grin. Because of course I invited her. Someone's got to diffuse the melancholy.

"I hate to leave you gals." Luke leans back in his chair, swigging light beer. "Black-headed grosbeaks aren't nearly as sarcastic as you, Evelyn."

"And nobody in Santa Fe looks quite as ridiculous in sweat-bands as you, Luke. Your absence will be a real loss for the community."

"Oh, Evie, stop!" Mom giggles.

That buoyant giggle. I'll miss it when it leaves along with Luke.

We all pause to *mmm* and *aah* as our waitress doles out sizzling hot cast-iron skillets of chile rellenos, stuffed sopapillas, and chalupas. Luke takes a fiery, cheesy bite and launches into yet another nerd-specific anecdote. Polar ice caps this time.

"Most people don't even *realize*," he says, wiping red chile off his chin, "but Earth's average surface temperature has risen nearly one entire degree Celsius over the past hundred years. And it's only getting worse."

His empassioned rage reminds me of my science teacher, Mrs. Krynsky, when we got this exact same lecture last year. I mean, and it *is* devastating. But, like, what is global warming in the face of my ghost-town heart? The way I can feel it hardening as I admit to myself what Luke's departure really means.

For nearly two weeks, he's been the buffer between Mom and me. Picking up where Dad left off, getting us both to chill. Having her brother-in-law here padded her sanity, I think. It still scares me that she drinks a small vineyard each night—that she'd rather do that than open up—but she's laughed more in Luke's presence. Cried less. Now he's leaving and I have a bad feeling her bar-hopping nights with Sharon are going to be fruitful and multiply.

"Pssst. Sam Winchester," Juana sing-songs accusatorily in my ear. "You're doing it again. What are you thinking about?"

"Huh?" I glance over at her and then stuff my face with Spanish rice. "I'm listening to Luke. Rising sea levels are a *serious* issue."

"Oh, totally." She mimics my so-called "Sam Winchester" contemplation, and I kick her shin under the table.

Once Luke has made it abysmally clear that the Arctic is well and truly fucked, he grabs a sopapilla and turns it into a Pollock painting with the honey bottle. "God, this food is delicious. I want to fill my suitcase with carne adovada. I want to swim laps in a bath of it."

"That sounds painful," I say.

JJ snorts.

Mom quickly motions to the waitress for another drink, then turns to me. "Evie, honey, tell us more about the photography class. You must be getting a feel for it by now."

"Oh." I shrug. "Yeah, I guess."

"You *guess*?" Her nostrils do this mini-flare thing that I'm sure only I can see. "Uncle Luke paid for you to be in that class. The least you could do is—"

"It's alright, Rita. She doesn't have to."

"Am I the only one who wants to hear about it?" she slurs too loud. "Fine. Never mind."

I glare at her, hard. On the verge of reminding her that, just because Dad's gone, doesn't mean she has to nag me twice as hard. Back in the old days, they'd at least take turns. Well, till recently. Actually, he was gone more and more—off with Bree, presumably. Was Mom pulling double duty for longer than I realized?

I pull back a little, swallowing my eye roll. "Okay, well, I guess we're learning about composition and symmetry, balancing the subject . . ."

Words come out of my mouth, but my brain gets off at a different elevator stop. Talking about depth of field is all I can do to keep my lip from trembling. I'm almost mad at myself—that I could miss his ever-pestering ways. But even the annoying thoughts have a way of worming their way back into good ones. The memory of Dad's lemon pancakes on Saturday mornings; Maurice Sendak stories at bedtime, read aloud until the pages fell out. Bear hugs. Bird books. Yes, we fought. Yes, he wanted me to be a math genius. Yes, he let Bree seduce him and nearly left us for her.

Thinking about it makes me want to puke, but instead I say, "I made a pinhole camera."

Mom looks impressed as she slurps sangria.

"Oh, yeah, I think I made one of those out of a shoebox once," Luke says. The fond memory elicits a classic Parker grin. "You poke a hole to let in the light at one end, then use photographic paper as film, right? Expose it for a couple minutes?"

"Basically."

"What about the people?" Mom asks. "You said Valerie was nice. Anyone else?"

"Violet," I correct.

"She's practically famous," Juana adds. "She has like two million followers."

"*Two million!*" Mom widens her eyes at Luke, and they feign gasps.

"Stop it." I snort. "She's not like that. She's actually really cool. And you would love Peter and Sten. They're completely adorable, even if they're too old to be my friends. Basically, so is everyone. Not that they aren't nice. Well, except Henri, he's kind of a dick. Actually, Ed's pretty much of a dick too. But there's also—" I pause, choking down my words. Because why on earth would I mention Declan Maeda's sense of humor or garage-band cuteness to my *mother*? I clear my throat. "Suze is fun. But, again, no spring chicken. She's like the Aunt May of the group—back when they cast actual old people to play May Parker."

Everyone laughs, even though I'm pretty sure Mom never watched a single Spider-Man movie.

After dinner, she and Luke move to the bar to finish their drinks while JJ and I drift outside out of boredom. We push through a sea of wait-listed diners and lean against the stucco wall, watching a couple of kids play rock paper scissors.

"Is your class really full of old people?" Juana asks, shifting her boobs in a striped tube top. "I thought it was going to be more college-y, for some reason."

"Spring Break Cancun: Art Class Edition?"

"Yeah," she laughs. "Something like that. You at least do Jell-O shots off your lens caps, right?"

"Oh, definitely. And we wear bikinis during critique."

"Phew."

I grab my phone out of my pocket and go into NMPI's app, where each class is supposed to upload our best images. At this point, there are photos of basically everyone, which makes it easier to describe Sten and Peter and their horse ranch in Tesuque; Ed's misogynistic overtones; the way Beth obsesses over germs. Juana's nodding, scrolling, mostly commenting on pointless stuff like the local Santa Fe landmarks. Until she sees Declan with his sun-dappled, angular features and that glint of auburn in his hair. She whistles.

"Ugh, would you stop?" I groan.

"Bitch, when you were comparing that lady to Aunt May, you did *not* tell me there was a stone-cold Peter Parker in your class. How old is he?"

"Declan? I don't know." I have to cover my cheeks with my

hands because I'm blushing like what-the-fuck, and it only gets worse the harder Juana stares at me. "Like eighteen? He's going to NYU in the fall."

"Why didn't you tell me about him?!" she shrieks.

The rock-paper-scissors kids' parents come and usher their innocent children away. I put an arm around JJ's shoulder and tug her down the wall a bit.

"Because there's nothing to tell," I say. Which is a lie. And I can't believe I haven't told her I made plans with him but . . . I don't want to make a big deal out of it. "Besides, you've been too busy partying. Wrapped around Melanie's little finger again. I barely see you."

"Says the girl in an intensive photography program." Juana wags a finger at me. "And I'm not wrapped around anyone's *any*thing. It's different with Mel this time. I'm serious. And I know I've been busy, but it's summer! Wild oats have to be sewn and whatnot. We can't all—"

Her spine goes rigid as she zips her lips.

We can't all be in mourning.

Is that what she was going to say? Or, I don't know, maybe her words aren't sledgehammers at all. Maybe it's all in my head. I take a shaky breath that ends in a sob, and Juana puts her warm arms around me. She strokes my shoulder blades in a way that seems to melt away my frustration. It's nice but weird, this newly developed maternal instinct of hers. I'm used to potty mouth Juana who burps in my face. The girl who once had sex in a bathroom stall of the very restaurant we are currently patronizing. But this works too.

"You okay?" she asks.

"I'm fine. Ish."

"Want to talk about it?"

"Not really."

She squeezes my hand and then slowly starts to grin—the maniacal kind that usually ends in a *muah-hah-hah* and mustache-stroke. "So, are you planning to tap that hot little photography-expert ass?"

"What?" My face flushes a blustering hellmouth red. "You know you sound ridiculous, right?"

"You like him." She pulls me close, dipping me back, cha-cha-ing with my rag doll body. *"You-oo-oo like him!"* she says, over and over again like it's "nanny nanny boo boo" and we're five-year-olds.

"I could have been friends with anyone," I mutter, flopping around in her arms. "Could have grown up anywhere. And yet the universe stuck me with you."

"You probably fucked up really bad in a past life. Stole from orphans or protested against abortion clinics or something." She twirls me back over to the wall, leaving me breathless and dizzy. "Anyway, stop changing the subject. Tell me about this *Declan*. What kind of name is that, anyway? I don't trust a name you can't rhyme. Like, take yours: Evie, bevy, heavy."

"Call me 'heavy' again and I'll deck you," I say, blowing her a kiss.

"Heavy as in deep. A la ve, touchy." She blows a kiss back. "Now do me."

"Juana, sauna, Madonna. Banana, but only if you say it fancy."

She shrieks with laughter, scaring away tourists with their chile-filled bellies. "Stop distracting me, Evie Parker. If you don't dish about this Declan-shmecklin guy soon, I'm going to—" She pauses, eyes zeroing in on a very, extremely old woman with curly purple hair sitting in a wheelchair about twenty feet away. "I'm gonna give abuelita over there a lap dance and the hottest, wettest French kiss of her entire life."

I burst out laughing and actually have to lunge forward to grab Juana's arm. In two strides, she's gotten close enough that the lady's grandkids are literally cowering behind her, maybe thinking Juana has a white van around the corner or something. The granny, luckily, is still totally oblivious to the whole thing.

"*Okay!*" I shriek. "I will tell you anything, as long as you don't defile any abuelas, okay?"

Juana shrugs, and I wonder if she would have done it. God, I hope not. We head across the gravelly parking lot toward my dinged-up silver Subaru and hoist ourselves onto the hood.

"Don't go freaking out," I warn, "but Declan and I are supposed to hang out this weekend."

Her jaw falls off her face and crashes into oncoming traffic. "Shut. Up."

"Don't make a big deal out of it. I'm not."

"But why? Don't you deserve a cinnamon roll after everything you've been through?"

I shrug, searching my brain for an answer she'll understand. "He's from Brooklyn. What's the point? Even if we did hook up, he's only going to leave at the end of the summer."

"Yeah, but—" She pauses for an almost R-rated eyebrow wiggle. "Think about what you two could do until then."

She puts her arm around my shoulder, tugging me closer so she can dig her chin into my collarbone. I can't *not* roar with laughter. It's a highly sensitive spot that, for some reason, always makes me have to pee. Ever since I told Juana during a game of Truth or Dare in fourth grade, she's used it against me.

"Stop it!" I shriek, tears welling up in my eyes. I'm still laughing, trying not to pee, when she finally backs off. "Jesus, JJ. You are cruel."

"Gotta be cruel to be kind." She bats her fake lashes. "So, that's it then? You're going to stay boringly platonic with your freckle-faced stallion because he's got a plane ticket for August?"

"Pretty much. Now, can we drop it?"

She tugs on her lip again. Asking Juana to drop the topic of crushes would be like asking Einstein to stop theorizing about relativity. Time goes by, and we watch the sun as it sets beyond some abandoned trains outside the old station. The light is a

silky hot pink, slowly fading into topaz. I look back over at JJ
and she's full-on staring at me.

"What?" I roll my eyes.

"I'm not buying it."

"You need another reason? Fine. Nothing is ever going to
happen with Declan because I doubt he's interested in fat girls."

Juana winces, hands forming a T. "Time out. Nobody calls
mi hermanita fat, not even you. You aren't fat. You're average—
and I mean that in the most above-average way possible."

"*You're not fat, Evie, you're beautiful*," I whine.

"Shut up, I didn't say that." She rolls her eyes. "Hips and
a hot rack are normal, some might even say sought-after,
attributes."

I laugh. "Could you not, with my rack?"

"Okay, but could you not, with the fat-shaming?"

"Okay, fine."

"Thank you."

I roll my eyes. Juana rolls hers.

Maybe I'm not *fat*, but I'm not thin either, and there's a lot of
middle ground. We've had this conversation a million times.
People that look like Juana don't understand. The way my
boobs would literally spill onto the sidewalk if I tried to walk
around in a tube top like the one she's wearing; how I can't *not*
think about my arms when I wave or the feel of my thighs as I
walk. My endless search for high-rise jeans to rein in my muffin top.

And just like that, I'm on the verge of tears. Because . . . jeans. I mean, no. I'm not literally crying over a pair of pants, but I threw my clothes away that night. In a heap of exhaustion, home from the hospital, determined to banish all reminders of what happened. If I'd known the mere mention of jeans would make me misty, I would have kept the best pair I had.

"Babe? Are you okay?"

"I'm fine." I try to laugh it off, but it comes out raw and hollow and heartbroken. "I think I'm too sad."

Juana nods, waiting for more.

"I miss him, but I don't get why he wanted to leave us. Bree's wandering around pregnant with his baby, and Mom is a scorching hot mess—which is partly my fault, because she doesn't *know* what he did to her. She's pushing me away, I'm pushing her away, we're both fucked beyond repair. It all ginormously sucks, and whether or not Declan's cute honestly doesn't matter. I don't want a crush. Look what that shit did for my dad? The way it ruined us. I'd rather be like this for a while longer. Feel my fucking feels and find a nonromantic way of channeling it. Like photography. Or luge lessons."

"Wait, can't you die in a luge?"

"You know what I mean."

"Barely. But don't go luging. Promise me."

"Fine. And promise *me* you won't push the Declan thing."

She crosses her heart with acrylic nails. "Consider it dropped."

"Thank you."

"I'll just help you focus on hobbies." She takes a chunk of my hair, tugging it playfully. "What's the polar opposite of luge—gardening? We'll get floppy hats and plant tomatoes and drink iced tea in the shade."

"Sounds perfect. And take up macramé."

"Macramé for the win."

I laugh, and Juana kisses my forehead.

The restaurant door swings open, and Mom comes stumbling out with Luke beside her. She's already got a cigarette in her hand, and she wastes no time lighting it, even though there are small children around, reaping the penalties of her craving. She looks tipsy, but she looks peaceful too. Before I can help it, I get a prickly feeling in my chest, seeing the two of them together. Him a little taller, her leaning comfortably against his arm. The way their words seem to fit together, flowing easily into laughter. There's nothing between them, I know. But it still *looks* like my parents, a million years ago. Back when they were in love.

Back when they had everything they needed to be happy.

CHAPTER 9

Because we're only "hanging out" and not on a "real date," I decide to invite Declan to my house on Friday night. Mom's with Sharon, as usual, and it seems way less formal than picking somewhere with menus and waiters and awkward eating—y'know, like a restaurant.

The downside, though? In the days since Luke's departure, my house has turned back into a dump. Something has to be done, and for twenty solid minutes, I flit around the house like Cinderella with a Febreze bottle, conquering cigarette smoke as I gather tissues and junk mail for the trash. I intentionally *don't* put on the SUPERNATURALLY SMOOCHY PLAYLIST that JJ and I made, instead opting for Beirut. Trumpets and haunting harmonies follow me into the kitchen, where I make a pitcher of ginger iced tea to calm my nerves. JJ must psychically sense my tension though, because my phone starts blowing up as I'm pouring myself a glass.

Is he there yet?

Did you brush your teeth and
moisturize?

Don't forget supernaturally
smoochy smooch!!

I roll my eyes at my phone and then look out the window,
surprised that Juana isn't in her living room with a pair of
binoculars. Her car's not in the driveway, so she's probably
off somewhere with Melanie. For a second, my gaze weakens.
Somehow I always pictured Dad using his birding binocs to
spy on me coming home from a date—having that awkward
what-are-your-intentions-with-my-only-daughter conversation
with some sweat-drenched dude.

Reason #863 why I miss my dad: He'll never walk me down
the aisle.

I clear my throat to snap out of it, cramming the tears back
into their cellar. This is not a date. Declan is not my future husband. And he does not need to see me crying when I answer
the front door. Deep breath, Evie.

Not yet. Now fuck off and
don't text again.

Love you too! 😘

Minutes tick by, and I remind my jittery-ass self that Declan wants a break from his grandparents as badly as I want a break from everything else. It is a simple, mutually beneficial hang. We're friends. Barely even acquaintances. I consider changing into a dress, but that seems too obvious, so I put on the jeggings Mom bought me for my birthday and a loose top with stripes on it. Then I freak out and don't want to seem like I'm trying too hard, so I change back into the same ripped jeans and white T-shirt I wore all day at NMPI. The shirt's sweaty, kind of? But fine. It's fine. It'll be fine.

Right on time, my not-a-date rings the doorbell, and I almost throw up on his face when I fling open the door.

"Hey," I say, winded.

"Hey," Declan says, normal.

I step aside to let him in, sucking my gut to my spine, bemoaning my ratty clothes when he's standing here in a blue plaid shirt unbuttoned over a Maryland: More Crabs than Bangkok T-shirt. If I'd known he was going to change—crap. His hair's damp too. Double crap.

"Thanks for the invite. Look, dinner and a movie." He hands me a DVD of *Rear Window* and a bag of gummy worms. "I realize I went out on a limb with something as primitive as a DVD, but they had it at the library. We could probably stream it otherwise."

"Believe it or not, you have stepped into the past, technologically speaking. DVDs are all the rage around here."

"Phew."

I point him toward the living room and head into the kitchen for two iced teas, reminding myself about *Rear Window* while I pour. It's the Hitchcock flick he mentioned on the first day of class. I examine the DVD cover, the stunning damsel in pearls and a sheer black dress. If Declan's into *that* type of girl, then this is definitely not a date. Which is fine. I'm fine with that.

I walk back into the living room and find Declan staring at a family portrait: a hiking trip when I was about ten. It's a cute enough picture—Mom and Dad smiling despite my death glare—but I'm suddenly sweating, desperate not to tell him I lost my dad or ruin the one normal thing I've got going.

"A*dor*able," he jokes, mimicking my feisty expression. "I bet you got in trouble a lot as a kid."

"What?" I feign a gasp. "Why would you say that?! I was an angel. I'm sticking my tongue out because I got a blister on that particular hike, and I didn't want to walk anymore. I'm pretty sure I got a piggyback ride the rest of the way up the mountain."

"Nice."

"When I *did* get in trouble, my dad used to keep this fish-bowl full of folded-up paper with different punishments on them. I got to choose. They'd say stuff like 'no TV for a week,' or 'clean the toilets,' or 'make grandma's lasagna recipe from scratch.' Total randomness."

"Like fortune cookies! I like that."

I shift awkwardly and gaze back at the photograph, remembering how Dad offered to carry me. The way he managed to tell jokes the whole way up the ravine, despite huffing and puffing. Because, I mean, I was ten. And I wasn't particularly delicate.

"You guys look happy," Declan says thoughtfully.

And we were, once.

I turn my back to the photo. "So, how are you liking Santa Fe? You've been here before, right? Visiting your grandparents?"

"Yeah, I love it here. Way more laid-back than grimy, non-stop New York. It's been great for my grandparents too. They moved here when I was a kid because of Jiji's cancer."

"Oh." My head ducks back. "I'm so sorry."

"No, it's cool. He's, like, totally fine now. Says the altitude cured him."

"Ah." I smile sagely. "Your grandparents are New Age."

"Yeah, but Jiji's legit. Started a website and everything. The Holistic Zone dot org? Heard of it?"

"The Holistic Zone?"

"Dot org," he clarifies.

"Oh, right." I nod. "It's my home page."

Declan laughs into the air. "Hey, it gets more traffic than you'd think."

"I bet. Are you their tech guy? In exchange for room and board?"

"I dabble in web design," he says, a hint of espionage in his voice. He takes a big gulp of iced tea and offers a refreshed *aahhh*. "Mostly, I spend summers here for company. My parents travel a lot. Literally, I haven't seen them in six weeks. They couldn't even make my high school graduation."

"Are you serious? Why?"

"They're filmmakers," he says. "Always off shooting."

"Sorry."

He shrugs and I shrug, and we both rock back and forth on our heels.

"You like Beirut?" he asks after a minute.

"I mean, I put it on, so . . ."

"Right. Duh. You know Zach Condon is from—"

"Santa Fe?" I cut in. "Of course I do. We New Mexicans tend to feel extreme pride for our local celebrities. Demi Lovato was born in Albuquerque. Georgia O'Keeffe lived in Abiquiú *and* Santa Fe. Tom Ford grew up here . . ."

"Ooh, Tom Ford? Fancy," He wiggles his eyebrows.

"You actually know who that is?"

"My mom used to model. I know all about fashion designers. Why do you think I dress so good?"

"Um, you dress like a tourist."

"And that look is *hot*," he replies. "It is kind of funny, though. My mom would *die* if she saw this plaid shirt Baba forced on me."

It's a joke, but I'm suddenly frozen. Pathetically caught off guard. I'm still not immune to the power that word has over me. I tuck my curls behind my ears, eyeballs antsy.

Declan frowns. "Did I say something?"

"No, it's fine."

I cough and bite my lip. Stare at the TV, the couch, the lamp. Anywhere but him, because I can feel those warm brown eyes burning into me. If I don't look, he won't ask. Don't look, don't ask. We drain our iced teas, and sweat dampens the base of my neck.

"So . . . *Rear Window?*" Declan says after a minute.

"Okay."

Next comes the awkwardness of who-sits-where and how-far-apart on the sofa. It ends up being kind of a B+ seating arrangement, with about an iPad's-worth of space between us as the credits begin to roll. Lips jumps immediately into my lap, desperate to lick my elbow. Declan keeps his arms folded in his lap. Anyone might think we seem comfortable. Friendly, natural. Nothing awkward about it. Nope.

The movie is from the 1950s and everything about it looks ancient. The characters are all hot and sweaty, and soon I feel my own temperature rise. Declan takes off his plaid shirt, tossing it across the room onto Dad's recliner. Grace Kelly nuzzles her nose along James Stewart's neck, and I notice that Declan's hand has fallen into the small abyss between us. His arms are freckle-free and creamy against the brown leather sofa.

I focus on the movie again. Grace Kelly is pouting in this wedding cake of a cocktail dress that no real human being would ever actually wear.

"I wish I were creative," she says.

"You are. You're great at creating difficult situations."

I reach into the bag with sticky palms, and there's only one gummy worm left. I consider eating it but don't want to look greedy, so I thrust it at Declan. He grins and rips it in half, handing me back the red gummy butt. James Stewart frantically spies on his neighbors from a wheelchair in his apartment. It stresses me out, honestly, watching this old guy strain and crane his neck to peer through a massive telephoto lens. He clocks their moves. Grows suspicious.

"I love this part," Declan whispers, leaning close so that his shoulder presses into mine.

"Look, in the courtyard," Declan quotes, brilliantly imitating James Stewart's fogyish drawl. *"Only one person didn't come to the window. Look."*

His voice and eyebrows go up for Grace Kelly's lines.

"Why would Thorwald want to kill a little dog?" he murmurs. *"Because it knew too much?"*

I stifle a laugh and watch Ms. Kelly as she dashes off to snoop in the killer's apartment. Declan winks like an Academy Award winner. He clears his throat, looking into my eyes with his big brown ones and those Marvel-hero bangs. My heart zooms. But I'm sweaty too, and I'm in my living room next to

Dad's recliner and my whole broken adolescence, and I've never had a guy over here before, and the zooming sensation in my chest is starting to feel more like heart palpitations. Faster, hotter, soupier, until I can't take it anymore and push Lips off my lap, jumping to my feet.

"What's wrong?" Declan asks, jerking forward in his seat. "It's the quoting along, isn't it? My friends hate it when I do that. I'll stop."

"No, it's not that." I back out of the room. "I'm thirsty. Aren't you thirsty? I'm so thirsty. I'm going to get some more iced tea." My back bangs against the wall, and I nearly collapse. "I'll be right back. You don't have to pause it."

I leave Declan to wonder what the hell is wrong with me while I go catch my breath in the kitchen. I lean against the counter; steady myself. Iced tea swims down my throat, and I polish off two glasses before slinking back into the living room. James Stewart is frozen, mid pained expression, reaching for his telephoto lens.

"You paused it."

"I had to. You can't miss this."

I sit back down, allowing a healthy amount of sofa cushion between us. Declan presses Play. It's good that he paused it too. James Stewart's apartment is being broken into. The bad guy is trying to kill him. Now my heart's racing for a whole other reason. By the end of the film, my stomach is in knots.

"So good, right?" Declan says.

"Actually, yeah. Even though James Stewart has two expressions." I pause to demonstrate them: *shock!* followed by *dread!* "And I can't believe Grace Kelly was such a doormat. Ada Fitz would never approve of her disregard for feminism."

It wasn't that funny, but we both laugh. Poking innocent fun at our classmates is kind of a thing. The laughter descends into steady breath. Declan starts to scoot closer, and I fly to my feet, accidentally banging into Dad's chair. The movie's over, gummy worms have been consumed.

I don't want a crush.

I don't want a crush.

My heart's not ready.

"Thanks for coming," I say. "And for the movie."

"Guess I better get going." Declan sends a quick text, then follows me into the hallway where I'm hovering like some weird Hobbit prison guard. "Jiji says he'll head over. This is better, anyway. He doesn't like driving too late at night."

"That makes sense."

I watch him wiggle back into his Adidas, and we walk outside, breathing in the crisp, piñon air. Hot as it was today, it's chilly now that the sun's gone down. The moon is waning, and it's pretty dark, but I don't flip on the porch light.

"Thanks for letting me come over."

"Yeah, it was fun."

My eyes drift up toward the sky. Mars. The Big Dipper. Pleiades, my favorite. The breeze picks up, and I shift my gaze off the stars. Declan's unabashedly looking at me, making my heart race. I don't want a crush, I don't want a crush. I swallow hard as he takes a step closer, but then a car rumbles up the dirt road, two boat-size headlights bathing us in light.

"There's my ride," Declan says—groans almost. "Thanks again."

"You're welcome, again. Thanks for the gummy worms. I ate way too many."

"You didn't." He smiles and then signals "one minute" to Jiji, who gives a thumbs-up before backing the Lincoln out of my driveway. "Can I see you again?"

I faint, mentally. "You're not sick of me?"

"Not at all."

I don't want a crush, I don't want a crush. I watch him grin and try to remind myself that he'll be gone in August. That I've never been on a date or had a boyfriend or even kissed a guy, and I might never recover if my damaged heart goes down this road. Not now. The timing sucks but I need to use my head, not my heart . . . If only my dad had been able to do the same.

Declan half smiles, reaching for a hug. Our chests fuse together. Is he making this harder on purpose? Am I? For a second, I stop overthinking, focusing instead on Declan's body. A weighted blanket, warm and soothing to my skin. Strong too—definitely Peter Parker *post* radioactive spider bite.

"See you Monday," he says into my hair.

"Mhmm," I say, forcing my eyes not to flutter shut. "I mean, yes."

He pulls away, jogging down the driveway and into Jiji's car. The smell of his cologne lingers in the air and on my shirt. I wait for a bend in the road to swallow their headlights, then walk back up the driveway and into my empty house.

CHAPTER 10

Juana's doing split kicks in the middle of the Sun Salutations Yoga Studio parking lot while we wait for her mom to finish a class. The cheerleading pertains to last night's date (non-date?) with Declan. One might say she's enthusiastic and reading *way* too much into it. I love Juana to pieces, but I wish she'd stop being such a romantic and start realizing that my heart is out of commission. But no matter how desperately I'm trying to protect what's left of it, Juana says "just friends" is fake news, and she won't stop with the dabbing and the cartwheels.

I switch some settings on Luke's camera and snap a few shots of her more balletic jetés for my "capturing movement" assignment, then hand Juana a gas-station chimichanga as she leans beside me against the car. She accepts it with a winded sigh.

"Is he a biter?"

"Excuse me?" I say, pausing to peel back foil.

"Like, when you kissed," she says. "Did he bite your lip, all seductive? Is he a nibbler or a tongue guy—I want details."

"For the millionth time, we did *not* kiss. We watched a movie and hugged goodnight. That's all. It was nice."

"Nice?" Her voice sours, regurgitating the word. "You make him sound like oatmeal. Sing out, Louise—I need metaphors! Similes!"

"Okay," I shout-whisper. Two pregnant women waddle past with their yoga mats, and I cough, not wanting them to overhear. "Declan smelled like dew on a summer morning, glistening from the soft, white buds of a honeysuckle bush. The way our shoulders brushed together during the movie was stronger than a bolt of lightning hitting the mast of a ship lost at sea."

"Ooh, that's *good*," she mumbles between bites. "A little bit Disney+? But I like it. Smolderingly PG. And, PS, you're ridiculous for not calling it a date."

I huff into my chimi, but my brain is abuzz, back in Mom and Dad's bedroom that night. Clothes neatly packed, drawers empty. If my own father could cheat, who's to say Declan wouldn't too? What if this is a pattern all the men in my life will follow? I'm drowning in insecurities, but I squeeze an extra packet of hot sauce onto my afternoon snack, swallowing down my food and my feelings.

Sunlight glints off the yoga studio's doors as they swing open, and Juana's mom comes sauntering out. I push myself off the bumper, crumpling my tinfoil wrapper into a tiny ball and waving as if I'm super excited to see her. Which I'm not, but at least it gets JJ off my back. Mrs. Lujan—aka the tyrant of Casa Buena, aka *call me Debbie!*—makes her way toward us in floral Lululemon leggings and a matching sports bra. Because *that's* how rock-hard her abs are—she doesn't even wear a frigging shirt to yoga. Back when she was at Chavez Academy, Juana's mom was prom queen. It has to have been like twenty or thirty years ago, but she still looks young, still walks around as if there's a bouquet of roses in her arms and a crown on her head.

I'm not trying to sound bitchy. Lately I'm jealous, wondering if my mom would ever consider trading in her Marlboros for a downward dog—saluting the sun rather than a pitcher of sangria. Thinking about someone other than herself . . .

"Juanita, tell me you are not sitting out here eating fried food," Debbie says, her überbleached smile wilting at the sight of our scraps. "You know what the dermatologist said."

"Oh, do you mean this deep-fried burrito?" Juana fist-thumps her chest to release a belch. "I rubbed it all over my face before eating it. Is that bad for acne?"

I bite back a laugh. Honestly, Juana doesn't even have zits. Debbie is just *that* concerned with appearances that she preemptively takes her daughter to the dermatologist and puts her on birth control and stuff to ensure that Juana's skin stays as river-calm and pristine as hers.

"Oh, Juana, stop," Debbie says, but her voice is playful. "Dad called while I was in the middle of a vinyasa. The mechanic says the beamer's ready. I need to be dropped off at the dealership."

We pile into the car, heads snapping against headrests as Juana peels out of the parking lot. We drive in silence down St. Francis, strip malls and business complexes whizzing past. Debbie's eyes meet mine in the rearview mirror, and her breath catches.

"Evie, honey?" She bites her lip. "I'm not sure if I should tell you this, but . . . after my class, I saw the new receptionist finishing her shift. She was getting ready to take the prenatal yoga class. I think it might have been Bree."

"*Mamí!*" Juana screams. Literally *screams*, swerving into the next lane. "That was a secret! Are you loca? Why would you do this to me?"

Her tirade goes full-on Spanish, and I sit there in the back seat, suddenly catatonic. Too preoccupied to be mad that Juana can't keep her mouth shut about anything and that Debbie is an even worse gossip. All I can manage are thin, raspy breaths. Dizzied by the juxtaposition of Bree's light, breezy name against the raked coals of my heart.

"I shouldn't have said anything." Debbie's grim face twists toward me in the back seat. "And don't blame Juana. To be honest, I might've already had an inkling. I saw Bree and your dad together, once. They weren't *doing* anything, but—I don't know—it stuck with me. Then, when Juana mentioned the baby, I thought I ought to tell you. I'm sorry."

"At least be useful," Juana snaps. "Tell us what she said. How did she look? What was she wearing? Are you *sure* it was Bree Hewitt?"

My heart thuds in time with her questions, quick and desperate.

Bree Hewitt.

At a yoga studio.

Working, exercising.

Steps away from me,

twice in as many weeks.

I'm lost in thought when Debbie goes, "Juana, green light. *Green light!*" and we lurch into the intersection. She exhales. "I didn't think to take notes, alright? I'm sorry."

"It's okay." I swallow back nausea. "It's fine."

"Are you sure?" Juana frowns. "Babe, I'm so sorry. I swear I will never tell my mom anything ever again, as long as I live."

Debbie groans overdramatically.

"You are sleeping on the couch of our friendship for a long time," I tell her. "But, I forgive you. It's probably better to have a heads-up."

"I'm sorry," Juana says again.

"Stop saying you're sorry."

"My friend Carol spoke to her briefly," Debbie offers at the next red light. "She recognized Bree from Cisneros and Associates, so she stopped to say hi. Apparently, Bree quit the firm recently—I think it was too much for her. She's doing some part-time work at Sun Salutations now, taking a few classes when she can. That's when I saw her, heading into a class. I think she had on a blue top."

The car swerves again as Juana tries to gauge my reaction in the rearview mirror.

"Juana!" Debbie screams. "You're going to kill us!"

"Sorry." She grips the wheel at ten and two and glues her eyes to the road.

"Thanks, Debbie," I manage. "For the info."

A frigid silence follows us the rest of the way to the BMW dealership. In the parking lot, Debbie takes her time, pulling the visor down to reapply her lipstick, pinching her cheeks, brushing her hair. I get out my camera, focusing on her lips in the rearview, her face blurring in the periphery. *Click, click*. She hears the shutter's tinny rattle and looks over her shoulder with a gleaming smile, head tossed back, stars twinkling in her eyes. *So* her daughter's mother.

"Mom, stop posing," Juana groans. "You're in enough trouble. Get out of the car."

"I'm having a little fun," Debbie groans back. "Can't moms enjoy life?"

"No," Juana says definitively.

Debbie finally leaves, and Juana launches into an endless stream of explanations and apologies. I focus on her mouth but tune out her voice, lost in my own thoughts. Am I supposed to feel *glad* that Bree is doing yoga? That she's getting exercise because unborn babies benefit from that shit too? Or, like, can I please be completely fucking disgusted that Sun Salutations would accommodate a home-wrecker? Literally. She wrecked my home. And now she's working on her tree pose.

It makes my blood boil. I have to flick through my camera roll just to distract myself. Tight shots of Debbie, oblivious to me, puckering her lips and smiling at her reflection. Further back, to the pictures of Bree, nibbling her muffin at the café. Laughing with a stranger, patting her belly. Suddenly I'm thinking about that movie Declan and I watched last night—*Rear Window*. How Jimmy Stewart photographed the killer's every move. *Click. Click.*

Click.

"Holy shit." I smack my hand tight over my mouth to keep from exploding, then scramble over the center console and into the front seat. "I think I have an idea."

Juana squints. "Does your idea involve pitchforks and my mother tied to a tree? Because I'm definitely down."

"It's not about your mom. Or you—you're both off the hook. In fact, maybe I should be thanking her. Because this is kind of like fate, right? That this is landing in my lap?"

"*What* is landing in your lap?"

"This!" I raise my camera, shaking it in my fist. "Voyeurism!"

Juana's eyebrows gravitate together in a perturbed pine-cone shape. "Sorry, what-now?"

"You know, watching people. A person, specifically."

She sucks her teeth as she pulls out of the dealership. "Did you take some gummies when I wasn't looking?"

"Oh, shut up. I'm talking about this fancy camera—one of Luke's lenses has this überclose zoom. It's for photographing birds and shit, but it would be great for photographing people *inconspicuously*."

"Who do you want to . . ." Her words slow up as her mouth widens. "*Bree*? You fucking stalker!"

"Am not!" I shriek. "But why does Bree get to strut around town with her lattes and her yoga mat, praised by strangers for her fertility? It's not fair."

"Agreed, but like, how is spying on her going to help?"

"Morbid curiosity?" I shrug. "All I want is to follow her for a while. See what she does. I mean, how hard can it be? Tons of people do it every day."

"Yeah. Those people are called stalkers."

"*Voyeurs*."

"Like I said, stalkers."

"God, Juana. Get on my side," I huff. "What's so wrong with wanting to find out more about her? If Dad hadn't died, he was maybe gonna move in with her. I think I'm entitled to see what all the fuss was about. Let me decide for myself if she was worth destroying their marriage and blowing up my life."

"But, like, *what*? We strap on fake bellies and join prenatal yoga?"

"Dude, no. We'll wait in the parking lot, hunched down in

the car—" I pause to demonstrate, and Juana snorts. "And when the class ends, we follow her to wherever she goes next. And I'll take pictures."

"Here's an idea." Juana flips her hair. "Why don't we, like, *actually* do some yoga, rather than watching someone else do it? Or, stop at Collected Works for a few self-help books. You've got to admit, this idea is craz—"

"I know this sounds ridiculous, but isn't being a stalker better than getting more depressed?"

"*Is it?*"

"It *is!*" I giggle, yanking her T-shirt hem. "C'mon, I'm serious. I really think it might help."

"So, you do this, and then you're healed."

"It will be my living, breathing Neosporin."

Her face sours, but deep down I know she gets it. This *is* the answer. I am 100 percent certain that learning everything about that heap of garbage will scratch the itch—no, cauterize the gash—left by Dad's death.

"Alright, then." Juana sighs, putting on her blinker. "But as soon as you start to make any kind of sad, crying face, I am hauling your ass out of there and taking you to Häagen-Dazs to regroup. Deal?"

"Deal."

"Welp, then I guess we're going back to the yoga studio."

I grin. "Nama-frigging-ste."

CHAPTER 11

The SUV is a sauna on wheels because JJ insists on cutting the engine to minimize her carbon footprint. As if you're allowed to care about the environment when you drive a frigging SUV. Even with the windows open, it's a breezeless hell, legs moist and stuck to the leather.

I squint through the windshield, fanning myself with one of the magazine perfume samples she keeps in her glove compartment. Prenatal yoga classes must be really goddamn decadent, because I swear we have been waiting in this parking complex forever. So long, in fact, that my mind starts wandering, eyes drifting around toward the other businesses that form a C-shaped plaza around us. There's a Fed-Ex, a pharmacy. Stuff like that.

"I'm hungry," Juana says. "Do you think Chopstix would deliver to a car?"

I reach under the passenger's seat, pretty sure I'm going to find—yup—ancient Doritos. I toss them over. "Here."

"But—"

The double doors next to the yoga studio swing open, and I slam my palm against Juana's mouth. We both freeze, momentarily forgetting that, yeah, that is not the entrance to Sun Salutations. It's the Chinese restaurant next door, but my breath catches anyway because *a pregnant girl walks out*. Average height, shoulder-length blond hair. My heart hovers in my chest until I realize my mind is playing tricks on me. She's like forty and on the arm of a burly man in cowboy boots and a sports coat. It's a false alarm, but I can't help being intrigued by them anyway, the way he holds the door for her; fingers brushing together as they cross the street. The camera is already propped on the dashboard, so I bring it to my eye, zooming in on their hands; her bashful smile. *Click.*

"That guy's wearing a toupee, for sure." Juana aims a nacho cheese–stained finger at his head as they stride toward a white Camaro. "His name is . . . Reginald de Cervantes. And he's a—"

"Haberdasher," I decide.

"Ooh, fancy. What else?"

"He's married to a trapeze artist named Jacinda." I pause and my heart rate spikes. "But that's not her. That's his mistress, Marietta LaRue. Which is why they're looking all skittish—afraid someone might spot them together."

The temp rises another billion degrees after that. Juana clears her throat and stops chewing. I rest the camera back on the dash, quietly wondering how I ended up here. Half-broken and noxious. Assuming the worst. That all men cheat and are out to destroy the women who love them. I mean, why did my brain have to make a beeline for that interpretation?

I feel my eyes begin to sting, a tightness hardening my throat. Is this me now? Feeling this way, thinking these thoughts? Because I have to hope there's more to it. Maybe my father did this to us . . . but what did this to *him*? What changed the clockwork of his brain and made him yearn for something other? How does someone *decide* to obliterate their family? How do they live with themselves?

But he didn't, did he? Maybe the strain is what killed him.

Everything inside me rolls forward and back, the epic tug of heartbreak. I wiggle free from my thoughts and grab the camera again, snapping a flock of Japanese tourists as they walk out with gift bags from a local shop selling chile ristras and smudge sticks. *Click-click-click.* Capture their smiles, the uniformity of their cluster—a museum of cedar waxwings.

"Hey, Evie?" JJ squeezes my free hand.

I nod, peering at the playback screen, deleting the crappiest images.

"Have you thought about tomorrow?"

I shrug. Tomorrow is June seventeenth, I think? Nothing comes to mind.

"I didn't know if—" She bites her lip, lowering her chin. "I wanted to see if you remembered about Father's Day."

"Oh." I freeze as a wind tunnel sucks the air right out of me. "I guess I forgot."

"That's okay," she says quickly, but it's too late. Already I'm falling, smothered by a lost-keys feeling. My brain rewinds further and further back until I remember that—"I forgot."

"It's okay, sweetie. I shouldn't have brought it up."

"No, I mean . . . last year." My eyes glaze over, heart thumping. "I forgot last year. Mom had this big ol' dinner planned for him. She told me to come home by six to help cook and set the table. But that morning, Dad and I got in an argument about my final report card—how he expected more from me—and I stormed off. Drove all the way out to Abiquiú Lake and sulked for hours. By the time I got home, Dad had already gone to bed. Neither one of us apologized. I didn't even care."

And, really, I didn't. But the pain on JJ's shadowed face makes me crumble.

I wish I could take it back.

Make it right.

Set the table,

make him dinner.

Make him stay.

"It's okay, Evie."

"It's not," I whisper, voice cracking. "I'm a bitch."

"No, you aren't." We don't have any tissues, but Juana grabs a black bandanna from the center console, blotting her own eyes before passing it to me.

"I *did* remember his last birthday." I sniffle the tears away, tucking my sweaty legs up into my chest, hoping this memory will count for something. "We made pancakes, and I bought him a monogrammed pocket protector. Because—remember?—he always used to carry all those pens?"

Juana laughs. "Oh my God, yes! The pens! Don't you wish there was a GIF of your dad, like, drowning in a shower of pens?"

We both laugh, but it doesn't last nearly long enough. We don't have the energy to feed the joke and give it life. Our laughter withers, and I can't help thinking about that pocket protector, wondering what ever happened to it. If it meant anything to him. My skin begins to itch and, more than anything, I want to think about something else right now.

"What about you and Manny? What do you have planned for Daddy Lujan tomorrow?"

"Same shit as always. French toast followed by a round of golf at Las Campanas. Every year he asks if I'll join him. I'm like, *I am not that kind of lesbian, Papí!*"

"But you'd look so cute in one of those argyle sweater vests."

She nods solemnly. "And a flat cap, right? I know. But it still isn't going to happen."

"Oh, shit." I gasp, and my spine stiffens. "Look."

Someone's propped the yoga studio's doors open and a brood of rosy-cheeked baby mamas are beginning to trickle outside, each of them looking all Zen as they walk to their cars.

Gales of laughter. Cooing over flutter kicks and acid reflux. It looks like a highlights clip from a reality show until we spot Bree, wisps of sweaty hair firing wildly around her face. Chewing on her lip, walking alone. Belly round and cheeks soft. And young—the other preggos must have a dozen years on her. She fumbles with her yoga mat and her straw handbag and almost drops everything as she searches for the keys to a beat-up blue Hyundai.

The car looks like crap. She looks like crap. Already a few pounds heavier than when I saw her on Monday.

"Talk about eating for two," Juana mutters. "How many babies is she *having?*"

"Juana, don't be a dick."

Under different circumstances it might be hilarious, but we're watching my dead father's pregnant mistress cradle her belly as she struggles to unlock the driver's side door, and it is brutally, tragically unmockable. Too bizarre to see her former-cheerleader tautness morphing into an inflated nest for future life. Too awkward to witness her klutziness. Her isolation.

I sink lower in my seat and lean out the window a little, zooming in, focusing my lens on Bree's messy bun and shiny, sapphire eyes. *Click.* Her yoga clothes are a bit more merciless than the hoodie and sweatpants I caught her in at the café. *Click.* I lower the lens, taking in her bump the size of a soccer ball. *Click.* The rest of the extra weight has gone to her thighs, her hips, her butt. That, I don't click.

Despite JJ's SUV being sandwiched between two cars in the back of the lot, I pull the camera in toward my chest and recline my seat a bit more. Bree hasn't noticed us, and she wouldn't know Juana's car even if she did, but there's no harm in being cautious. Legit doubling down on the voyeurism angle. Breath held, we watch as Bree dumps her bag and mat in the back seat, then wedges herself behind the wheel. I swat Juana's arm to start the engine.

"We're really doing this?" she whispers.

I nod, anxiously zooming in and twisting the focus ring on Luke's camera.

Bree makes a right on Don Gaspar and so do we. What we're doing is absurd. Untenable. More illicit than anything, including that time I stole lip gloss from CVS when I was twelve or all the times Juana and I smoked pot in the arroyo behind my house. This is so intense we're not even playing music. SUPER-NATURALLY STALKERISH hasn't been created yet, and, right now, I need to focus—my camera, my brain, all my attention.

"Think she's going home?" I ask.

Another coral sunset fades into navy blue and our task gets easier because Bree has a broken taillight. We're tracking a cyclops-mobile, and the cyclops turns left into—

"McDonald's?" Juana says. "Who goes straight from yoga to Mickey D's?"

"And sits inside," I add, watching Bree skip the drive-through and head for the fluorescent, saturated-fat zone.

"Maybe she's ordering a salad?" I suggest, although I don't know why I'm defending her.

"Yeah, I'm sure their salads are really effing fresh," Juana mutters. "Be real, Evie. There's no point in McDonald's without fries."

Her stomach rumbles, and I shake my head. "Don't even think about it."

"Fine." She tips the end of the Dorito bag into her mouth.

I balance my camera on the dashboard and peer through the viewfinder, switching the camera to autofocus. The lighting is almost aggressively bright, illuminating old acne scars. *Click.* Cheeks dimpling as she orders. Luke's lens is so good that I can see every detail of the gnawed-on wreckage of her cherry-red manicure. Bree pays with crumpled bills and gets loose change in return, then finds a booth near the window closest to us. She stares out, vacantly. *Click. Click. Click.*

"Is it me," Juana asks, "or does she look really down in the dumpsicles?"

It's what I was thinking too, but I won't let pity cloud my hatred. Instead, I focus on the realness of Bree Hewitt through my lens. Her lips clenched around a straw. The girl who tore my parents apart. Barely an adult, preparing for a baby of her own. Is that how she kept her claws in him? Binding him to an unborn baby? It's a sick thought, and I'm not proud of it, but I have to believe she is capable of anything.

After a minute, Bree goes up to the counter and comes back

with her tray. Elbows on the table, fists under her chin. Most people dig in, but Bree takes a minute. She stares down her burger and fries. Regret tugs at her lips. Like maybe my salad theory might normally be true. A creeping feeling draws my chest down onto my spine.

This isn't how I thought it would be.

Juana must feel it too, because she reaches over the gearshift to squeeze my knee. For a while longer, we watch in silence. Chew, swallow, repeat. Fry after fry, bite after bite, ketchup painting her lips. *Click.* The conflict in my gut grows. Bree isn't supposed to look this pathetic. I mean, she *is* pathetic. And I want her to be frigging miserable. Want her to burn and writhe and suffer the way Mom and I have. So I keep clicking, feeding my rage.

Fries demolished, Bree crumples her trash and then stares at it. Like she really, honestly might cry. She doesn't, exactly, but she does frown, lips fluttering as she exhales. I've never regretted gorging on junk food, but I used to get that look when I failed a math test. Dad drilled it into me so hard, wanted me to succeed so badly. I should have done better. Should have tried harder. Never meant to fail him.

"She's coming back out, duck!" Juana shrieks.

We both sink below the dashboard, inquisitive foreheads bobbing back up. Bree doesn't go straight to her car, though. This old lady walks by with a cute little pug, and Bree squeals. She says something, and when the lady nods, Bree puts one hand below her belly in order to squat onto the ground and start fluffing up the dog's fur. The dog licks her face, and Bree laughs. *Click.* She scratches behind the pug's ears, and her smile practically bursts for the first time all night. For ten seconds, it's like she's a different person. Is this what my dad saw in her?

Dog Lady moseys off, and Bree stands up; no choice but to get in her car.

Juana reaches for the key, but I grip the steering wheel, shaking my head. "Wait, don't."

We sit there, breathless and frozen, until Bree is safely out of sight. Then JJ starts up the car. We pull out onto the road, silently agreeing to call it a night. I got what I came for. Saw more of Bree Hewitt than I ever imagined wanting to. On the way home, I stare at my camera screen, scrolling through tonight's images. They're not bad, actually. Bree's loneliness, my use of thirds.

Back at home, we sit in Juana's driveway for a few minutes, melancholy and motionless. I look into my best friend's soft, brown eyes, not wanting to be mushy but wanting her to know how grateful I am for her friendship, even if she *did* rat me out to Debbie. Because, way beyond that, if there is one thing the past month has taught me, it is that we are sisters, no matter what. I should tell her that I'd walk through fire for her. But I think she already knows.

So, instead, I say, "Thanks."

"It wasn't so bad." She grins. "In an uncomfortable, hot, starving, probably illegal kind of way."

"Right?"

We slink out of her car and hug before going our separate ways. I'm halfway across the street when I turn back. "Oh, and happy Father's Day. Y'know, to your dad, tomorrow."

She flinches a little before smiling. "Thanks, Ev."

The words put a lump in my throat but, somehow, saying them out loud almost feels like I'm saying them to my dad.

CHAPTER 12

I chase Bree in my dreams that night. Running through rubber cement, voicelessly screaming that she ruined my life and set fire to my family. McDonald's fries rain down from the sky, forming puddles of ketchup that splatter on my skin and soak through to my battered soul.

And when I wake up? It is frigging Father's Day.

"Morning." Mom glances up from her newspaper at the sound of my slippered feet scuffing dismally into the kitchen. She's hunched over a cauldron of coffee, last night's mascara crumbling beneath her eyes. God only knows what time she got home; I was already fast asleep.

"Hungry?" she asks. "Luke made me buy one of those canned cinnamon roll tube things, then left before eating it. Should be out of the oven in a minute."

"Sure." I pour myself a coffee and pause before sitting across from her, not sure I can do it. Like, whether or not I can bring myself to meet her eye after what I did last night. Who I saw.

She must notice my indecisive hovering, because she throws me a weird look, her bloodshot eyes narrowing. "Everything okay?"

"Yeah," I say quickly. "Didn't sleep well, that's all."

The oven timer pings, and Mom is all of a sudden more motherly than I've seen her in weeks. Mitts over hands as she pulls the cinnamon rolls from the oven, sliding them gingerly onto a plate that she sets down between us. She doesn't open the packet of icing that you're supposed to drizzle on top. Like some kind of monster.

It's nice, though. Effort, at least. And the sheer coziness of it snaps me out of my daze. I sit down at the table, cinnamon steam dancing in the air between us. "You were out late, huh?"

There's an inside joke to her smirk, but she doesn't say anything.

We fall into silence, nibbling.

It's Father's Day, I want to say, but don't. *Remember how I forgot last year and you were furious with me? Remember how I promised I'd make it up to him this year?*

"Any plans today?" Mom asks.

"Not really," I mumble.

I stare into the brown abyss of my mug, wondering if this is a set-up. If she's looking to pick a fight over my lack of Sunday ambition. Or if, like, maybe this is her delicate way of broaching the Father's Day subject. Because I don't have plans, but maybe *she* does. Maybe we'll spend the day playing Monopoly in his honor, sharing memories over chocolate chip cookies. I'll forgive her for pushing me away when what we should have been doing all this time is grieving together.

Instead, she says, "How's photography class? You're being pretty secretive with your work. Don't I get to see any of it?"

"No!" I shout. Way too loud.

So unnecessarily impassioned that Mom jolts, a frown tightening her face. "Jesus, Evie. Calm down. I was only *asking*. God forbid you *actually* share your talent with your *mother*."

She pushes her chair back from the table, huffing as she walks to the sink. She needs a cigarette now, and it's my fault. I provoked her. I open my mouth to apologize but then quickly clamp it shut. My insides are rattling to tell her *why* she can't see my progress—that I've been shooting Bree and need to come clean about it—but the fire in my belly turns to fear, which quickly plops into a vat of anxiety at my cold feet.

"Sorry," I mumble. "It's taking me a while to get used to Luke's camera. There's more buttons on that thing than our stereo remote."

"Well, of course it's going to take practice, Evie. Skill doesn't land in your lap." There's a familiar pinch to her voice. Whatever the cinnamon rolls were supposed to do, their magic is gone, replaced by our usual cranky bullshit. "And don't forget to send Luke a thank-you note. I will not have him thinking his niece is ungrateful."

"I will, Mom. God."

Even though, yeah, no. I totally wasn't planning on writing him. My eyes jerk toward the ceiling and land back down on my balled-up fists. Because she's doing it again—judging me, nagging me, never letting me off the hook for fucking *anything*. It's not even the grief talking. It's just *her*, which makes it almost impossible to forgive.

She stubs our her half-smoked cigarette and out of nowhere starts quietly bawling.

"Mom?"

"I'm fine," she sobs. "It's nothing!"

I should run to her, but it's like my whole body is paralyzed. I've heard her at night through the walls like this, but she hasn't cried *like this* in my presence in weeks, and it feels like a punch of déjà vu to the gut. Silent in the waiting area; lemon-scented bleach on linoleum floors. *We did everything we could. I'm so sorry for your loss . . .*

I wring the thought from my bones and use the guilt of her tears to propel me from my seat. I have to do something, so I rip a square of paper towel from the roll by the sink and hand it to her.

"Thank you, sweetie. I'm sorry for losing it like this." She snivels, pausing to blow her nose. "I promised myself I would hold it together today. I decided that if you weren't going to bring it up, I wasn't going to bring it up. But you've clearly forgotten, and—"

"Excuse me?" My lip curls as I stumble back. "You think I *forgot*?"

"Well, I wasn't—"

"Today is Father's Day. Is *that* what you think I forgot?"

Her face goes pale, arms dropping down by her sides. "You remembered?"

"Of course I did. God, I can't believe you."

Now she's backpedaling, an apology drizzling down her soggy cheeks. "Well, you've been so busy," she whimpers. "I guess *I'm* the one who didn't remember. Not until yesterday, when I got a call from the Compound, reminding me of our brunch reservation for today. I must've booked it two months ago. I wanted to do something special. To make up for . . . well, y'know. How it didn't go so well last year."

"You mean, how badly I fucked it up?"

Mom winces and I groan into the air. All I can think is, *Why am I doing this?* Five minutes ago I was desperate for this conversation. Monopoly and chocolate chip cookies. Grieving together. And yet here I am, ruining it. Breaking it like I break fucking everything.

"Evie, stop. I—"

"Come on, Mom. I'm only saying what you're thinking, arent' I? Well, for your information, I *did* remember. Sorry there was no parade to cancel, but I'm not an asshole, okay? I wouldn't forget."

Except for how I did. At least Juana's not around to rat me out.

"I'm sorry," Mom says, but there's a glint of irritation in her voice. "I didn't mean to piss you off so much."

Which obviously pisses me off *more*.

Rather than watch my guilt spin us into yet another squabble, I grab two cinammon rolls and turn to leave. "I'm going to my room."

"Oh, Evie, you don't always have to sulk. We could still have a nice day, without blowing up at each other."

"Yeah, great plan," I mutter, but I'm already gone.

I stomp up the stairs, slamming my bedroom door so that the whole house recoils. My heart pounds. *Could* we have had a nice day? If I had swallowed my pride, ignored her assumptions? I look down at the cinnamon rolls, already cold and stale. Naked without their glossy white icing. Evidence that Mom was trying, baking, making an effort. And I ruined it.

I should have opened up, but I didn't.

I drop the plate on my desk, reaching for my phone, ready to do something I haven't been able to bring myself to do in all the weeks since Dad's death. I scroll past my texts with Juana, past the ones between me and Mom. A few from Declan, Georgy, Luke. Past the dozens of condolences and weeping bitmojis from sypathetic classmates, until I find the last few exchanges I had with my father.

Your curfew's still 11 right??

> OMG it's literally 10:40 rn. The movie just got out and I'm waiting for JJ to get out of the bathroom. Then we r driving home. Ok?

Yeesh. I was only checking.

> Yeesh?! 😠😠

I smirk a little. For some reason, Dad really doubled down on the word "yeesh," and I always took the time to give him shit for it. My heart sags as I get to our last conversation. Three days before he died. A regular bullshit Tuesday.

> Mom wants you to pick up cilantro on your way home.

Shoot. I've got a meeting.
Might miss dinner.

> She says WHY DIDN'T YOU TELL ME THAT BEFORE I STARTED MAKING ENCHILADAS.

She said it in CAPS LOCK?

yep

Ok, I'll try.

And that's it.

I drop the phone onto my chest and flop back against the pillows. *Did* he try? Did he rearrange his meeting and make it home with cilantro in time for Mom's green chile enchiladas? Or was it just the two of us sitting quietly at the kitchen table, picking at a casserole baked for three? The fact that I can't remember breaks my heart.

No, I take it back. What really breaks my heart? Knowing he was probably with her.

Chapter 13

Georgy calls on me to go first on Monday, but there is literally zero chance of me letting NMPI critique my photos of Bree. So I show everything else. Reginald de Cervantes and Marietta LaRue; the museum of Japanese tourists. Sneaky angles and covert details. And the photos aren't bad. Honestly. Even judgy Henri, with all his skill and superiority, seems genuinely intrigued by the lighting, the cropping, the je ne sais quoi.

For the first time in my life, I almost wonder if this is what it feels like to have a calling.

"Very stripped and cinematic," Georgy says, stroking a cherry blossom tattoo on her forearm. "Let's focus on this gentleman—what do you all see?"

Everyone looks at Reginald, chest puffed out, dimple carving a hole in his chin. In the photograph, he's looking sideways at Marietta, haloed by a neon green Heineken sign from Chopstix's front window. With Luke's lens, I was able to catch a bit of electric green bouncing off his brown eyes and illuminating his sweat-dampened forehead.

"The timidity in his eyes," Ada murmurs. "So palpable. I wonder about his childhood."

Ada's German accent is everything. I mean, it's like she's Freud or something, and now everyone's nodding profoundly, imagining Reginald with buck teeth and a bowl cut, stuffing crayons up his nose.

"Great observation," Georgy says. "Anyone else?"

All of a sudden, Beth pipes up, her arms crossed tightly around a crisp, white blouse. "Isn't anyone else bothered by this? I'm sorry, Evie, but it makes me very uncomfortable that you photographed these people without their knowledge."

I start to blush, slouching down in my seat.

Georgy stands, newly energized. "An honest response and a valid observation. Technically, Evie hasn't done anything wrong. Her subjects are in a public parking lot. They have no expectations of privacy, and she's not trying to profit off them. Evie, what was the goal here—were you trying to elicit an uncomfortable reaction in your audience?"

"Oh, um. No? Or . . . I guess? I wasn't really thinking about it."

"What *were* you thinking about?" she prods.

And I shrug. Because I'm not going to tell them I was thinking about Bree. Waiting to follow *her*, photograph *her*, invade *her* personal space. Now, I'm beyond flushed. Scorched, flustered, shrinking into the couch. Maybe I hate Beth for putting me on the spot, but I'm the one who took the pictures. I'm the one who crossed a line.

"I get Beth's point," Violet says. "But I love the results. It's a vivid slice of life. Total Americana."

I mouth a *Thank you*, and she winks back.

"I simply love these pictures," says Suze. "Anyone else think Evie's work is getting more adventurous? It's only been a couple of weeks, but look at these bold new choices. You should feel proud of yourself, honey!"

To be fair, Suze is probably lonely for her own kids, praising me out of some kind of displaced necessity, but it's still really sweet. I flash her a warm smile.

"This is outside that business complex on San Mateo, right?" Peter asks. "I love how you captured the auras of your subjects. Hauntingly intimate."

"Oh, honey, I love that," Sten says, squeezing Peter's bicep.

Hauntingly intimate.

My photos.

Just, like, take a minute to absorb that.

The projector goes dark, and I do my best to focus on Suze's dramatic self-portraits as they flicker onto the screen. Everyone has a lot to say, complimenting the emerging depth of her style, the risks she's taking. We switch to Ed's industrial landscapes, and the banter goes on. Declan's shoulder presses into mine as he leans toward my notebook, scrawling on a clean page.

I had fun on Friday.

My eyes whip over to him. There's a smile on his rosy lips that has my insides defying gravity. My smile says, *Me too,* and I wait a few seconds before brushing this effervescent feeling aside. Did my parents ever look at each other the way Declan is looking at me right now? When I was little, maybe. But I can't remember that far back. What I remember most is the arguing. Eyes narrowed, irritated.

You okay? Declan writes.

I realize my eyes have glazed over, lips slipping into a frown. I take a deep breath to recalibrate, then nod. We both look back at the projector screen, and I momentarily lose myself in Violet's low-contrast, edgy fashion images. She's got an incredible eye. A minute later, Declan's pen is poised at my notebook again. He's drawn a cute little cartoon of a floppy-eared puppy underneath.

Thinking about puppies always cheers me up.
What about you?

I chuckle quietly and then pause. What *does* cheer me up? Happiness feels so obsolete lately, I barely remember how I ever attained it. But then an image pops into my head, unexpected yet comforting.

Nancy Drew books, I write. Old school mystery solving.

Right away he doodles a pretty girl with a fifties bob haircut and a magnifying glass pressed up to one eye. Damn, he's a good cartoonist. He draws a bubble over the girl's head, and writes, *Gee willikers, Evie. Could'ya help me find the hidden staircase?*

Aw, shucks, I write back. I'd be delighted.

CHAPTER 14

The technical assignments crunch my brain and, for most of the week, that's all we do. Fancy studio lighting, complicated gear. It's cool and complex and feels very professional, but it's also hard to understand why I have to fumble with a handheld light meter when the one built into Luke's camera already measures light fine. Georgy's pretty insistent that handhelds offer more detail than built-in meters, and she says she wouldn't be doing her job right if we didn't at least explore the technique. So, yeah. Brain crunch.

Friday's adventure is another field trip. Canyon Road, this time, which I'm not all that into. The whole touristy gallery-hopping scene riddled with overpriced coyote paintings and horse head sculptures. But it's a welcome break from the classroom setting. I live on the opposite side of town, so I only ever come down here with Juana and her parents for swanky art openings because they're *collectors*. Oh, and on Christmas Eve.

That's when the roads are closed off, sidewalks lined with candlelit paper bag farolitos. Everyone sings Christmas carols and sips hot apple cider and says hi to strangers. It's like some old-fashioned alternate universe.

We spill out of the NMPI van into a dusty parking lot, and my visions of Christmas are obliterated by the 90-degree heat trying to strangle me. The sky is a bright, Gatorade blue, not a cloud in sight. Christmas is a million miles away.

"Alright, gang. This is going to be fun," Georgy says, ushering us onto the narrow sidewalk. "You've all got your cameras, but, really, I want you to mill around. Beth's reaction to Evie's work on Monday got me thinking. We should explore what the masses consider to be art. See if we *agree*. I'd like next week's images to reflect on today's findings, so make sure you get a few shots of your inspiration, in addition to whatever else. Think of it as interpretive dance."

"Interpretive dance?" Beth blanches, and I'm right there with her.

Suze nods. "C'mon, Beth. Let your hair down."

"I know you've got it in you," Sten adds, shimmying his shoulders. "We all saw those hips shakin' when Nina Gold banged her tabla drums."

Everyone laughs, acting ridiculous, mimicking Nina's unfettered technique. It's kind of become this inside joke with our class. Anytime things get heated—like Ed and Ada arguing, or Henri's being an all-around snob—someone starts banging the imaginary tablas. Yes, it's dorky. But, yeah, I'll take any opportunity for an impromptu laugh.

We break off into groups, and it's like youngsters vs. oldsters. I follow Violet, Declan, Ed, and Ada along rows of sandwiched-in, one-story adobe galleries. Canyon Road is just as popular as the plaza but in a different way. Downtown, Native Americans line the sidewalks and portals, selling their intricate, handcrafted turquoise jewelry atop colorful Pendleton blankets. On Canyon, the sidewalks are too narrow for street vendors. Instead, tourists wander like lost cattle, marveling and taking pictures. Today, Afro-Cuban jazz pumps out of a particularly vibrant shop. As much as I thought I was going to hate this, it's not horrible exploring my own city. The smell of honeysuckle and fire-roasted green chiles; a gumball machine's worth of color popping through gallery windows. For a while, we amble, eventually turning down a gravel driveway toward an enclosed sculpture garden.

Corrugated steel windmills swirl in the breeze. Ed and Ada stop at a large, rose quartz waterfall sculpture, and Violet snaps a few pictures of them making up from an earlier fight about hair clumping up the sink drain.

Declan and I stroll a bit farther.

"Some of this stuff is incredibly ugly," he says.

"Agreed." I notice an older couple in matching neon, waving their selfie stick in front of a carved wooden Native American.

"This town is so saturated with tourists and art that no one can afford."

"It's the same in New York." Declan pauses in front of a life-size, bronze bear statue, ushering me in front of it. I smile self-consciously and flash a peace sign. "My parents love dragging me to art openings in Manhattan. Everything's a billion dollars, whether it sucks or not. I kinda love it, though. Growing up like that—seeing so much art. It's why I want to study photography at NYU."

My insides twist irrationally. Not because he knows what he wants to do—I mean, it's great that he's so confident while my future cries in a black hole somewhere—but, like, the reminder that he'll be leaving at the end of all this. Back to Brooklyn; Santa Fe in his rearview mirror. I shake a few layers of panic from my limbs and snap Declan's Marvel-hero bangs as they sweep across his eyes. Who cares that he'll be leaving? Not me.

We pick up the pace again, blanketed in easy silence. Bodies close but not touching. Well, not touching until Declan's thumb grazes the side of my hand. I swear I feel it all the way down to my ankles.

"Hey, want to go in here?" I ask.

I lurch away from him and into a bright, airy gallery, and Declan trails after me. The cozy main room is full of abstract paintings the size of postcards. They're nice to look at, but more importantly, studying them allows me a minute to compose myself. Stop thinking about Declan's smooth hands; the lavender bliss of his laundry detergent. I'm almost back to normal when he hands me the gallery's brochure, offering a hoity-toity smirk. I smirk back, and the two of us mill around, keeping a small but notable distance.

We land in front of a blurry mound of russet paint, flecked with white. The tag says it's made from organic beeswax and red chile powder. I give it three stars and move on to a series of acrylic inkblot paintings, which are actually very pretty. Blues and golds punch the canvas. Purple coalesces with bronze. I hold up my camera and snap a quick pic.

We stop at a yellowish-gold inkblot, and I feel Declan's breath on the back of my neck. "This one's cool."

"Yeah, I think it's my favorite," I whisper back.

Our bodies drift closer, notable distance be damned. His upper arm presses into my shoulder. I suck in my stomach. Both of us freeze, barely breathing. My heart flutters. My heart has never *fluttered* before. It's weird. Weird and cool and exciting and warm and new and—

"There you guys are!" Ada barrels into the room with Ed and Violet, and they've picked up Sten and Peter and Suze along the way. "We thought we'd lost you."

"Nope, not lost," Declan says casually.

I stumble back, heat on my cheeks.

"Good afternoon! Welcome to the Conn Gallery."

All eight of us turn toward the high-pitched crackle of a

perky gallerist, and I first notice her shoes—platform wedges lined with ominous silver spikes. I know those shoes. I *know* I know those shoes. My eyes spring up, and her platinum pixie cut confirms it. Loudmouthed and eccentric. This is Nell Cohen. She's old, in her fifties at least; the owner of a costume shop off Old Santa Fe Trail. Hoop skirts and Musketeer capes, stuff like that. Last summer, Juana and I did some part-time work there, and for three excruciating months, we were subjected to Nell's giant, blaring volcano mouth.

"Evie Parker?" she says, eyes popping out of their sockets. "I thought that was you!" She leans in for a hug and then stands at arm's length, green eyes boring into me. "Oh, I miss having you and Juana around. We had so many laughs last summer. Remember that thing? With the epaulets? God, that was funny. You should see the jokers working for me now. One of them won't take her headphones off and the other has a drug problem. I'm thinking about staging an intervention, but I don't know if that's too extreme. What do you think?"

Pop Rocks in a deep fryer. That's what I think of when Nell speaks. Every time.

"I . . . really can't really answer that," I say, shifting awkwardly. "Nell, what are you doing here?"

"What? Oh, I'm part-time. The regular manager is in the hospital with gallstones—can you imagine?" She tries for a commiserative smile with Ada, who offers a most excellent scowl. "Are these your friends? I should really be practicing the gallery spiel. Let me see if I can remember." She stares at the ceiling and starts rattling off information none of us need, and the caged feeling in my chest starts to fade. There's no reason to be nervous, just because two of my worlds are colliding. Finally, she finishes, gesturing to the round splatter that Declan and I were cozied up beside. "The artist collected her pigments from a mine in Afghanistan. She literally risked her life for her art."

"Wow. That's dedication," Sten mutters.

"Right?" Nell shakes her head in agreement. "Anywho, feel free to look around. Tell me if I can answer any questions."

The group disperses, but Nell stays beside me, resting gentle fingers on my arm. "I was so sorry to hear about your dad. So unexpected. How are you handling it?"

A flush turns acidic in my chest. Nobody's actively listening to us, but the gallery is about the size of an Altoid box. There's no way they can't hear her condolences filling every crevice.

"Oh." My voice wobbles. "Thanks . . ."

I try for a furtive glance around the room, but we're way past that. Violet's eyes are sinking onto me. Sten's gone sheet-white. And Declan. He chokes out a cough that makes my guts capsize.

Because, that's it.

The door is closing,

I can feel it.

Maybe he won't find out the kind of man my dad was or the pain he left behind, but a grief-soaked girl is probably a deal breaker for a summer fling. It doesn't matter if I'm afraid of opening myself up to love—that's out the window now.

He knows I'm broken.

That I'm scarred and

scared to move on.

"Were your parents separated before he died?" Nell asks, her kaleidoscopic face bobbing around me.

"What?" I stammer.

"I heard something about your father," she adds. "And his receptionist?"

My chest implodes, shoulders narrowing in on themselves. Is this what it feels like? To have the blood drained completely from your body?

"How awful," she goes on. "Poor Rita—your mom's really been put through the wringer, hasn't she?"

"Hey," Suze snaps. "I'm guessing that's none of your business. Wouldn't you say, *Nell*?"

Nell cuts short as Suze sidles up beside me. Violet warms my other side.

"I'd watch how you talk to her," Violet adds, voice tough and full of starch. She raises her phone and hits record on Nell's stricken face. "Dredging up people's pain and turning it into gossip could get you fired for emotional assault."

"What?" She stumbles back. "I didn't mean—"

"Come on, Evie." Peter extends his wings around Suze, Violet, and me, ushering us toward the door. I feel his chest rise and fall as he offers Nell a disappointed tut.

My head is spinning when we topple onto the too-bright sidewalk.

"What a cow," Ed mutters.

"Honey, are you okay?" Suze sounds softer than I thought her voice possible. "We had no idea you were going through such a big loss."

Violet hugs me. "If there's anything we can do . . ."

Gnats flicker in my vision, heart pounding. I can't handle this—being babied and peppered with questions. They mean well, but my mask's been ripped off, and I'm ruined.

"I'm sorry, you guys. I can't. I have to go."

"Evie, wait." Declan calls after me, but I lurch down the street, bobbing and weaving between tourists. Where I'm going doesn't matter, as long as I get the hell away from every human being on the face of the earth. I want to strangle that blabbering bitch in spiked heels, but I force myself to keep running.

Eventually, I wind up in a quiet, residential neighborhood and try to catch my breath. Rough stucco scrapes my back as I slide down a wall, sinking to the ground. I can't get Declan's face out of my head. The pity melting off all of their stunned faces.

Hey, it's Georgy.

I look down at my phone screen through blurry eyes.

I heard what happened. Are
you okay?

Am I okay. *Fucking great,* I think. But don't actually type it.

We're all back at the van.
Want us to wait, or pick you
up somewhere?

I want to throw my phone down the sewer drain. I can't deal with their worry.

No thanks. I'm going to get a
cab home.

But your car is at NMPI. Are
you sure we can't give you a
lift?

I whimper at my additional patheticness. I mean, to hell with my car—let them tow it. I'm never going back there.

Promise you'll be safe. Okay?
Luke would kill me if anything
happened to you (so would I).

All I manage is a thumbs-up in response.

My tears dry up, but I stay on the sidewalk for another hour or so, mulling over my options, trying to decide what to do. Honestly? I could sit here forever, swathed in my own misery.

Miserable because, not only does my class know, not only do I loathe Nell Cohen, but the secrets I'm keeping from Mom are starting to give me brain freeze. Do I seriously think I can keep this from her forever? I mean, I've tried so hard to protect her, but what's to say Mom won't see our pregnant nemesis with her own eyes? What if the faucet is on full blast and all I'm doing is pressing my hands over the spout?

On a whim, I start typing again. To Mom, this time. Propelled by an infectious burst of guilt. *Mom, we need to talk.* Delete. *Mom, there's something I have to tell you.* Delete. *Mom, I know Dad was having an affair, but I also know he was packed up and ready to move out. Don't hate me for keeping the HUGEST SECRET OF ALL TIME.*

Delete.

Delete.

Delete.

Obviously.

Even the thought of pressing send on this razor-burn realness has me queasy and jumping to my feet, shaking loose my hands. I nearly combust when my phone starts buzzing again, but it's only Juana this time. Thank God.

Guess where I am right now?

10,000 WAVES

How jealous are you?

I roll my eyes. Juana's at Santa Fe's fancy Japanese spa. Great. Congratulations.

> I honestly don't care right
> now. Sorry, but I'm having a
> shitty day.

A hot second later, my phone rings. "Tell me everything."

So I do. It takes me a full four blocks to get the whole story out, starting with a sentence-by-sentence replay and then moving on to my angsty emotional interpretations.

At the end, Juana groans. "God, I hate Nell Cohen. Just hearing her name is giving me indigestion."

"She's heinous." I grab a pebble off the sidewalk and hurl it into some bushes. "Like, why did she have to say all that in front of my class? I was starting to like those guys—or, at least, I liked that they didn't know. Nobody thought I was a sad sack with a dead dad."

"You're not a sad sack."

"Or judged me because of his nasty girlfriend."

"His girlfriend is *not* your problem."

"Yeah, but they used to think I was normal."

"You *are* normal," Juana yells into the phone. "Look. You've got to stop thinking any of this is your fault or that you're going to end up cheating and being cheated on. You aren't your parents. None of us are, thank baby Jesus. And don't even think about Bree. I know we stalked her last weekend, but you can't let her get in your head like that. You need a Bree Hewitt enema. Or, wait, I mean a lobotomy—we don't want Bree Hewitt crawling up your ass!"

Before I can stop myself, I'm laughing. JJ too.

"I can't believe I'm about to say this, but I'm not even in the mood for a spa day right now. Want to hang out?"

"No, you should stay. What are you even doing there?"

"Nothing."

"Juana . . . ?"

"I came to see Melanie. She works at the restaurant, but I missed her break."

I think about rolling my eyes, but the two of them have been back on for a few weeks now. Maybe it really is different this time. "You *sure* I'm not messing up your plans?"

"Shut up, of course not. Meet me at my house. We'll watch *Supernatural* and snuggle all night long."

"Only the funny episodes?" I ask.

"Only the funny ones."

Chapter 15

I end up conking out in a sleeping bag on Juana's floor, bathed in candy wrappers and Winchester dreams. Morning creeps closer to noon and JJ's barely stirring, so I head for her private bathroom to wriggle out of my clothes. Showering at the Lujans' is the best because Debbie buys all these deliciously expensive bath products. I choose a Moroccan oil shampoo that moisturizes my scalp and calms my nerves; a sugar scrub to tackle yesterday's shame.

"Juana, where's your blow dryer?" I yell, wrapping a striped towel around my curves.

She pokes her head into the bathroom and looks me up and down. "Why don't you air dry today? Scrunch those curls."

"Because you have a blow dryer. And I want to blow dry my hair."

"Nah." She pulls my slippery arm back into her bedroom, holding out a stretchy, blue maxi dress with tiny purple flowers. "Cute, right? I stole it from my mom's closet. It's way too young for her—despite what she may think—and you need clean clothes anyway. You should wear it to the park, no?"

One of my eyebrows curves toward Canada. "What is happening right now?"

"Nothing, except trying to help you stop dressing like you work at a gas station."

"Excuse me! I do *not* dress like—"

"Okay, a really nice gas station that sells cappuccinos and artisanal chocolates . . . but still. You'd look gorgeous in this. Come on."

"Juana?" I cross my arms. "Why are you trying to dress me up and take me to the park? Are you going to propose?"

"Okay. Look." She sits at the edge of her bed, pulling her phone out of her pajama pocket. Except, no. Not her phone. *My phone.* "You got a text while you were in the shower."

"And?"

"And it was that Declan guy."

My stomach drops. "Juana Joy Lujan, what have you done."

"He wanted to see how you were doing."

"So you read the message and put my phone back in my bag. RIGHT?"

She doesn't smile so much as bare her teeth for a dental exam. "Come on, don't be mad! He used so many emojis. Teenage boys are so cute when they try to emoji flirt. I couldn't resist. I told him you'd meet him at Rose Park."

"You told him wh—"

"I know you hate me right now, but there's not much point to being shocked. He's sweet, Evie! You think everyone hates you, but clearly they don't. Just, like, give him a chance. Besides, he's already on his way, and a lady never cancels."

"Ladies cancel all the time."

"Welp." Juana shrugs and practically lassos the dress over my bewildered head. "Not this lady."

———

Rose Park is tiny with—you guessed it—a small garden of multicolored rose bushes in the center and a few massive pine trees here and there. The way this summer has been so dry, a lot of the grass is dying and the pine trees look a little anemic. Miraculously, the roses are doing fine. They're beautiful, actually.

Curious that Juana would suggest such a romantic landscape for this meeting.

I get out of my car, and Declan's already there, lying on the patchy grass, propped up on one elbow and reading a weathered paperback. He spots me and leaps to his feet, tossing a novel called *Lullaby* onto the ground.

"Hey, what's up? I'm glad you came."

"You can thank Juana. She kind of stole my phone to text you while I was in the shower."

"Really?" He smiles. "How Cyrano of her."

Which is probably exactly what she was thinking.

"Should we . . . ?" Declan gestures toward the grass and sits back down. I settle a couple feet over, arms crossed in an unsuccessful attempt to flatten my boobs.

"You look nice, by the way."

I blush. Not to sound *whatever* or anything, but I actually do. The sky-blue rayon matches my eyes and cozies nicely up against my curves. Presumably Declan still thinks of me as the girl with depressing family drama, but at least I look good while he's thinking it.

"How was the rest of class yesterday?"

"Fine. Mostly everyone was worried about you."

"You mean, gossiping about me," I mutter.

"No way. More like appalled by that lady. You should have heard the way Suze tore into her after you left. It was kind of amazing, actually. I should have filmed it. Side note, do *not* mess with Suze Wilkinson."

I flash a gentle smile. "Thanks."

Declan chews on his lip for a second. "Evie, I'm really sorry about your dad. I had no idea. I get why you kept it from us, so I'm sorry we all know, but if there's anything I can do, you know I will—we all would, I mean."

His concern seeps through my skin and pierces my heart. I force a nod, looking down at the grass. Cars whiz by, birds chirp. We pretend what happened yesterday didn't change everything. But it did. Of course it did. This was a terrible idea.

I shouldn't have come. More pity isn't going to do me any good—least of all his.

"Do you do top fives?"

I look at him and blink. "What?"

"It's something me and my friends do back at home. Like icebreakers."

"You want to do *icebreakers*?" I literally cringe, and Declan laughs.

"Hear me out. They're more like boredom breakers. I'll start." He clears his throat. "Favorite words. I like the word tomfoolery. It's a classic and it's totally underused. Mellifluous, unconscionable, nefarious. And . . ." He pauses, a grin stretching his lips. "Puppies."

"Puppies."

It's not a question. A judgment maybe, but not a question.

"Those playful, popping Ps—it's onomatopoeic."

I fight a smile. "Yeah, I guess."

"You *guess*? Tough crowd."

"Okay, Mr. Icebreaker. Do another one."

"You're not ready to chime in?"

"It would be unconscionable."

"Touché." He grins. "Okay. Top five comic book movies. *Spider-Man: Into the Spider-Verse. Black Panther. The Dark Knight.* Can't forget the *Guardians of the Galaxy* franchise. And, of course, *Wonder Woman.*"

"Of course," I snort.

"What?" He cocks his head. "You didn't like *Wonder Woman*?"

"No, I actually loved it. All those Amazon women are such badass warriors. In fact, I loved all of those movies. Except *The Dark Knight*. Which I didn't see."

His nostrils flare to the size of tennis balls. "That is. Tragic. Gonna have to remedy that. But okay, let's see if I can think of something a little closer to home. How about a Santa Fe top five? One, green chile, obviously. And then there's red chile, obviously. And you obviously can't leave out the green and red chile combo—"

"Christmas," I say, feeling my voice perk up. "Obviously."

"Right. Christmas." His eyes lock onto mine. He smiles, flicking his bangs out of his face. "Four, I like the view from the top of Sun Mountain. And, five, I like . . . you."

You.

A tornado whips through my chest, stealing my breath. Three simple letters to knock me off my feet, off my game. I'm shook to the point of speechlessness, but I sit up a little straighter, worrying less about my boobs and more about the beating heart beneath them.

"*Aaand*, crickets." Declan laughs. "Sorry, that didn't sound as cheesy in my head."

"That's not it," I manage. "The thing is I . . . I—" *I what?* Because I can't tell him how scared I am. That my heart hurts too much to unlock. "Look, it's very honorable of you to take pity on me or whatever, but—"

"Pity?" he yelps. "That is *not* what this is about. I mean, I'm incredibly sorry that you lost your dad like that. Georgy said it was only a month ago, so I mean, holy shit. But that's not why I like you."

I blink and my eyes sting. I'm too ashamed to tell him how broken I am. *Why* I am. But the truth is delicate and messy and rough, and my pain goes so much further than death; it spans a whole other ocean. Maybe Declan doesn't pity me, but he doesn't see me either. Not yet.

"After he died, I found out my dad was having an affair."

Declan lowers his head.

"That's what Nell was talking about—my dad and his receptionist. And, no, my parents weren't separated. Bree was his mistress or whatever. And now she's pregnant."

"Shit, Evie. That's intense."

"And I should probably mention that I've even followed her a few times. Y'know, to give you a clear picture of how disturbed I am."

Declan's eyes bulge, but I raise a palm before he can answer. "Don't. I just needed to explain. That if I act weird around you, that's why. And I can't even believe I'm admitting this, but . . . I like you too." I pause to cringe. "God, I suck at crushes at the best of times. But, the thing is, you're only here for the summer, right? It's a bad idea. I don't think I could handle adding heartbreak to what I'm already suffering through."

He starts to nod, eyebrows drawn. "Okay."

"Okay?" I feel my fluttering, contradictory heart fall.

"Yeah. I mean, I get it. I kind of wondered what that woman from the gallery was talking about. No wonder you don't want anything to do with me and my witty banter." He pauses, smiling through a blush. "I still like you, though. From the first day of class, you seemed cool."

I swallow, staring down at the grass rather than his warm, hazel eyes.

"Plus," he adds, "you're like the only reason I'm surviving this summer. My parents dumped me with Baba and Jiji so they could fly to Laos for a new documentary. It's always been like this. I'm a total afterthought."

"You're not an afterthought," I whisper. "But I'm sorry."

"I'm only telling you because hanging out has been good for me."

"Me too."

He blinks. "Then, maybe, if it's okay, we could kind of be friends?"

A breeze whips past, and I let a tiny piece of my heart loose in the air between us. I look at Declan, all lanky and concerned. For the first time, I see storm clouds in his eyes.

"Like a buddy system," I say with a tentative smile. "That could work."

He smiles back and the heaviness around us starts to lift.

"I'm sorry you got dumped with your grandparents."

"They're not that bad. They're just old."

"Now that we're buddies, should we stop talking about old people?" I ask.

"Abso-frigging-lutely." He laughs with relief. "I'd give anything for a conversation that doesn't involve FaceTime or require the other person putting in dentures."

"Aiming high, Maeda!" I smirk. "So, what do you want to talk about?"

"It's your turn for a top five—you ready?"

He lies back on the grass, hands laced over his chest. I sigh and lie back too. Next to him, but not too close. I glance sideways at him. "Right. Top five. And I can pick anything?"

He smiles with his eyes closed. "Anything at all."

CHAPTER 16

It's a struggle, getting myself to even *consider* going back to NMPI after the bullshit Nell Cohen pulled on Friday. My photographs though. They convince me. After an entire weekend glued to Luke's camera, I want to see them up on the projector screen. So, despite my shame, I roll myself out of bed. Force myself into the shower. I even put on a cute top, celebrating my curves rather than berating them. Which has nothing to do with my new "buddy," Declan.

Nope, nada.

I'm halfway out the door with coffee and a Pop-Tart when I notice a figure beneath a blanket on Dad's recliner. It's Mom, obviously, still in yesterday's clothes. There's a photo album in her lap, an empty wineglass nestled in the crook of her arm. I'm tempted keep walking, but . . .

There was a Pop-Tart between my teeth *that* morning too. I was in a rush, as always. Barely capable of so much as waving goodbye.

You're going to be late.

Ohmygod, Dad. I paused to roll my eyes, swallow my bite. *That's why I'm literally racing to the front door right now. See?*

Yeesh. Sorry.

Yeesh yourself. 'Bye.

The door slammed behind me, and then I was gone. He was gone.

I'm in just as much of a hurry this morning, but I pause. Swallow. Walk closer. Mom stirs when she hears my stainless steel thermos clink against the coffee table.

"Evie?" She wipes saliva from the corners of her mouth. "What time is it?"

"Nearly nine?"

She swears under her breath and lunges for her phone, firing off a quick text. A reply comes in a second later, and her shoulders release. "Okay, good. Sharon's covering for me."

"Why are you sleeping on a chair?" I ask softly.

She looks down. Like she hadn't even realized. Her cheeks flush as she moves the wineglass onto the floor. "Oh, I was up late. Looking at old albums. Remember our trip to the Four Corners? I found the cutest picture of the three of us at Mesa Verde. You were probably too young to remember."

I bite my lip. Because I *was* too young. I don't remember it at all. I wonder how much I'll continue to forget, the older I get.

"You on your way to the photography institute?" Mom rubs her eyes and sits up a little straighter. She looks around, out of sorts. Almost like—I get the feeling—she still wakes up some mornings and expects to find him here. Whistling while he shaves, chuckling at podcasts.

My chest sinks, and I have to pump it back up manually with a forced inhale. "Yeah, I'm on my way out. There's a fresh pot of coffee in the kitchen. Want me to pour you some?"

She shakes her head no, but I do it anyway, returning a moment later with black coffee in her May the Floss Be With You mug. It's practically scalding, but she devours a mouthful anyway.

"I should go," I say. "See you tonight."

"Tonight?" She winces. "I'm supposed to be doing something with Sharon tonight. Is that okay? I assumed you'd be out."

"On a Monday?"

Her lips part slightly—maybe to backtrack? Apologize?—but I quickly shake my head. "No, it's fine. You and Sharon have fun. I'm eating dinner at Juana's anyway."

"Are you sure? Because if you want—"

"No, it's fine. I seriously don't care."

"Evie, I can tell you're—"

"I'm not!" I shout. Because, I mean, I *am*, but what good will it do, calling out her selfish bullshit. I sling my camera bag over my shoulder, feet quick as I back away. "I've got to go. I'm going to be late."

You're going to be late.

Dad's words ring in my ears, all the way down the driveway
and to my car.

Tears tiptoe up my throat,
but I swallow them down
and put the car in drive.

———

Emotionally, I'm a worn-out chew toy when I walk into class
twenty minutes later. And it doesn't help that all eyes instantly
glue onto me, full of puppy-dog woe and compassion. Before
I'm even able to dump my stuff on my usual loveseat, Violet's
beside me, squealing, surrounding me with her swan-like
arms.

"I thought about you all weekend. Let's exchange num-
bers—I can't believe we haven't already."

"We're all so sorry to hear about your daddy," Suze adds.
"Here you are, coming in to class, day in and day out, and going
through *this*."

Sten nods. "We had no idea. I mean, we heard about Victor
Parker's death—his firm handles our taxes, so they sent out an
email. But we didn't know your dad personally or that you
were his daughter."

I wince. My most tragic life experience, emailed out in a
newsletter.

Their delicate intentions crawl over my skin like spiders.
Not one of them mentions the Nell-induced elephant in the

room, but they must be thinking it, right? Desperate to know if my dad had a *thing* with his receptionist? Or, I don't know. Maybe they know already. Maybe it was an attachment on the email Sten and Peter received; they're just too polite to say it.

"I'm sorry about Friday," I say after a minute. "And for lying to you guys."

"You didn't lie." Ada frowns. "It's called compartmentalizing."

"It's your business," Peter says, eyes heavy. "We only wanted you to know we're here for you."

"If there's anything at all we can do . . ."

"I feel like I missed something. Is Evie not okay?"

We all look over at Henri, who said it. His French accent is so deadpan, I'm honestly not sure if he's kidding. Actually, I am sure. And he's not. Everyone else seems incensed, appalled by his insensitivity. But. I don't know. It makes me laugh. I mean, ladies and gentlemen, I present to you Henri: a beacon of sympathy. Pretty soon Violet and Declan are giggling too. Then Suze and Peter, even Beth, until it's run its course and we all refocus on Georgy.

"On that note," she says, "let's get to it. After gallery hopping on Friday, you were supposed to complete your own interpretations. Let's see what you came up with."

Henri surprises no one by volunteering to go first. The lights dim, and the screen fills with still life photographs of fruit and flowers, eerily identical to their oil-painted counterparts. They're good, technically, but nothing special. Georgy suggests finding more creative still life objects and lowering the camera's ISO speed. Then there's Ada's ethereal portraits of Ed, really taking Georgy's "interpretive dance" directive to a whole new level.

We reach the end of the submissions, and Georgy smiles at me. "Do you want to show anything, Evie? You don't have to."

"I didn't really do the assignment. But—" My fingers still shake, no matter how many times I hand Georgy my thumb drive. "I took a bunch of random pictures this weekend."

Thumbnails pop up on the screen. Most of my Sunday was spent walking, exploring new hiking trails. Dusty-red landscapes and brittle piñons; portraits of my limbs and soul. I even managed to take some pictures of a hawk.

Funny how Dad's love of birds feels almost like his legacy.

Georgy repositions her glasses and starts clicking through. The hawk came out blurry. My landscapes are nice but uninspired. The warmth of boredom begins to seep under our skin. Then . . . stops. We get to my self-portraits, and the air crackles. People comment on the framing. The light. The way my head is turned away, hair obscuring my face.

"I love how you blend into the wooded area around you," Ada says.

"Like camouflage." Declan looks at me and winks.

"I love the colors."

"The drama."

"The mood."

Henri says something about my "young clothing" (his words) being an intriguing contrast to the harmony of nature. Which I'm not entirely sure isn't an insult.

We break for lunch, and I'm the only one who doesn't follow the gang down to the café. Taking my time instead to retie my shoelaces, waiting till no one's in the room but Georgy.

"You okay?" she asks, pulling a stack of papers from her bag. "I'm glad you came back today. I honestly wasn't sure if you would."

"Neither was I."

She hands the stack to me, motioning to each empty seat in the room. "I liked your self-portraits. Is that what you feel the most comfortable with? It's a great way to express yourself, and you show a real talent for it. It can be tough to get the focus right, but—"

"Hey, could I show you something?" The words rush out of me, hot and fast over hers. "Sorry to interrupt you. I didn't want to show this stuff in front of everyone, but I kind of wanted your opinion."

"What is it?"

My eyes wander up to the ceiling, searching the slanted wooden vigas for my thoughts. How do you tell someone you barely know that you've been stalking your dead father's pregnant girlfriend? I mean, you don't. But it's like a switch has flipped inside me. I've spent so much energy fearing everyone's reactions, but what if Georgy doesn't care? What if my whole bunch of weirdo classmates are here for me, like they said? Still, better to make Georgy my focus group.

Rather than stumble through a sticky preamble, I opt for handing her the SD card from my camera and putting last weekend's images up on the screen. And then, there she is: life-size and chromatic. A flush bleeds out from my core, all the way up to my cheeks. There's something about seeing Bree magnified. Alone in the parking lot, a streetlamp illuminating her face. Shadows clawing at her cheeks. Projected this big, I can see a scar above her plump upper lip. Concealer masking the zit on her chin.

"Wow," Georgy breathes. "This is fantastic."

"You think?"

"Absolutely. You've done something incredible with the highlights and shadows." She pauses, eyes landing on me. "There's a lot of emotional context too. Is that . . . ?"

"The woman my dad was sleeping with?" I bristle, squinting down at my fingernails. "Did Luke tell you?"

She hesitates, then nods. "And she's pregnant?"

"It would appear so."

"Have you spoken to her?"

"Are you kidding?" I almost laugh. "I'm not talking to that slut."

Georgy's eyes widen. "Sweetie, I know you're hurting, but—"

"But what? She slept with my dad. Who was *married*."

She opens her mouth, then shuts it, then clears her throat. "I know. Really, I do. But if you could take a step back," she says softly. "Maybe try to be objective."

I follow Georgy's gaze back to the projector. Bree fumbling with her car keys, glancing over her shoulder as she walks into McDonald's. Grim and glaring at a ransacked tray of fast food. Her eyes are empty and big as cereal bowls.

"Now. Look at her. What do you see?"

"Someone pathetic." The word is harsh on purpose, grating because it can be.

"Or . . . lonely?"

We're both quiet for a minute, comforted by the hum of the projector. When I don't respond, Georgy ejects my thumb drive, and the screen goes dark.

"I know you're hurting," she says, voice gentle. "And I know it's impossible to see it from her side. But maybe acknowledge the fact that she's got one? Maybe she *is* horrible. Maybe she has beguiling ways and ulterior motives. I don't know. I have lived through a lot of relationships though, and I can promise you nothing is ever as black-and-white as it seems."

My jaw hardens in response, a lump forming in my throat.

"Speaking purely as an artist, these are beautiful images. You've really captured the tension through use of light." She pauses to untwirl her bun, fingers dancing through her hair. "But we both know you can't move forward with this as a project at NMPI. Why don't you wrangle a friend to be your subject? You may not feel it right now, but what really stands out about these images isn't the distance, it's the empathy. Maybe there's something there."

Empathy.

The word rocks back and forth in my brain. Flickers like a candle till I can almost feel its spark. I do not empathize with Bree Hewitt. I mean, I can't. She's a monster. But I smile anyway, thanking Georgy for her time and for placating my flimsy confidence. She pats my shoulder and grabs her purse, heading outside to make a phone call. All I can do is stand there in the empty classroom, laying out my thoughts like solitaire.

Bree is sad . . .

Bree is lonely . . .

Bree is hurting.

I am sad . . .

I am lonely . . .

I am crushed.

The both of us, aching over Victor Parker.

I finish distributing the handouts and sink back down into my seat, thinking about my photographs of Bree. The anger fueling me and feeding my shutter finger. But what if Georgy is right? What if I'm starting to see past Bree's yearbook picture and short skirts? The word "home-wrecker" still comes to mind, but her smile and clumsiness distort me.

Maybe Bree is more than just one thing. Maybe we all are.

CHAPTER 17

"Did you ever see an eighties movie called *Stakeout*?" Declan whispers.

It's Saturday night, and I bet we are the only people in the history of time to haunt yoga studio parking lots while on a date. I mean, not-a-date. Our buddy system in action. Bree's clunker is parked near the front of the lot, and we're in the back. In my Subaru this time, because Juana is on another date with Melanie—which is good because it meant she didn't ask me a thousand questions about my plans with Declan.

"*Stakeout*," I ponder, reaching for another Twizzler in the jumbo pack between us. Side note: I'll say this about our buddy system, it's nice not to feel self-conscious about eating in front of a boy. "I don't think so. Who's in it?"

"Charlie Sheen's brother. Emilio Estevez." Declan swings his Twizzler around like a lasso. "That's what this feels like. Eighties detective romp, *Stakeout*. I call Emilio. You have to be Richard Dreyfus."

"*Who?!*" I squeak. "Can't we pick a movie with a strong female lead? Like, what about *The Girl with the Dragon Tattoo*?"

"In which case I'm Daniel *Craig*? Uh, yeah. I'm good with that."

I suppress a grin and get quiet again, scrolling through my Spotify, ultimately settling on The Weeknd.

"I saw him at Madison Square Garden."

"Really?" I rein in a gasp. "I desperately wanted to see him in Albuquerque last year, but my dad wouldn't let me."

"Fish bowl punishment?" Declan asks, smirking a little.

I try to smirk back. Because he's right, but now I'm stuck remembering a C+ in math followed by a fight about my lack of ambition. My blood bungees up to my earlobes. Like, it was okay for him to have an affair, but I couldn't go to a fucking concert without straight As.

Declan clears his throat. "Do you miss him?"

"Who, The Weeknd?"

He rolls his eyes, and I frown. "Yeah . . . I miss him all the time."

There's a pause, and Declan gently touches the back of my hand on the gearshift. I let my fingers flex. An invitation. Every nerve tingles as Declan's fingers slowly bend, soft and curving around mine. My heart races, but I keep still. This is not buddy-system behavior. This will not keep my heart in one piece. But it feels peaceful, and I ignore my brain in favor of a warm, lazy breath.

"My dad told good knock-knock jokes."

"Yeah?"

"I mean, as good as a knock-knock joke *can* be."

"Hit me," he says, palm still pressed against mine.

I pause, trying to think of a good example. "Okay, knock knock."

"Who's there?"

"Grape."

"Grape who?"

"You should see a doctor if your poop is gray!"

Declan winces with laughter. "Well, I mean. That was a joke." He snorts again. "Okay, knock knock."

"Who's there?"

"Interrupting chicken."

"Interrupting ch—"

"Bcaw! Buck-buck-buck-bcaw!"

"Oh my God, that was horrible!" I shriek. "Not even the joke—which is a knock-knock classic—but that atrocious chicken impression."

"I think you'll find I am an impeccable chicken."

"Sure you are."

Our laughter fades, and Declan's eyebrows slowly draw together. "Do you ever wonder why he did it?"

"Why do you think I'm here?" I glance at Bree's car. "My dad was a good person, okay? Yes, he was a drill sergeant about homework, and I guess he cheated, but he was decent. He went to my dance recitals and soccer games. Taught me all about birds and took us on family hikes."

"Sounds like he loved you a lot," Declan says. "Even if he . . . you know."

"That's just it, though. I don't understand *why* he'd YOU KNOW. Like, I hate that I have to *remind* myself of his goodness. I'm sick of having to replace bad thoughts with better memories. And, I mean, what if he really was just—" I force a sharp inhale to pump the brakes, but the thought has already formed. *A dirtbag. Selfish.* I shake my head, and my lip trembles. "There has to be a reason," I whisper. "I *need* there to be a better reason."

"Of course."

"And my mom," I add, swallowing back tears. "The fact that she stuck around has to count for something, right? That it couldn't have been my dad's fault? Otherwise, I mean, why would she knowingly let him do this to her? That *can't* be who he was . . ."

Declan shakes his head. Maybe he agrees or maybe he's trying to walk me down off this ledge. Because I am on a fucking ledge here.

I wipe my eyes before the levee breaks and force a laugh. "I'm fun to be around, huh?"

"Actually? Yes." He smirks, but his eyes sag.

"Are your parents still in Laos?" I ask softly. "Have you talked to them?"

"No, but their Instagram feed's nice." His jaw muscles flex. "Next best thing to, like, *actual* communication."

"Were they always like this?"

"Pretty much. Always on a shoot or preparing for one. A few years ago, Mom got pregnant. I guess it was an accident, but she was excited. Kept talking about how she was going to pull back from work, focus on family. I got excited too." He pauses, bangs drooping down over his eyes. "Then she lost the baby, and Dad signed them on to a project in Mozambique the next day. He's super driven. I seriously think he was relieved when she miscarried."

I barely know how to respond, so I squeeze Declan's hand instead. Not flirty like before. But, like, in solidarity. We're both quiet for another minute, looking toward the front of the parking lot, wondering if Bree is ever going to come out, not really caring either way as my palm molds to Declan's.

It's weird to think about Declan's dad being relieved about a miscarriage. Weird and incredibly sad. It makes me wonder how my own dad felt about having another baby. Did he *want* one? Was I not enough? Was he really going to discard one family to make room for another?

The fact that I'll never know splits my heart into a thousand empty pieces.

"Evie, look!"

A light flashes as the studio doors swing open. I lift my camera off the dashboard, lens poised. Mommies-to-be waddle out. Same as last time, separated into different flocks and cliques. All except Bree. Slouching and sweaty, she is the last preggo to emerge from the studio. Her mousy, messy hair is in a bun, and she's got two lumps protruding from her body—one lump is the baby, the other is her boobs, smooshed together in a sports bra under her gray sweatshirt. For a minute, she lingers on the sidewalk. *Click.* She yawns into her palm, acrylic nails scratching her nose as she blinks up into the evening sky.

Declan rests his elbows on the dashboard. "What is she doing?"

It's hard to answer because she's not doing anything. Avoiding *everything.* The rest of the parking lot empties, and Bree gets her keys out of her straw bag, walking slowly to her car. She's nearly there when she trips, smacking down against the asphalt.

"Oh my God, what happened?"

Declan shakes his head. "Did she trip on her shoelace?"

"I don't know!"

"Use the camera," he urges.

Of course. I zoom in and focus. Bree lies flat for a second, slowly pushing up on one arm. She's not crying, but she looks dazed as she rubs the back of her head, reaching down to feel her ankle. The longer she rocks, the more agony she seems to be in. I glance behind her at the yoga studio, but it's gone dark. The parking lot is empty.

"She needs help. Right?"

Declan nods.

I hold out my fist for rock paper scissors, which is what

Juana and I would do in this situation, but Declan's eyes only widen in horror.

"Well, *I'm* not going," I whisper. "What if she recognizes me? How do I explain what I'm doing here? Maybe we should call 911 and run."

"Run?" he chokes. "Come on, Evie."

Five seconds pass. Ten. He won't quit staring at me. Glaring at my soul. With a groan, I reach for the door handle and ease onto the sidewalk. I suck in a massive lungful of air before jogging across the parking lot. Bree's still clutching her ankle, trying to get up off the dirty concrete. Her eyes almost pop out of their sockets when she sees me, but I don't let myself think about it. I've got to be a firefighter. Go in, get the job done, and then get the hell out.

"Hey." I squat down to her level, looking at her ankle rather than her face. "Are you okay? Does it hurt?"

"Yeah," she says. "Like a bitch."

Her voice isn't how I remembered. Not bubble-gum bright or My Little Pony–pink. I'm struck by the licorice iced tea–ness of it. The fact she sounds human.

"What about your head?" I point.

"Headachey. Hey, how did you—"

"Me and a friend were . . . smoking." I pause, cheeks burned by my shitty lying skills. "Can you move?"

She lets out a frustrated grunt. "Not really. Can you put your arm under me—like this?"

My pulse skyrockets as I cradle her rib cage. The way I'm

forced to meet her gaze and stare into the wide-open sea of her eyes. On three, I hoist Bree's lumpy body up to standing. She's five foot five, the same as me. Her body is tougher, though. Round, yes, but yoga-fied. Toned and cheerleader-y despite the added flesh. My arm slips to her waist, grazing her belly, and I *can't*. I can't do this, I can't do this, I—

"I couldn't have done that on my own," she says finally. "Thanks."

"What about *that*?" I blink down at her basketball bump. "Is it okay?"

Bree pauses to spread her pink-and-yellow zebra-striped nails wide across her waist. She's quiet for a minute, her eyes heavy. Seconds pass. Years. All I want is to run back to my car and drive to Mexico, but I'm trapped, still supporting the majority of her weight. I stare hard at the pavement, listening to her hum, hearing the sound of her hands as they swirl circles along her gray cotton sweatshirt.

"Well?" I ask.

"Hold on." She presses a little harder below her left ribs, then smiles. "Yeah, I just felt the little guy kick."

My heart stops beating. "It's a boy?"

She flashes a small smile.

"What about your foot," I say—anything to change the subject. "Is it broken?"

"I'm pretty sure I twisted my ankle. Used to happen to me a lot."

On the cheerleading team, I think. I start to let go of her waist but she wobbles. "Do you need an ambulance?"

"No, no. It's not that bad. But I'm not sure I can drive home on it."

With her free hand she grabs her cell, looking down at the screen like it's going to turn into a flying carpet. Nothing happens. I watch her watch it, and the grim reality becomes more and more clear. The way she scrolls through her contacts, passing one name after another. Does Bree honestly have *no one* she can call?

"Uh . . ." I start, but my words fizzle. She obviously needs a ride. The devil on my shoulder (Juana in a Catwoman outfit) says, *Let that home-wrecking puta call a cab! You don't owe her anything.* And the devil is right: I don't owe Bree shit. But then the angel (Juana in tennis whites) argues, *It's the right thing to do. She needs a ride, show some mercy.*

"Are you calling someone?" I finally ask.

"I'm trying to think. My last Uber driver was super sketch. I'm not sure—"

"Look, do you need a ride?"

It's more of an accusation than an offer, but Bree's eyes shine. "Really?"

I shrug.

"Oh my God, thank you!"

Part of my brain shuts off while she reels off her address— the part with any sense of self-respect. Every inch of me came here out of anger, and now my arm is around her waist. Propping her up, driving her home. If I could see my own face right now, I'd punch it.

I pour Bree's fragile body into the passenger seat and sprint across the parking lot to where Declan is pacing, arms crossed over a Land of the Midnight Sun T-shirt. "Is she okay?"

"She needs a ride home," I pant. "She's all alone. You should have seen her scrolling through her contacts. I don't think she had anyone to call."

"And you're driving her?"

I nod, and Declan pulls me toward him, wrapping his arms around me. He feels warm and strong and certain, and I didn't know I needed this until my cheek presses into his chest.

"How can I help?" he asks. "Follow behind in your car?"

I raise my chin to look at him. "You don't drive."

"I don't have my *license*," he specifies. "But my aunt Jody taught me to drive at her cabin upstate. I'm pretty good. Never once hit a deer."

"How reassuring."

It's a bad idea, but we're already in it. Too late to turn back. I kiss my car keys for good luck and toss them into Declan's hopefully capable hands. He settles into the driver's seat and does all the good-driver stuff like adjusting the seat and the mirrors. I leave him to it, scurrying back to Bree's car.

I slide in behind the wheel without a word, and the car smells cantaloupe-sweet and breezy as it wheezes to life. Pearl

Jam blasts through the speakers, plunging nails through my broken heart. Because, I mean, fucking *Pearl Jam*. Dad's favorite. Now I'm cruising down Cordova Road and I'm thinking about hours spent suffering through *Ten* and *Vitalogy*; the T-shirt I removed from his suitcase and returned to the drawer. In all my hours of speculation, I never really thought about music being something they bonded over. The fact that their interests might have intertwined and overlapped.

"Make a right onto Pacheco," she says, glancing quickly at me.

Streets whiz by. A few drops of rain hit the windshield but they dry up before I can find the wipers. Typical. The rain doesn't care how badly we need it. Bree and I are both stiff as boards, breath catching as we bite our tongues. She must know that I know that she knows. My palms sweat onto her leather steering wheel. The seat belt crowds her belly. She shifts and tugs at it with each breath. Every block or so, my eyes dart to the rearview mirror, keeping an eye out for my silver Subaru. Declan is one car-length behind me, always.

We stop at a red light, and Bree cracks her knuckles. "Can you believe this weather?"

"Mm-hmm," I answer.

"God, I wish it would rain."

"Mm-hmm."

There are shell beads hanging from her rearview mirror. Loose change in the ashtray. I spot an empty McDonald's apple pie wrapper near her feet and blush at the memory of two weeks ago. Guilt bruises my dignity. I swallow and glance at her back seat through the rearview. A Game of Thrones novel, her yoga mat, a glittery gray scarf. The scarf is pretty, but at the same time, it bugs me. Almost like I know that scarf—like I *have* that scarf. I nearly swerve off the road when it hits me that I *do* have that scarf. Dad bought it for me. Last Christmas.

"Are you okay?" Bree asks.

"Fine," I manage through gritted teeth.

But I'm not fine. Not at all. We have the same scarf—*the same fucking scarf*—and my brain is on fire, wondering if he was really the type of guy to buy his mistress and his daughter matching gifts. I wince, and something cruel and sharp twists my heart. A brutal truth etching into my ribs. I've tried so hard to excuse him, to blame her, but—I swallow back tears— maybe my dad really *did* know what he was doing. Maybe the affair wasn't all on Bree.

Regardless, I'm gonna fucking shred my gray scarf.

"This is me." Bree's voice jolts me back to reality. She points to the newish apartment complex across the street, directing me toward her parking spot. "I'm on the third floor," she says, apologizing almost.

Which is when I realize: she's telling me she needs help getting up there. And, Jesus God, I don't think I can. I honestly might scream if I am forced to spend another second with this glittery-scarf-owning, Pearl Jam–loving—

"Hey, you guys okay?"

Declan knocks on the passenger side window, and Bree shrieks.

"It's okay," I say. "That's Declan. He was driving behind us in my car."

She glances at me quickly, and I give a quick, *I promise he's not a serial killer* look, which seems to satisfy her. She opens the door, letting him help her onto the curb.

"I feel so dumb for falling down like that. Pregnancy has turned me into such a klutz. I used to be able to do triple back-flips in my sleep, and now I fall down if I sneeze wrong."

"That sucks," Declan says, and I glare at him for being nice. We are not here to be nice. Or, I mean, that is the *only* reason we're here. There's no need to be cordial too.

I slink behind like a fool with Bree's purse, listening to the sound of her breath and self-deprecating mutters while Declan helps her up the stairs. The back of her neck is long and scarf-worthy. Does she also have the watch Dad bought me for my sixteenth birthday? The noise-canceling headphones I got on my fifteenth? Thinking about it makes me sick.

"I don't know how to thank you," she says, outside her apartment.

Declan waves discreetly and shuffles back down the stairs, abandoning me without permission. I flex my jaw, glancing at Bree's door. Is this where my dad would go while Mom and I waited at home? The two of us, suffering quiet dinners, thinking he was working late and crashing on the office couch. Did he really think he could have it both ways?

"I should go," I hiss.

"Evie, wait. I wanted to—"

"*I said, I have to go.*" I stumble back, nearly tripping down the staircase as I lunge for the banister. Away from apartment 3C. Away from Bree and her bump, her scarf, her everything. Because, like an avalanche, it's suddenly asphyxiating me. What I just did. Who I just helped. And . . .

My name. She said my name.

By the time I reach the sidewalk, I'm a desperate mess of tears. Full-blown blubbering sobs. It's embarrassing, and I try to run past Declan, but he takes a wide step and pulls me toward him. I bury my face in his chest, huffing and heaving until I can't hear her voice anymore, telling me she's having a baby boy. A tiny human who will share my blood in some despicable, biological way.

"It's okay," Declan whispers, stroking my hair. "It's gonna be okay."

He proves his driving skills yet again, navigating my car to his grandparents' house while I stare dully out the window. I've stopped crying, but my breath still shakes in my chest. The sheen on the sidewalk outside Baba and Jiji's house suggests they got more than five drops of rain. Nice to know it landed somewhere.

"Do you want to come inside?"

"With your grandparents?" I scoff. "No thanks."

He nods, and I don't stop him when he takes my hand. "Are you okay?"

"Not really."

"You did the right thing, helping her."

I wince and pull away. "I know you mean well, and I know I dragged you on that stakeout to begin with, but I really don't need your encouragement right now."

"Are you mad at me? For suggesting you help an injured *pregnant* woman?"

"Yeah, I'm fucking mad—okay? I didn't want to come face-to-face with her. I wanted to call 911!"

"Come on, Evie. You wouldn't seriously have done that."

"Oh, like you're an expert on my moral capabilities," I say, but my voice is softer. Sullen rather than raging. "I didn't think it was going to be like that. I keep expecting her to be horrible, but. She's not. She does yoga and eats McDonald's—that's literally all I know. Oh, and she likes Pearl Jam." I pause to sniff back tears. "Frigging Pearl Jam, Declan. He cheated on my mom—ruined our family—for a pretty girl who likes grunge rock. It's not fair." I stomp my feet and scream into the car. "It's not fucking fair!"

A dog barks, and I sink below the dashboard.

"It's *not* fair," he says softly. "But as much as I dislike Pearl Jam, I don't think you can credit them for breaking up your parents' marriage."

"Will you be serious?" I bark. "Something changed tonight. I *helped* her. I heard her voice. It honestly broke me."

"I know."

I don't think he has a clue, but whatever.

It's just . . . for so many weeks, I've tried to excuse him. Only seen *her* as the problem. The office tramp, asking for it in her slutty skirts and stilettos. Shit. I wince at the thought of it now—not her clothes, but my brain. That I could blame a skirt for my dad's bad decisions. God, I am the worst. Seriously. My steering wheel is more feminist than me right now.

The front door opens, and Baba steps outside, squinting with her palm up to her forehead, shielding her eyes from the motion-sensor light. Declan swears under his breath.

"I gotta go. And I know you don't want my opinion, but maybe you should take tonight as a sign. You have every right to be angry, but following Bree isn't going to take that away."

My jaw stiffens. I don't want to agree with him, but I'm not entirely sure he's wrong? I don't know. It's complicated. And maybe it's too impossible to explain that facing Bree *changed* me. Tonight, I ripped open a seam, and now all I want is to pick at more loose threads. Find out *everything*. He's right that I'm angry . . . but I'm okay with that.

Declan unbuckles his seat belt. "Thanks for letting me tag along, Lisbeth."

"Wait, what?"

"*The Girl with the Dragon Tattoo*." He shrugs, like, *duh*. Which is too cute, honestly. Nothing like Daniel Craig or whatever his character's name was supposed to be. But Declan Maeda is probably cuter. To me, anyway.

"Yeah, okay." I smirk a little, pushing him toward the door. "Thanks for being a private eye with me. While it lasted."

"It was unlike anything I've ever experienced. See you Monday."

With a wink, Declan scurries up the path. I look back down at my camera for a minute before hopping back into the driver's seat. Because of Bree's twisted ankle, there aren't many pictures, but in the ones I did snap, she's got a melancholy sheen. Ignored by pregnant classmates sauntering toward expensive cars and doting husbands. Hugging her yoga mat; locking the studio doors.

Bree, alone.

Bree alone.

Bree *alone.*

What the pictures don't show is that look of gratitude when I offered to help. The way she tried not to burden me with a heavy torso as I helped her into the car. Her low, summertime voice and those last few words as we stood awkwardly outside her apartment.

"*Evie, wait. I—*"

I what?

I'm sorry . . .

I loved him . . .

I never meant to hurt you?

I hate myself for wishing I'd let her finish that sentence.

CHAPTER 18

I cringe at the sight of Sharon's Mustang in our driveway when I get home. Like my evening wasn't bad enough without walking into *Moms Gone Wild*. But, alas, that is exactly what I get. The living room is a mess of empty wine bottles and Tostitos bags. Right in the epicenter is bronzed, brunette Sharon, dancing to Springsteen while Mom sings off-key into a hairbrush. White wine sloshes out of their glasses and onto the rug.

"Hello?"

Neither of them hears me. They're too busy "Dancing In the Dark."

"Mom!" I shout.

"Oh, Evie!" Her voice swims in slurred surprise. She clunks her glass down on the coffee table and smothers me in a teetering hug. Her nicotine breath is garlicky. They must have ordered pizza. "Hey, sweetie. I thought you were doing something for your photography class tonight."

"I was. It ended."

"Dance with us!" Sharon merengues over in a pink bandage dress to steal my hands. "You're getting so pretty, Evie. Have you lost weight?"

Because of course she would say that. It kind of rolls off me, though. To the point where I almost wonder if I've stopped giving a shit. Or, like, maybe actually *started*? Not that I'm about to have an existential chat with drunk Sharon.

I offer a saccharine smile. "Thanks, Sharon."

She winks a "you're welcome" before sauntering off to the bathroom.

I lower the volume on Springsteen and look back at Mom, who is weaving like a skipped record. "What are you doing?"

"What do you mean?" She fumbles with a cigarette pack. "Dammit, where did I put that lighter? Help me look for it, sweetie? It's the silver one Grandpa gave Daddy. It's got to be around here somewhere."

For a second, I try to play along, scanning the coffee table like a magpie. But her ignorance slashes open my skin and leaves a trail of guilt on the carpet. All night I've been watching Bree—young and pretty and pregnant—while Mom stands here, disintegrating. And it's my fault. All of it. She might be different now, if I hadn't unpacked Dad's suitcase. If I'd told her about Bree's pregnancy, maybe she would be moving on with her life rather than drowning in it.

"Would you stop looking for the fucking lighter?!"

Mom balks. "Evie? What's the matter?"

"God, Mom. *Everything* is the matter. I'm trying to protect you, but—"

"Protect me? From what?"

I shake my head, sucking the truth back in through my pores.

"Evie?" Her spine stacks on top of itself. It's the most alert I've seen her in weeks. "What do you think you're protecting me from?"

"Nothing," I mumble.

"Sweetie." She hesitates. "I think we need to have words."

Goose bumps prickle my arms. *Have words*—that's what Dad used to say. It always sounded so ridiculously formal, and it sounds even weirder coming from her. She pats the sofa cushions, and we sit down like strangers on the same job interview.

"I know you're disappointed in me lately, and I'm sorry. But if you knew what I'm up against." She pauses, almost smirking to herself as she reaches to refill her glass. "Believe me, there's a lot more to it than you realize."

"No, there isn't." My breath balls up in my chest and then fires. "I know about Bree."

Mom freezes mid-pour. "You . . . what?"

"I overheard you on the phone. Talking to Sharon after the funeral, and—"

"How much did I say?"

"You called her a bitch, and said you didn't want her in your house."

"Oh, sweetie." Her expression twists, fingers squeezing her forehead. "Why didn't you say something? We could have talked about it."

"Because you're so easy to talk to?" I scoff. "Look at you lately! You mope all day and drink all night. Missing him has made you almost dysfunctional."

"You think *that's* what this is about?! You think I'm acting this way because I *miss* him?"

"Well—" I hesitate. "I mean. Don't you?"

"Jesus, Evie. Of course I miss him, but I'm also furious with him!" The words barrel out of her, and the next second she's sobbing, shoulders bobbing uncontrollably. "He was cheating on me. You don't know what it feels like to be cast aside like that. To devote twenty goddamn years of my life to a man who decides *Bree* is the one who makes him feel young. You know why I didn't make him feel young anymore? Because I'm fucking not! I'm middle-aged! We were supposed to be middle-aged together, warts and all. But *nooo*. And now he's gone, and I still have to see her around town? Buying produce at fucking Whole Foods?"

I blink. Mom's never sworn this much in her life, and I'm lost in her words. Trying to catch them midair and make sense of them. "You've seen Bree?"

She nods, punishing her wine, necking the entire glass.

"If you've seen her, does that mean you *know*?"

"Y—" Mom stops short. All the color drains from her face. "Oh God, have you seen her too? Since she started . . ."

Started to show, she means. Since it became obvious to all of Santa Fe that Bree Hewitt is pregnant. I manage a terse nod. "Yeah, kind of."

"Damn it. I tried so hard to keep it from you, sweetie. I need you to know that."

"But why?" I ask. "Why didn't you just tell me?"

"Kids aren't supposed to know that kind of stuff about their parents. What good would it have done?"

"It would have changed everything!" I wail. "I've been killing myself, trying to keep you from finding out."

"Oh, honey." Her face softens into a disappointed smile. "That's sweet, but it's not your job to protect me. I am well aware that your dad was having an affair. And now that affair is due—in two months."

Mom goes about refilling her wine again while the living room spins around me. My whole world is ablaze, and she's raising her glass in the air, toasting her misfortune. One more drink and she'll need her stomach pumped.

"Mom, would you stop acting like this is *okay*?" I shout, jumping to my feet, limbs on fire. Because, I mean, her stubborn denial is infuriating. Giving me hives, pushing me over the edge.

"Honey, why are you getting so worked up? This had nothing to do with you."

"Are you kidding?! He was leaving us. How can you think it wouldn't affect me?"

She looks up at me, squinting. "Evie, what are you talking about?"

"Dad's bags were packed," I murmur. "If he hadn't died, he would have been gone by the end of the day. You're oblivious if you didn't see it coming."

There. I said it.

I fucking said it, and I half expect my chest to crack open. For relief to flood out of me and whoosh through the air. But there is no victory lap. I'm dizzy and panting. Mom is sobbing. Breaking in the exact way I knew she would.

"What are you talking about?" she asks again. "Who told you that?"

"Nobody told me. I . . . I found his bags." I lower my voice and my eyes, arms snaking around my waist. "I got home from the hospital before you, and his suitcase was on the bed, already packed. His clothes, his whole half of the room. I unpacked everything. It all went right back where it was supposed to be."

I don't look up when I'm done. Don't think I can stomach the hurt and betrayal in her eyes. She's quiet for a second, choking on tears.

"Did he—did you—" She shakes her head. "Did you really do all that?"

"Yes," I whisper.

"Why on *earth*, Evie? Jesus. What the fuck did you think you were doing?"

"I did it for you. To protect you."

She covers her face with her hands, sobbing uncontrollably. I've got tears of my own now; a spider web spinning tight around my throat. What have I done? All my certainty, my altruism—okay, so it wasn't altruism, but now it's mold. There are no words for this cinder block rot in my gut.

"Rita?"

Sharon clears her throat from the doorway, tiptoeing toward Mom. The room goes on mute. She obviously heard everything; the glower she shoots me could burn toast. "Why don't I make you some tea."

Mom wipes away tears to make room for a fresh torrent.

"I'm sorry," I tell the ground. "But you needed to hear it. I'm tired of keeping it all inside. Watching you act like this—especially if you knew. Like, you *knew* he was a dick and you stuck around anyway. I don't get it."

My words are acid, eating a hole between us. And it's my fault. Maybe Dad broke her heart, but I'm the one grinding it into pieces. I wish I could rewind time so far back that we're all at the dinner table, laughing at his silly, terrible jokes. A family. But I'm never going to feel that safe again.

"Mom, I—"

"Please don't say any more."

"But—"

"I said *stop*," she screeches. "Please, Evie, I'm begging you. Just stop."

Her sobs turn hysterical, and I duck back, sucking in my quivering lip.

"Maybe I should stay at Juana's tonight," I say, baby voiced and five years old.

Rather than answer, she turns her back to me, burying her face in a cushion to muffle the sound of her pain. After a minute, Sharon comes back in, resting a protective hand on Mom's shoulder.

"Why don't you give her some space," she mouths, head jerking toward the door.

I sniffle and stare too hard at Mom, silently begging her to—to what?

Forgive me?

Ask me to stay?

Tell me I am still loved?

But she says nothing. *Does* nothing but cry drunk, defiant tears.

So I do as I'm told, stumbling into the hall, fumbling to put on my sandals. I should probably grab spare clothes, but I'm too numb. Let me fester in these clothes and die in them.

I slink across the street but can't bring myself to ring Juana's doorbell. There will be plenty of time for "I told you so" speeches about my lack of honesty with Mom. Instead, I wander over to our tree. It's been years since I was limber enough to climb it. I lower myself onto the soft, cold ground, tucking my knees up into my chest. Feeling the darkness all around me.

Chapter 19

Every bone in my body tells me to stay away from Bree Hewitt, but I've got nothing left to lose. After a week of heavy, gray clouds that feed my mood but never end in rain, the sky gleams blue on Saturday morning, and I take it as a sign to use Luke's telephoto lens.

Not that I haven't been using it for class. The 70mm is better for self-portraits, but the telephoto lens has really helped with all my stylized, film noir portraits of Juana, who, I swear to God, suddenly thinks she's on the cover of *Vogue* every time I photograph her at night, shrouded in headlights or streetlamps. The results aren't bad, and my classmates seem to genuinely like my work . . . but it's not Bree, and she's all I can think about since Mom threw me out. Okay, so she didn't "throw me out," but I still haven't been home except to pick up clothes. Haven't uttered a single word to her in seven days, and it all boils down to one thing: Bree.

If Dad hadn't hired her
slept with her
impregnated her.
If I hadn't found his suitcase
unpacked his things
kept his secrets.
If I'd *known* Mom knew.
It could have gone differently.

I can't change the past, but I *can* hide behind my camera and let my festering thoughts play out. I can imagine the inside of her apartment—maybe a small threadbare sofa and a laptop on a rickety IKEA coffee table. Bare walls painted a rusty, puke green and dirty laundry everywhere. I can't control the past, but I do know where Bree Hewitt lives, and I'm hoping she'll be home at 8 a.m. on a Saturday. Double hoping that she'll be heading out soon, somewhere I can follow.

I wait in the back of her parking lot and pull the telephoto lens up to my eye. From down here, I can almost make out the metal C in 3C, showing me which door is hers. *Click*. I switch out the lens for a 35mm, turning the camera on myself. It's hard to get the focus right when you're not looking through the lens. I take about twenty self-portraits and like about two of them. I photograph my hands on the steering wheel; my eyes in the rearview mirror. There's a cardinal on a nearby branch, so I put the telephoto back on, focusing on the bird's gnarled beak.

A door slams, and I look back up in time to see Bree standing in her doorway, pulling a white cardigan over a striped maternity dress as she locks the door. There's a cane in her hand. It's the kind you'd get at the hospital, but hers has a million rhinestones on it, maybe decorated after an old injury. I hold my breath, narrowing the aperture as Bree limps down the stairs. She gets into her car, and the engine roars to life, a flurry of gray smoke billowing from the tailpipe.

Arctic Monkeys seems right for this mission, so I throw on SUPERNATURALLY DANGEROUS and keep my car a decent length away from Bree's as she heads out of the apartment complex and toward town. She eases into the left lane, forgetting her signal. She turns right, I turn right. We end up on South Guadalupe, and she finds a spot on the road, then hobbles into Bluebell Café, the first place I spotted her pregnant. My heart sinks into my chest at the memory.

My lens bobs around until I find her inside the café. Lucky for me, she drops her stuff at a table right by the picture window before heading to the coffee counter. My heart thumps while she's gone. Wondering what she'll order, who she'll meet, if it's wrong that I'm craving this.

She reappears at the table with a cup of tea and biscotti and cracks her knuckles. *Click.* Checks her phone. Yawns. Her clothes are nicer than her yoga wear. Not formal receptionist clothes, but her dress is cute. The purple brings out her eyes. *Click.*

A middle-aged couple comes up to her table, and Bree

smiles at them. I'm struck by the way she shakes their hands. Like she's interviewing for a job or something, which maybe she is? There's nothing relaxed about her demeanor. Not nearly as eager as the woman, who starts babbling a mile a minute while the guy goes off to the counter. Bree swallows a lot. She nods and laces her fingers over her belly. *Click.* When the guy returns, he's got two coffees and a cinnamon roll that he places in front of Bree. She shakes her head.

Who the hell *are* these people? With their sitcom style and anxious grins. The way Bree's so guarded is making me nervous. I take a thousand photos of their stilted, boxy gestures.

And just like that, it's over. As soon as they're gone, the smile drips off Bree's lips. Her shoulders curl in, both hands clutching her belly.

It's almost as if I've been expecting it when a tear slides down her cheek. Quiet, private sobs. Not for public consumption—not for me. All my pent-up breath rushes out as I toss my camera onto the passenger seat. I glare at it, waiting for it to explode. I'm about to start the engine when a glint of white catches my eye through the windshield.

I see Bree.

Crossing the street.

And waving at me.

She limps closer, an Ace bandage wrapped tight around one ankle. My heart bashes into my chest, desperate for a way out. Quickly, I push the camera onto the floor, tucking it underneath the passenger seat as far as it will go. I'm still afraid she might see it though, so I meet her on the sidewalk before she can bend down toward my window.

"Hey," she says, sniffling and wiping her cheeks with the back of her hand. "I thought that was you. What are you doing here?"

"Tomasita's," I stammer, pointing behind us. "I, uh, I'm meeting someone for lunch."

"At ten in the morning?" She giggles, wiping her eyes again. "Are you . . . okay?"

"I'm fine." Her eyes flit briefly back to the café. "Hormones, I guess."

"Oh."

"I'm glad I ran into you." She raises her cane, jiggling it so the rhinestones sparkle. "I wanted to thank you for helping me the other night. It's lucky you showed up when I fell—not that I'm *surprised* I fell. Pregnancy is *not* my friend all the time. I'm so klutzy and hormonal and exhausted compared to how I used to be. I'm doing my best, though. Which is why I'm on my way to Whole Foods. Hey, have you ever heard of hemp seeds?"

"What?" I blink wildly. "Um, yeah? I guess?"

"I'm supposed to be buying ingredients for a prenatal smoothie. One of the teachers at the yoga studio says it'll help with my energy. She told me to buy kale, ginger, spinach, yogurt, tofu, and hemp seeds. Isn't that what *pot* comes from? I can't believe I'm about to make a pot smoothie for my unborn baby!"

If Juana was the one cracking the jokes, I'd be 100 percent laughing along with her, but right now I am sweating, fidgeting, wondering why Bree's still talking to me or what I did to deserve this.

"I'm trying to be good," she goes on. "Folic acid, prenatal yoga, childbirth class. Not that I have a partner." She switches her cane from left hand to right, babbling about childbirth class like it's detention. How much she's dreading it, how showing up solo will be so embarrassing. All I can think is: *Maybe you should have thought of that before.* It's making me squirmier and squirmier, my heart running a marathon inside my chest.

"So, yeah, I'm off to spend half my paycheck on smoothie ingredients. Healthy, healthy, healthy—that's my new motto. Don't tell my OBGYN, but I still sneak in some Mickey D's. I love fries. How could anyone not, right?"

I blush, remembering that night. The way McDonald's fries didn't seem to make her happy at all. More like isolated. Misery sprinkled in salt.

"I have to go," I say. But I can't meet her eyes, so I look at her belly, the way her fingers swirl around it. It's almost hypnotizing until Bree gasps. She grits her teeth, pressing her belly button. "What is it?" I ask. "What happened?"

"The baby's kicking up a storm." She grins. "I swear he's trying to knock out one of my ribs."

He. There it is again.

"Want to feel?"

"What? No." I take a step back, banging against my car. "This shouldn't even be happening. I have to go."

Bree frowns. She looks at me. Really looks at *me*, for the first time. Like she's waking up from a coma and finally sees how massively fucked up this situation is. She takes a step back. "Thanks again for your help the other night. It was nice of you. I mean, considering—"

I shake my head for her to stop, then spin around, practically diving into the car.

Bree doesn't move. She's still standing there, face falling like a game of Jenga as I peel out of the parking space and drive off. For three blocks, I think I'm going to cry or puke or maybe both. *Touch her belly?* Does she actually think I want to *feel* that thing? That I'm *okay* with it?

Something new squeezes my heart that I can't quite place. Different from anger, different from guilt. Yes, Bree approached me, but I'm the one who followed her. I'm the one who got out of the car.

I press my foot hard against the gas pedal, hurtling too fast back to Juana's where I run up to her room and throw myself under the covers beside my still-sleeping best friend.

"You okay?" She's groggy when she sees me, eyes scrunching together.

"I talked to her," I whisper.

"To who? Your mom?"

"No. Bree."

She sits up, cottonmouthed but alert. "Wait, are you serious? What did you say to her?"

"Nothing," I sob. "She asked me to feel the baby kicking. She wrecked my life, and she stood there talking about smoothies. She acted like we were friends! She had the audacity to, to, to—"

"Come here." JJ pulls me close, tangling her legs with mine. "You've gotta stop following her, babe. It's too much. You're only hurting yourself. And it's not even productive. You said yourself that you're not showing the photos to your class. There's a *reason* you're hiding it from everyone."

She grabs a tissue for my tear-stained cheeks, rubbing my back while I cry. Whether or not she believes it, my best friend tells me everything is going to be alright. With a quick text, she cancels her plans with Melanie, and then she is mine. For the day, the weekend, eternity. We'll devote ourselves to pretending Bree is a problem that can be solved through *Supernatural* and junk food. That there could possibly be an easy solution to this ache in my heart.

CHAPTER 20

There's an end-of-summer gala in the works at NMPI, but you'd think it was the fucking moon landing. Suze and Beth turn into giggly schoolgirls, gabbing over who's the most talented while Peter and Sten discuss themes and location ideas. Violet's thrilled too, adding the news to her Stories, but I can't help slumping down in my seat. My pictures of Bree are obviously never going to see the light of day, but are my portraits of Juana good enough to exhibit? Am I brave enough to plaster my own face all over the NMPI walls?

"How big are we printing these?" Ed asks, knees splayed wide. "My industrial landscapes should really be thirty-six by thirty-six, at least."

Violet rolls her eyes. "Is size really that important, Ed?"

I snort, and Georgy stifles a grin. "I'll ask the manager if there are stipulations."

Declan nudges me with his elbow. "Nervous?"

"No," I say. But yeah. Giant pile of yeah.

"I'm pre-embarrassed for whatever humiliating comments my grandparents make about everyone's work. Baba's going to have no idea what to do with Ada's toilet bowl still lifes."

I laugh . . . then secretly cringe. Like, will I have to invite my mother to this? Will we be on speaking terms by next month? The more I retreat into my photography, the less likely that seems. Not that I don't miss her. In fact, I miss her to the point of watching her through the blinds sometimes. Occasionally using my telephoto lens to zoom in on her new clothes, her fresher face. Mom's doing pretty well, it looks like.

Correction: doing well without me.

"What are you going to show, Evie?" Georgy asks.

Everyone looks at me, and my face burns.

"The pics of your best friend are awesome," Violet offers. "You should show those."

"And your self-portraits," adds Beth. "Maybe a combination of the two?"

Which is nice of her to suggest. Honestly, she'd probably have me put on a watch list if she knew about Bree. So, rather than elaborate, I nod and turn everyone's attention on Declan. "What about you?"

"Um." He grins, almost bashful. "I want to keep shooting my grandparents."

Everyone emits puppy-dog *awwwws*, and Declan's cheeks redden.

"I know they're ancient and into buttons and obsessed with teaching me how to play this Japanese card game, uta-garuta. But they've been there for me way more than my parents. I want to make the time count."

More *awwwws* crescendo. I smile and bump Declan's shoulder, allowing my body to stay pressed against his. It's sweet that he wants to make his final project about them. Immortalize them, almost. So sweet I could kiss him, the thought of which is becoming harder and harder to ignore.

"Ooh, look at the lovebirds!"

"Beth," Violet groans. "Let a moment be a *moment*."

"What! I'm only saying they look cute together."

Sten rests his head on Peter's shoulder. "Remember being young and in love?"

"*I* do," Suze sighs. "Isn't young love the best? God, you two are so adorable I could *die*!"

And there it is again: die.

I swallow hard, waiting for that sinking feeling. For the memory of loss to drag me somewhere dark and infectious.

Only, I keep waiting. I feel . . . okay. Well, not *okay* okay—I am furiously blushing under the collective gaze of a dozen busybody photographers. But they mean well. They mean for me to be happy. And sitting beside Declan, his body warm and close to mine, I wonder if maybe I could be.

———

I drive Declan home after class, even though Baba and Jiji are perfectly capable in their boat-size Lincoln. The four of us exchange a few polite words in the Maedas' pristine kitchen, and then Declan tells them we're going to study in his bedroom. Which isn't really *his* bedroom. Back in New York, I imagine exposed brick walls, an old-fashioned typewriter on a refurbished postmaster's desk. Records, leftover Euros from spring break in France, maybe even a pair of vintage skis or something. Hunter S. Thompson, without the gonzo weirdness. Here, though, at the Maedas' adorable little house, it's got a much simpler vibe. White walls, potted orchid on the nightstand, a twin-size bed. The only thing *Declan* is the Leica camera on his dresser and the sticker-covered Mac it's plugged into.

"Want to listen to music?"

I nod, and something indie starts playing through tinny laptop speakers.

We sit awkwardly on the floor, painfully avoiding his bed, which is the only other seating option. It's not just about Baba and Jiji in the next room. I've never been in a boy's bedroom before. And no, Juana's little brother's bedroom doesn't count. My heart is racing, knowing I told Declan I don't want anything more than friendship. I mean, I do want friendship. Friendship is great. But I can't concentrate on anything except his smile as he sits down beside me.

Whatever band is playing, the music is chill and stops me

worrying about the bulge of my cleavage in this V neck T-shirt. Still, I pull my camera out of my bag to fill the silence.

"Want to see what I've been working on?" I hold it out to him, scrolling through thumbnails, past Bree at the café, till I find this weekend's pictures of Juana. "I'm thinking about doing a film still portrait series. What do you think?"

He takes the camera from me and starts flicking through images. There's a vignette of Juana at the laundromat, camera placed in the back of the washing machine barrel. Another one of her glancing over her shoulder, haloed by the fluorescent, blue glow of a television screen. It's not easy to see the depth and moodiness from this tiny little display screen, but Declan gets the idea. His eyes are wide when he looks back at me.

"These are amazing."

"You think so?"

"Definitely." He nods. "They'll look great printed."

"Thirty-six by thirty-six—right?"

We both laugh. And I'm still smirking, heart bobbing inside my chest, when Declan *kisses* me. Our lips bounce together for two warm, cozy seconds. Long enough for my whole body to catch fire, full of thunder and lightning bolts and power outages.

"Sorry." His eyes dart down as he pulls back. "I know I wasn't supposed to do that."

"It's okay." I shake my head, pausing to tuck my hair behind my ears. "Guess you really liked my pictures, huh?"

He laughs. "Guess so."

Silence settles over us, and there's a quick twinge in my heart. The fact that Declan is leaving at the end of the summer; the fact that I don't want to fall in love. At the same time, I haven't felt my heart like this—alive and pumping inside my chest—for such a long time, and I like knowing it's still there. So, when he leans toward me again, I let my eyes drift shut . . .

"Hey, are you still taking pictures of Bree?"

"What?" I pull back, eyes popping open. "Why are you bringing up *her*?"

"I saw the new pictures on your camera. You followed her to the coffee shop?"

"Could you not talk about her before kissing me?"

"Sorry, it's just—" He opens his mouth, shuts it, opens it again. "I should tell you something."

"About Bree?" My eyes widen. "I really don't want to talk about her right now."

"Don't be mad—"

"Okay, never start a sentence with 'don't be mad.'"

"Okay, but I really *don't* want you to kill me when you find out I saw Bree last week."

"You *WHAT*?" I scream.

We both glance at the bedroom door for a second, wondering if Jiji's going to bust in on us, but the walls are actually pretty thick. Our eyes lock again. Declan puts a hand on my knee. Like he's worried I'll flee, which, yeah, maybe I will.

"I was on Jiji's bike," he explains then snickers. "You should have seen me, tooling around town on this rusty turquoise Schwinn from the seventies. Too retro to even be retro. Anyway, I saw Bree at that gas station by her apartment complex while I was getting a Coke. I said hi, she said hi. And we talked. She invited me back to her place."

My hand flies up over my mouth. "You went to her *house*?"

"She made tea," he says. As if that justifies anything. "We talked. Well, mostly she talked—that is one seriously chatty lady."

The room goes dizzy around me, nausea creeping up my throat. Declan explains how nice Bree seemed. How lonely. How she offered her side of the story—the way things really happened.

"*Really* happened?" I crab crawl away from him, practically panting. "What, like I know a *fake* version? Did she tell you she *didn't* get knocked up by her boss and convince him to walk out on his family? Does Bree think my life *isn't* destroyed because of her?"

"No. I mean, I don't know." He shakes his head. "I think it's complicated."

The room gets smaller and smaller; the fade-out at the end of a movie. I jump to my feet, and Declan scrambles up after me.

"Evie, are you okay?"

I won't answer. I can't, I'm too tongue-tied. Brain clogged, wondering how this afternoon went from top five status to bottom of the barrel. All because of *her*, perpetually out to get me.

"Say something."

"Like what, that I thought you were on my side? Because I did. What about our buddy system? Is this what you call *protecting me*? Going behind my back? How could you do this to me?"

"That's not how it was. I bumped into her, and we talked, that's all. It just happened."

"*Just happened*?" I bellow. "You didn't have to talk to her. You could have thought, *Oh, hey, there's Evie's slutty enemy,* and then hopped back on your Schwinn and ridden home. But you didn't. You betrayed me."

"Come on, you're blowing this way out of proportion." He groans, watching me grab my bag, my shoes, my camera. "You're mad at Bree, not me. All I'm saying is, maybe you could—"

"Are you seriously suggesting that I hear her out? After everything she's done to me?"

"She's not a monster."

"Right, and I guess she's not a slut either," I add, knowing it was a shitty thing to say.

"Don't you want to find out? Isn't that why you're following her? Why should she take the blame when—I'm sorry, but— your dad had just as much to do with it as she did. She's been dealt a shitty hand, that's all I'm trying to say."

"Why the hell are you pushing this?"

"Because you don't need to hide behind your camera. She's an actual person, Evie. Same as you."

I stomp over to the door and glare back at him, hungry for him to feel the way I do right now. "This is some kind of desperate transference thing, isn't it? You wish your parents cared this much about *you*? Look, I'm sorry they're assholes, but that doesn't give you the right to meddle in my life. If you want to fix something, fix your own bullshit."

"Jesus, Evie." Declan's bangs sway like grass over the tears in his eyes.

This. *This* is why I never wanted to fall for him. One of us was bound to get hurt, and now we both are. I collect the remaining shards of my shattered heart and sling my bag over my shoulder, still tasting Declan's ChapStick, cool and fresh against my lips. It's too late to explain how badly I'm hurting or how painful it was, being asked to feel Bree's baby kick. And yeah, I'm not naive—I know she has *her side* and that I haven't given her the benefit of the doubt, but would it make any difference? She's not a slut, and I'm an asshole for suggesting it, but it's no easier to admit that my own father was a sleazebag.

I clench my jaw, pushing his bedroom door wide. Baba looks up from the kitchen counter, eyes widening as she takes in the flush on my cheeks.

"Evie?" She rests a knife on the cutting board. "Is everything alright?"

Without answering, I slither past her and Jiji and storm out the front door, leaving everyone slack-jawed and spiraled in my wake.

———

I drive aimlessly, angrily, for almost an hour before winding up at the train park. That's not its real name, but there's a big locomotive parked behind the playground, and I guess the nickname stuck. I used to come here when I was a kid, and it still allows for pretty decent meditation.

At first, I don't get out of the car. I'm too upset, too guilt-ridden. Why did I say those horrible things to Declan? More importantly, why did he go behind my back? Running into Bree randomly is one thing, but *going to her apartment?!* I mean, was she flirting with him?

Am I a bitch for thinking that?

I stare through the windshield at the climbing structure where I used to spend so many hours playing while Dad read the paper or did work on a nearby bench, looking up every so often to cheer me on or give me a time check. I think about his face, kind and warm when he wanted to be and so serious and distracted when he was busy consulting people's tax returns. Did he make time for Bree? Make her feel special? Is that the "her side of the story" that Declan was referring to?

A couple of boys catch my eye, chasing each other up and down the slides. The only other kid at the playground is this girl. Five years old or so, sitting on a swing. I wonder if the boys are her brothers and maybe they made fun of her, because she looks sad. I can see myself in her too. Lonely, unhappy, misunderstood. My lips droop as I watch her, bare feet dragging along the wood chips. Not just me, though. The girl reminds me a little of Bree too.

Lonely, unhappy, misunderstood.

The girl grows bored of her own boredom and begins to swing faster, higher, happier. I watch for a while longer, and when another girl comes to swing beside her, I start my car and drive away.

Chapter 21

Declan stomps out of NMPI after class on Tuesday without so much as blinking in my direction. Not only that, he wouldn't even sit beside me in our usual loveseat. He's so pissed, he'd rather sit across the room beside Henri, of all people. Which, I have to admit, stings.

"Trouble in paradise?"

I glance dismally at Violet. "I don't know *what* you mean."

Her lips sag for me. We link arms, walking outside and over to a turquoise-painted bench near the monastery entrance. "Come. Tell Auntie Vi what happened."

"It's too complicated." I flop over my knees like a rag doll, and Violet pats my back.

"You poor sweetie. Listen. I have had over a dozen boyfriends in the last seven—no, six—years. I almost eloped to Paris, I am the inspiration for at least one Grammy-winning song, and I've had my heart broken more times than I can count. Believe me, I know complicated. Now, overshare."

"There's kind of a lot of backstory."

"Do I look like I have somewhere to be?"

I half smile. After the hours I've spent lamenting my woes to Juana, it's actually kind of refreshing to tell it all to someone with a smidge more life experience. I mean, her eyes full-on *bulge* when I mention the suitcase, and she's practically gasping at the part about Declan going to Bree's house, but she doesn't look judgy. Which I appreciate.

"*Wow*," Violet says after an indulgent exhale. "I didn't want to speculate too much, after the woman at the gallery mentioned your dad's receptionist, but . . . I kinda figured it was something like that. I'm so sorry. You've been putting on a real brave face."

"You're not going to scold me for stalking my dad's mistress?"

"Are you kidding?" She laughs. "I'd probably do the same thing. I mean, it's not like I haven't Insta-stalked ex-boyfriends and then subsequently their new girlfriends. That shit is normal."

"Really? You don't think I'm crazy for—"

"No 'crazy' talk." She shakes her head. "You're grieving, honey. It's okay to think with your heart, as long as you aren't doing anything dangerous. Like, don't go getting yourself on the receiving end of a restraining order, but you have every right to be curious about that girl. She was obviously important to your father, and if you want to find out why, trust your gut."

I nod slowly, and it's like my whole body exhales. For the first time, someone doesn't think I'm completely messed up for having this morbid interest in my father's mistress. She actually *agrees* that I deserve to know more about Bree. It's such a relief, I could fucking cry. But I don't. Instead, I wrap my arms around her, inhaling the blooming jasmine of Violet's perfume.

"See?" she says, hugging me back. "I told you Auntie Vi could help."

"What about Declan?" I ask. "I can't forgive him for talking to Bree."

"Sweetie, making up with Declan is the easy part. He likes the hell out of you."

I blush, and she chuckles.

"I know it seems like he went behind your back to talk to her, but he obviously meant well. He's a good guy."

"He kind of is, isn't he?"

She nods, and her dangly wooden earrings rattle. "So you said some shitty things about his parents—he'll get over it. He's got to realize you didn't mean that stuff. Did you?"

"Of course not."

"So then apologize."

"Well, when you put it like that." I roll my eyes.

"It isn't as hard as it sounds. *I'm sorry.* Say it with me: *I'm*—"

"Sorry," I finish.

"See? You're a natural."

We both laugh, and Violet takes a chunk of my long, wavy hair, humming as she weaves it into a braid. When she's done, she pulls me to my feet, admiring her work.

"Hey, what are you doing for the Fourth tomorrow?" She digs a rental car key from her bag, and we walk toward the parking lot. "Most years, I'm somewhere fabulous. I need something flashy for my social feed, unless fireworks are illegal in this dry-ass town."

"Pretty frowned upon," I say. "But my friend Juana and I always go to Pancakes on the Plaza. It's hectic but awesome. We stuff our faces and listen to boring speeches about our forefathers, blah blah blah."

She hops into her car and laughs. "You make it sound so appealing!"

"There's also mariachi bands? And a craft fair, and a classic car show. Oh, and American flags everywhere. I'm telling you, we've got the best flags. People love our flags."

"Okay, okay. I'm sold."

With a giggle, Violet pulls out of her parking space, grin faltering as she rolls to a stop beside me. "Hey, I really am so sorry for everything that you're going through. It's a lot. And I know you're mad that Declan spoke to Bree, but the boy *does* have a point. Whatever you may think of her, she's going through a lot too. You're not the only one hurting. Just sayin'."

She leaves me with that, gently tapping her car horn as she drives out of the parking lot. I let out a long, murky huff. A year ago—I mean, shit, even a couple of weeks ago—I probably would have ripped into her for offering advice about how to live my own life.

Now, though?

I let Violet's words form into dough in my mind, kneading the idea that I'm not the only one hurting. That maybe it's time I faced Bree Hewitt, once and for all.

———

I pull into the Sun Salutations Yoga Studio around 5 p.m., feeling bold enough to snag a spot near the building. Through the glass double doors, I can see her behind a large wooden desk. Her skin looks tan in the warm glow of lights. Hair straightened, collared shirt buttoned to the top. Professional. That's how she looks. The way I used to see her at Dad's office, chirping into the hands-free headset, offering still or sparkling to potential clients.

Before I go in, I play out a few possibilities in my head: she's shocked to see me, she's thrilled, she's furious and asks me to leave. Honestly, I can't see the last one happening, which is a small but not insignificant comfort.

Out of habit, I grab my camera off the passenger seat and inch onto the pavement. The sidewalk steadies my shaking legs. I duck into the building, and Bree doesn't see me at first. She's talking into a cordless phone, telling someone about an upcoming spiritual retreat in Taos. Panpipes cover "Old Town Road" through the stereo.

I clear my throat, and she looks up.

"Hold please." Her hand goes over the microphone, eyes bulging. "Are you—did you come for Vinyasa Flow?"

"No, I—" My throat's so fucking dry, I can't swallow. "Can we talk? For a minute?"

"Really?" She hesitates, cheeks turning pink. "Give me a second. You can sit if you want."

I edge over to the water cooler and bring one of those crappy little cone cups into the beige seating area, grabbing a copy of *Yoga Journal* to read while I sip. Boring article after boring article. One's called "Seven Steps Toward Enlightenment," and I skim it looking for tips. Step number four: allow your thoughts and judgments to arise and dissipate by themselves. Yeah, right. I toss the magazine down and tap my foot against the floor. There's a scent in the air. This pumped-in, chamomile-and-rose-petal, yoga studio *essence*. It's soothing, and I can't avoid relaxing a little.

Bree drops the phone in its base and limps over, leaving a healthy space between us on the couch as she lowers herself down.

"Can I get you anything?" she asks. "Tea? A glass of water?"

"No."

"Okay."

Silence. "Old Town Road" segues into a panpipe rendition of "God's Plan" by Drake. Under normal circumstances, I would question whether God really thought Drake and panpipes were a quintessential part of His "plan" . . . but I'm too nervous.

"You do photography?" Bree asks, nodding at my camera.

I tug the strap around my neck. The weight of this camera is the only thing grounding me. "Kind of."

"Cool. I love photography. Do you know Diane Arbus? She did a lot of black-and-white portraits in the sixties, I think. There's that one with the twins? They always reminded me of the twins from *The Shining*. Did you ever see that movie? I had nightmares for weeks."

God, she talks a lot.

"That's not really—" I pause to clear my throat, furious with my heart for doing football drills inside my chest. "Declan told me he saw you the other day. He said you guys talked, and I sort of thought maybe it was time we talked too."

"Okay," she says, but then . . . nothing. She tucks her chin, rubbing her belly. Not that I necessarily expected a big ol' open-your-mouth-and-*share* fest, but the fact that she's gone mute makes me anxious. How dare she clam up when *I'm* the one going out on a limb?

"This was a bad idea." I start to push up off the sofa. "I should go."

"No, don't," she says quickly. "I'm really flustered. What do you want to know?"

"Is that my dad's baby?"

Shit. The words surprise us both, but I've never seen Bree look more hurt.

"Is this about the paternity test, again? Because you can forget it."

"Wait, what?"

"I'm not after money," she snaps. "I already told your mom I'm not lawyering up, okay?"

"You spoke to my mother?"

"Not exactly." She sighs. "I saw your guys' lawyer. He came by about a month ago."

"My mom sent her *lawyer*?!"

"She didn't tell you?"

I shake my head and look away, guts rumbling as I shudder. Mom didn't just *know* about Bree and not tell me, she actively pursued her. Tried to punish her. I'd be appalled, but, I guess I'm kind of doing the same thing. We're more alike than I thought—in the most screwed-up way imaginable.

"I made it perfectly clear that this isn't about money. I'm doing some bookkeeping, and I've got this." She extends one arm like the yoga studio is the grand prize on a game show. "My brother sends what he can, when he can, plus I have some savings."

"But, so, my mom thought—"

"That I'd sue you." Bree's voice is quiet but harsh. Clearly frustrated. "This baby doesn't need your money. He needs a dad. Suing you won't bring Vic back."

The word "dad" sets fire to my bones. How badly do *I* need a dad?! Not that Bree cares. I swallow hard, reminding myself why I'm here. What I need to know.

"I swear, I had no idea about any lawyer stuff. My mom and

I aren't even talking. The reason I came . . ." I pause, nostrils flaring as I inhale. "It's like, I used to not know anything about you—and why would I? But now you're *everywhere*. I feel like I'm losing my mind, and I really need you to tell me, okay? Like, why him? Why did you have to choose *my* dad? He had a wife and a daughter. Didn't you think about that?"

"Of course I did." Her voice bites into me. "What do you take me for?"

"That's the whole point!" I explode. "I have no fucking idea!"

I glance around the waiting room, my head ducking back. The place is still empty, but it somehow feels wrong to swear in front of the mini Ganesh statue on the table.

"Look, I know how hard this must be for you," Bree says delicately. "To lose your dad like that. And then to find out about me on top of it? God, it must have been torture. But it's been hard for me too. My whole world ended the day he died. I keep thinking it's going to get better, but it doesn't. I feel like it's never going to stop hurting."

Her suffering hangs in the air, weighed down by chamomile and panpipes.

"You know I have nightmares, thinking about his face?" she says. "It scared the shit out of me, seeing him all tight and red like that. The way his eyes—dammit." She covers her mouth. "Sorry, you shouldn't be hearing that. Sometimes I worry the baby's going to start having my same nightmares. The doctor says he won't, but I can't help it."

All I can do is blink. Because holy shit. That's what I forgot: Bree was the one to call 911. She's the one who saw him go from being totally normal to literally *dying* of a heart attack. I've envisioned it a thousand times, but she actually saw it. I can't help shuddering.

"I didn't think about that," I murmur.

"I'm sure you've had plenty of horrible thoughts about me, but I want you to know I'm not awful. I didn't *choose* your dad. It wasn't spiteful or whatever. Vic and I just kind of happened. I met him at the library."

My goose bumps multiply every time she says his name. Nails on a chalkboard.

"I'm studying to be a CPA," she says. "I was standing in front of the accounting and finance section—probably looking completely overwhelmed—and he handed me a book. *The Tax and Legal Playbook.* He said it was worth a read, and—"

I squirm instantly. "I don't want to hear this."

"It's nothing gross," she swears. "You said you wanted to know how we ended up together, so I'm telling you. We started talking. I mean, I thought he was cute. Don't you think he looks like Jensen Ackles?"

Okay, now I'm about to puke. My dad: cute? And did she seriously just make a *Supernatural* reference? I mean, no. One hundred percent, in no possible universe does my dad resemble Dean Winchester. Period. But the pure fact that she knows that actor kind of throws me off track. I fold my arms into my lap, trying to focus on her words rather than the image of Bree and Dean, hunting demons in his black Chevy Impala.

"We got to talking. I mentioned that I was studying online to get my degree and looking for a job in an accounting firm to get some extra experience."

"*Extra experience?*" I mutter.

That throws her off. "It's not like he hired me on the spot because of my tits."

I open my mouth to apologize, then close it.

"Getting that job was totally legit. Through HR and everything. I had no idea it was going to bring Vic and me closer together, it just did. At first, we'd walk to Starbucks together on breaks. Talking about music and politics. Then dinners. And it kind of . . . happened." She pauses, and her chin dips down. "And I knew he was married. But. I don't know. I don't know, he didn't act like it, I guess."

I try not to gag as her words wash over me. Battery acid on my soul. It's gross and painful, and I don't want to hear it, but I don't stop her. Can't *not* allow my heart to keep crumbling. Especially when she tells me my dad had regrets about his life—dreams dashed because my parents had me so young.

"Oh, so it's *my* fault?"

"Of course not," she says. "But you have to understand that Vic went straight from college to supporting a family."

"*My* family—what's so wrong with that?"

She shakes her head. "Nothing. But he didn't get to travel, or join the Peace Corps. He wanted a lot out of life. And, I think, maybe that stuff got put on the back burner when he had you."

The back burner. As if my dad's life was an underbaked casserole.

"I don't think he would have changed any of it for the world," she adds, pausing to catch my eye. "He loved you, Evie. But he liked having someone to talk to about things he missed out on. I could listen to him talk for hours. About statistics, about birds—"

"You *liked* that about him?"

The studio doors swing open, and we both glance up.

"Crap, I'll be right back."

On her good foot, Bree walks gingerly over to meet a perky, pregnant couple by the desk. I sink back against the pillows, wondering if this innocent (still creepy) library story could be true. It sounds believable. Typical "my dad" behavior, wanting to show off his knowledge and offer book recommendations. Painfully typical, actually. More than that, it's painfully fucking selfish. Knowing how Mom stayed at home for him, kept her vows, while he just, like, saw a pretty girl and went after her.

My cheeks suddenly roast with guilt. That I could spend so much energy judging Mom for going out with Sharon, flirting with strangers. And why not? If Dad was allowed to do it, why shouldn't she?

Up at the front, Bree explains pricing packages to the couple, and I can't help noticing she's good with people. The perfect receptionist. Disarming in a Bambi sort of way. She hands a clipboard to the guy and continues chatting with the woman. The guy though. His eyes keep flicking over to Bree. Up and down her chest; those full, pink lips. How unfair it is that men think they can just *do* that shit. Does it happen to her all the time? Was my dad yet another dude who thought he had a right to her body? Or I don't know. Maybe he didn't and that was what set him apart.

She's about to come back to the couch when the doors swing open again. I try not to groan, but it's almost impossible. This conversation isn't going to reach any kind of meaningful conclusion if pregnant yogis keep barreling in, lining up at the front desk.

I grab my camera and stomp over to Bree. "You're obviously busy. I'll go."

"Wait." She shoves pens and clipboards at her customers and offers me a kind of hopeless, guilty smile. "Since you're here— *tonight*—there's something else I wanted to talk to you about."

I look down at my phone. Like I have somewhere super pressing to be. "Fine, one more minute."

"Come here." Bree sneaks around the desk, motioning for me to follow her toward a chart of really fucking uncomfortable-looking yoga poses hung in the corner of the room. "Look, this is going to sound completely off-the-wall, but I'm signed up for the pregnancy education class. It's twice a week, and it starts tonight, and . . . I don't have a partner."

I'm blank at first. Because of course I have no idea what—*ooooooh*. My jaw barrels to the ground. Now I get it. "You've got to be kidding. No fucking way."

Her expression capsizes, but she nods. "No worries. I shouldn't have said anything."

"Yeah, you definitely shouldn't."

"It's just, Vic always talked about wanting the two of us to be friends."

"Friends?" I scoff. "Did he know we were in school together? You didn't want to be friends *then*."

She lowers her head. "I had no idea about that until way, *way* later. Yeah, that was *definitely* a shock."

"And yet, it wasn't grounds for calling it off."

"Look, I know it's unconventional, but stranger things have happened. Your dad and I made each other happy."

Happy. The word makes my heart lurch and sink to my knees.

"He was nervous to tell you, and I can see why. You're kind of . . . prickly." She winces apologetically. "But he loved you a lot, and he really thought we'd get along. I know these aren't the circumstances either of us was thinking, but—"

"But nothing!" I shout. One of the ladies by the desk looks over, plucked eyebrows carved in suspicion. I flash her some stink eye before lowering my voice. "You can't use my dad as leverage. The answer is no. I don't owe you anything, and my mom would seriously kill me. Ask someone else. Literally anyone else in the entire world."

"You don't think I want to?" she snaps. "My parents haven't spoken to me in nearly a year. My brother is deployed overseas. It's not like I have a million options."

"It's still not my problem," I say. But for some reason, I wasn't expecting that, and I blush. "What about friends? You were a cheerleader in high school—aren't you people supposed to mate for life?"

"Not all cheerleaders are popular." She sighs miserably. "I had a few friends, but they're gone. California, New York. Nobody stuck around after high school. There's Clay and Dierdre, but—"

"Who the hell are Clay and Dierdre?"

She looks dismally down at her belly. "They answered my ad. Y'know, for an adoptive couple? I mean, how am I supposed to do this on my own, right? I never imagined giving up my own baby, but I don't know what I'm doing anymore. And they seem nice, I guess? Dierdre wanted to do the childbirth class with me, but I freaked. I'm honestly not sure I can go through with it."

"The class, or the adoption?" I ask softly. All I can think about is Bluebell Café. The woman laughing too hard at Bree's jokes; the guy wooing her with pastries. "What did you tell them?"

"I told them not to come. I made up an excuse."

"Do they know you're having second thoughts?"

"I don't want to scare them." She lifts her chin, and I wonder who she's trying to look brave for. "They seem perfectly nice, but what if I can't do it? I'm scared that if I go through this class—watching their sappy, smiling faces practice breathing techniques, both touching my stomach like it belongs to them—I'm scared I'll start to hate them and then I'll back out."

The longer I look at Bree, the younger she seems. Scared and innocent and in way too deep. Going against Clay and Dierdre out of spite sounds exactly like something I would do.

"Look." I puff out a big hunk of air and stand my ground. "I get that you don't want to do Lamaze with Dierdre or whatever. But that doesn't give you the right to ask me."

She forces a brave smile. "You're right, I get it."

"Okay, good."

When she looks away, I stare at her profile and the soft curve of her lip as it trembles.

"Sorry," she finally says. "I guess I got too excited when I saw you walk in. I thought it was a sign. But I was wrong. Vic always made fun of me for being so optimisitic."

I wince.

Good ol' Vic and their inside jokes.

"I have to go," I say quickly. "It was a bad idea to come here."

Before she can answer or try to stop me, I walk past her and head for the door. Already she's under my skin though, infusing my thoughts with her sadness. *Walk away, Evie—she's not your problem.* I mean, she's a *huge* problem, but she's not my responsibility. And yet, I can't stop thinking about this baby. It isn't *its* fault my parents fell out of love or that my dad thought

Bree was for the taking. This baby might end up being adopted by strangers, but for now, it's still a little piece of my dad. Possibly the only piece I have left.

I step aside as a few more couples straggle in. Bree swallows her tears. Her smile is fake and fractured, but I doubt anyone can tell besides me. Her chest puffs full of air, and she heads back to the desk, handing the newest couple a clipboard as she points out bathrooms and emergency exits.

I should leave, but I'm mesmerized by these expecting couples. Their animated introductions and similar due dates. All of them have stuff in common—their age, their cute tops, their masseuse or financial advisor. Even the hippies go to the same astrologer. It's impossible not to see what it does to Bree. Desperate and alone are probably not things Bree expected to be at the age of twenty-two, but she has about as much control over it as the heart attack that killed my father.

The doors to one of the studio classrooms swing open and out struts this lightning bolt of lime-green hair, piled up in a high bun. She's a black-clad yoga ninja, aggressively clapping like her dog's run off too far in the park.

"Welcome, mommies and partners! We're ready to get started if you want to make your way into the studio. There are pillows and blankets and blocks and straps. Use whatever you need to feel comfortable."

Respectable people—happily married, perfect couples—go waddling past the front desk and into the studio. Lime Head looks back at Bree, and a frown dangles from her lips. It is the exact same look of pity I've been getting all summer, and it sends chills through me.

"Come on, sweetie." She extends her hand toward Bree, then pauses, noticing me by the door for the first time. "Oh, hi. I didn't see you there. Can we help you with something?"

"No, sorry. I'm leaving."

I push through the doors and stumble out onto the sidewalk, fresh air stinging my lungs. My heart beats differently as I get into my car, rewinding our conversation as I drive. Wondering if I got the answers I came for or if all I feel is more broken. A brain full of rattling chains. I have to remind myself that Bree being alone is not my problem. It is not my fault that I said no to her ridiculous request. Because, I mean, that happened, right? My dad's mistress seriously asked me to be her *birth class partner*?

A red light sneaks up on me, and I slam on the brakes, gasping. Not gasping because I almost hit the car ahead of me, but because—the part that's really fucked up?—a tiny piece of me might actually regret telling her no.

Chapter 22

The annual pancake breakfast is the one day of the year Juana willingly wakes up at 6 a.m., and she's in a disturbingly good mood when she pokes me.

"What?" I grumble, opening one eye.

"Pop quiz: What is the 'bloody show'?"

"Ew!" I shriek. "What are you talking about?"

She snorts, holding her phone out toward me. The screen is full of gross pregnancy terms and diagrams. "If you're going to be Bree's birth coach, this is the kind of shit you gotta know."

"Ugh, I never should have told you." I push her bony ass off the bed, and she bumps onto the floor with an *ouch!* "I didn't say I was going to do it. I said I had *regrets*. I have a lot of *regrets*. Being friends with you, for instance, is a lifelong *regret*."

"It's just so fascinating." She jumps up and throws a pair of denim short shorts over yesterday's underwear, eyes still glued to her phone. "Oh my God—did you know some babies are born with teeth?!"

She starts chattering like a wind-up doll, looming toward me. It's impossible not to laugh. "Would you shut up already? I feel weirdly sorry for her. Don't ask me why."

Juana sighs meaningfully but says nothing as she trails me into the bathroom.

"Look. Bree's all alone. That's all I'm saying." I put tooth-paste on both of our toothbrushes and hand hers over. "The only people willing to help her are the douchy-sounding adop-tive parents. *Clay* and *Dierdre*."

Juana makes a gagging sound and then spits into the sink.

I spit too. "It's not like I'm going to deliver the baby."

"Of course not." She rubs my shoulders, which are hard as rocks. "Shit, I don't know. Maybe you were right about healing. Maybe helping Bree would be therapeutic or something."

"Thanks, Sigmund."

She tips an imaginary monocle. "Quite welcome. Look, I'm not saying you should do it. But if you're having so-called *regrets,* maybe you're right to trust your gut."

"You're not going to try and talk me out of it?"

"I tried that already, remember?"

I snort.

"Besides, if she's telling the truth, your dad wanted to get the two of you together."

"I don't think this is what he had in mind."

"Of course not, but . . . if Bree was really that important to your dad, she wasn't going to go away. Whether you like it or not, she was sticking around. So, now it's your choice. Do you want to be a part of each other's lives or not? Personally, I'd say hell no." She pauses. "But then, there's the baby. We haven't really talked about it, but, I mean, what's in her prego belly is kind of a biological part of you, right? And it's not going away."

Not. Going. Away. Those three words scrape against my heart till it's raw.

"Sorry, babe, it's way too early to be this existential. Do you still want to go to the Plaza this morning, or no?"

"Yeah, sure. Give me a minute."

She closes the door gently on her way out, and I stand in the bathroom for a while longer. Staring at this stranger looking back at me in the mirror. This stalker, who might honestly be considering teaming up with her prey—aka the girl who destroyed her family, aka a sad girl, lonely for the same reason.

I sigh at my reflection. Not a stranger, just . . . not who I thought I was. Nothing's the way I thought it would be. I splash water on my face and pair a cute top with denim shorts that acually look pretty damn good, then Juana and I drive downtown. We're already too late for a good parking spot, so we park over on Quintana Street and walk half a mile to get to the Plaza, which is rammed.

Our historic little town square is kind of a mess on Fourth

of July, crammed with a thousand times more people compared to the usual spattering of tourists and locals milling around the ancient adobe buildings that used to be houses for Spanish bigwigs. Sometimes I wonder what it must have been like back in 1600. Like, I don't know a single person who's not proud to be a New Mexican but, like, there're all these statues celebrating the conquistadors who pillaged indigenous people back then—it's fucking horrible. At least, I think it is. Activists finally tore down the bullshit "Union heroes" versus "savage Indians" monument on the Plaza, but I'm not sure the teens scoring weed and playing hacky sack in modern times give a shit. For the festivities today, the whole place is overflowing with picnic tables and, like I told Violet, flags everywhere. People laugh, and kids whiz past in every direction. It's Armageddon, and we're all here to carb-load.

After ten million years of waiting in line for our pancakes, we find a couple of seats, and Juana pulls a can of Reddi-wip out of her bag, swirling a creamy, white tornado on top of her plate.

I laugh at her and she shrugs. "What? I didn't haul my ass out of bed at 6 a.m. in order to count calories."

"Fuck it, neither did I," I say and drown my plate in syrup. We clink plastic forks and then start to chew. And chew, and chew. And chew. "Did they taste this bad last year?"

"Why do we keep coming back for this?"

"Tradition!" we both yell, snorting back giggles.

We poke our rubbery pancakes in silence for a while until JJ all of a sudden elbows me. "Dude. Your mom's here."

"Shit, does she see me?"

Juana's eyes bulge, but she shakes her head. I slump down in my seat, following her gaze. My mom is in profile, her head merrily bobbing from side to side as she enjoys a pancake breakfast of her own. And now I know why Juana looked so shocked. Mom's curls are out of their usual messy ponytail, now lightly frizz-controlled and fanning her face. Her floral sundress doesn't look familiar, so it must be new. I know it's only been a couple of weeks, but my heart aches to see her. She looks good too. Happier. Maybe even sober. I mean, to be fair, it's eight in the morning. But she doesn't look hungover, which is worth noting.

Nobody else at her table looks familiar. No Sharon. None of the other dental hygienists. And I definitely don't recognize the bald guy on her right. He cracks a joke, and Mom covers her mouth to laugh. The other people laugh too, but not nearly as hard as Mom.

"Oooh." Juana whistles. "Do you think Rita's got a new boyfriend?"

"No way," I mumble. "I mean, do you think?"

"Are you going to talk to her?"

I hesitate. "She looks busy."

Mom starts to scan the crowd, and part of me wonders if she's looking for me. Like, maybe she does want to talk . . . but then she waves at some people she and Dad used to be friends with. I'm not even a blip on her radar.

"Well, you were right about the flags."

I turn toward the sound of Violet's voice, all prepared to scoot over for her, when I see Declan standing beside her. He's cradling a plate of pancakes and OJ, wearing a Made in Nebraska T-shirt. Aviator shades mask his expression. I feel my heart flutter a little as he combs his bangs across his forehead, choosing to look at Juana rather than me.

"Hey, I'm Declan."

"*Oh.*" A grin swallows Juana's whole face. "So *you're* Declan. Nice to meet you. I'm Juana. And don't even bother telling me you're Violet Rutherford, because I already know. I love that picture you posted of the cactus flower yesterday. You know, you should come by Casa Buena—that's my parents' store. We could use the press."

"I'd love to!" Violet cheers. Like, actually *cheers*, which instantly has me squinting at her. "You know what, I'd love to hear more about this Casa Buena place. Will you help me find the bathrooms and we can talk about it on the way?"

She does this meaningful eyeball dance that bounces from Declan, to me, then back to Declan again, and Juana squeals emphatically. "The *bathroom*?" she says. "Oh my God, yes! Y'know, I didn't even realize I had to pee until you said that? Wow. It's like, we've barely met and already we're on the same cycle."

I roll my eyes. "That's your period, smartass. Not your bladder."

She waves me off like "whatever" and links arms with Violet. "There's actually a bathroom in my parents' store.

Fortuitous, right? While we're in there, I'll show you some of my favorite local crafts. Everything at Casa Buena is so—"

"Crafty?" I supply.

Declan snickers.

The two of them skitter away, and he snatches the seat across from me before another pancake-eating vulture can swoop in and steal it. He pulls off his sunglasses and those magnetic hazel eyes stare back at me, glinting in the light.

I use my plastic fork to slide maple syrup into sticky piles that ooze out of formation instantly. "So, are you a big fan of pancakes?"

"Everybody likes pancakes." He furrows his brow like he's going to say something else, but then he looks back at his pancakes. A triangular wedge disappears into his mouth, and his nostrils expand. "Whoa. This is . . . not a pancake."

"What do you mean?" I bite back a grin. "What is it?"

"A clay pigeon? A Nerf ball?"

"I was gonna go with Band-Aids, but a Nerf ball captures the texture better."

We both laugh, and I think maybe we're going to gloss over our fight. There's no rule that says we need to whimper apologies when we aren't even together. And yet, here I am, staring awkwardly at the ugly vinyl tablecloth out of guilt.

"Okay, look." Declan leans so close it doesn't feel like we're in a crowd of thousands. His bangs fall in front of his eyes. "I need to say something."

"Declan—"

"Just, hold on. I practiced this speech in the mirror." He offers a weak smile. "At least let me get it out."

I hold my breath and nod.

"I'm sorry for everything you've been through this summer. It's horrible. And I shouldn't have gone to Bree's house. You were right to be mad at me. I thought I was helping, but I was butting in. It was pure jackassery, and I'm sorry."

"Good," I say. "You should be."

"Well, I am."

"Well, good."

He exhales up into the air, and I sneak a glance at his Adam's apple, the way it juts out from his neck. When he looks back at me, his eyes are warm and apologetic. So are mine.

"I'm sorry too," I murmur. "It was shitty of me to bring your parents into it. You didn't deserve that. I'm really sorry."

"Thanks."

"You know—" I almost swallow the words, then don't. "I went to see her yesterday."

"Wait, *Bree?*" he gasps. "You did?"

"I'm not gonna lie. It was kind of brutal."

"I'm so sorry."

"I don't really want to get into it, I just thought I should tell you. Since you're so damn interested."

He winces. "I really am sorry for butting in."

"I forgive you. Don't do that shit again, though."

"Promise."

Declan stretches his long arms above his head and gives in to a big smile, all rosy-lipped and genuine. It's a really nice smile. Maybe our fight is finally over, but I still don't know what it means for us. Here is this perfectly adorable boy sitting across from me, possibly making doe eyes at me, and it's getting harder and harder to remember why I want to keep my distance from him. It really doesn't seem like he wants to break my heart. But I don't know. We only have a handful of weeks left. He's still going to leave; I still have my fragile heart to protect.

But I guess he can't actually read my indecisive mind, because he reaches across the table, sliding his hand along the underside of mine, tickling my palm. It feels good. Okay, maybe he can read my mind, and he's trying to nudge it. I look down at our fingers, looped and purled together. Yes, he's leaving, and maybe I'll miss him, but . . . at this very moment, I feel light. Not something I've felt a whole lot of lately, and I don't want my brain to scare it away.

So I let my heart unwind a little, feeling my chest rise and pull slowly toward his. Even though there are elbowy strangers on either side of us, stuffing their faces, I let gravity pull me closer. I let my heart flutter and race and, finally, I surrender to a warm, sticky, maple-syrupy kiss.

Chapter 23

I'm full of determination when I walk back into Sun Salutations on Thursday night. Because I know it makes no sense but at the same time, what *does* make sense at this point? All this stuff with Bree has evolved in ways I never would have imagined, and it kind of boils down to: yeah, I sort of feel for her. Maybe it's time to try giving myself a break about it.

Real talk? This is a decision Juana and I made at four in the morning after two cans of Pringles and a new mug cake invention. So, my clarity is hazy.

I walk in and the lobby is already full of the same pregos from Tuesday's class. They're huddled over on the sofas, acting as if they own the place; chatting like besties already, gaily laughing about what fun it is to be happy twenty-four hours a day. I mean, presumably.

"What are you doing here?" Bree asks, looking up from her desk.

"I'll do it," I say. "I'll take the class with you."

"Wait. *Really*?" She almost claps, but my death stare takes care of that.

"I've got one condition." I pause. Inhale. Lift my fancy camera onto the counter. "I want to take photos for this other class I'm taking. Deal?"

It's the one stipulation Juana and I came up with. Kind of like my security blanket.

"Deal."

"And if it gets too intense, I can leave at any time."

She nods solemnly. "Also deal."

The studio doors open, and the lime-haired lady starts ushering everyone in. She flashes me an odd smile, like maybe she remembers my loitering ass from the other day.

"That's Ziggy," Bree says, moving at super speed to shut off her computer and organize her desk. "FYI, she's a bit wacky."

A whoosh of "what have I gotten myself into" buzzes through me but I clutch my camera and follow Bree into the classroom. Maybe "classroom" is a little too official though, because this place is *nothing* like school. Everyone's got their favorite seats picked out from the first session, squatting on bouncy balls or yoga blocks, forming a circle on the floor around Ziggy—who, by the way, is a master at Intense Eye Contact. I don't know what the hell they did in the first class on Tuesday, but this second one launches right the fuck in with these really specific demonstrations of various childbirth scenarios.

"It might be very internalized." Ziggy's eyes flutter shut,

and she hums, low and soft, rocking gently on all fours. Then her eyes pop wide and predatory. "Or your labor could be intense!" she yells. Actually *yells*. Her bloodcurdling screams bounce off the walls, all the way into our hair follicles as she crouches into a sumo squat, with eyes squeezed shut and palms smacking against the floorboards. The whole class squirms, and I seriously consider calling backsies on this whole fucking thing. I glance nervously at Bree, sitting beside me with her legs crisscrossed. She looks even more terrified than I do.

"Or—" Ziggy comes out of her screaming trance and flashes a coy, sultry grin. "Childbirth can also be a *very* pleasurable experience," she says, and basically has an orgasm in front of us all.

One dad takes notes.

Bree and I exchange a look, and when she snorts with laughter, I raise my camera to snap a quick picture of her dimpled smile. She blushes, and I do too.

It's weird, almost, the fact that I'm using Luke's 18mm– 55mm lens on her rather than the telephoto. I'm close enough to take actual portraits and see the details naturally. A subtle dusting of freckles on her cheeks, the bright whites of her eyes. It's nice having more control over the lighting—to feel like I'm not hiding for once.

Ziggy lists the various signs of labor, and I snap a photo of Bree's eyebrows furrowing. The way she tugs on her lip with one hand, practically writing a memoir with the other. Her ridiculous acrylics glide across the page. *Click.*

The labor-signs talk goes on for a good long while, and Bree leans over to me. "My mom was in labor with me for thirty-seven hours."

"Emergency C-section," I whisper back, pointing at myself.

Ziggy drops her dry-erase pen and points at me. "Did you say emergency C?"

"Sorry," I say. "I'll shut up."

"Don't apologize! This is an open environment. We're all here to learn and share. And I'm glad you brought this up. While many of you may have your heart set on a natural childbirth, you all need to be prepared for possible alternative realities."

Bree's back stiffens against her bolster pillow. Automatically I stiffen too. It hadn't occurred to me how scary that might sound, to be ripped open like that. All the moms-to-be turn pale as Ziggy warns them about tangled umbilical cords and hemorrhaging and enlarged heads—it's all really reassuring. *Thanks a fucking lot, Ziggy.*

In the middle of it, I notice Bree holding her breath, hands protecting her belly. It's so obvious how much she loves this baby. How badly she wants to keep it safe. Doing yoga, making hemp smoothies. And yet, she's thinking of giving it away.

I almost say something but then catch myself. It's not my place to ask why she's considering adoption. Clearly, she seems to love it—him, it, the baby—but what do I know? Maybe raising kids is too expensive, maybe it's too hard to do alone, maybe she misses my dad too much to do this without him.

One of the moms raises her hand to ask about something called dystocia, and Ziggy freaks everyone out *more* by describing the way a baby's shoulder could get stuck inside the vagina after the head comes out. I mean, holy shit. I'm grossed out and horrified, but Bree actually gasps. Without thinking, I reach over and squeeze her hand. It comes as a surprise to both of us, but when she flashes me a timid, appreciative smile, I can't help jerking away. It was an impulse, nothing more.

"Sorry," I whisper.

"It's okay," Bree whispers back.

We look back at Ziggy and don't speak another word.

———

When it's over, I help Bree roll up yoga mats, folding and stacking the rough, colorful, Mexican blankets. She's more meticulous than I would have thought, making sure everything's lined up perfectly. My dad was like that too.

"Did you get any good pictures?" she asks after a while.

"Ziggy's pretty photogenic. Did you hear her? She asked me to send any good shots for the website. She said she'd give me fifty bucks."

"That's great!"

"And I got lots of moody, rolling-your-eyes shots of you whenever Ziggy was grunting."

"It's impossible *not* to," she says and promptly rolls her eyes.

I snicker.

We walk out into the waiting area, and Bree turns off the air conditioner and stereo and sets a few alarms. I linger by the door, pretending to check my phone. The two of us walk out into the warm July evening.

"What are you up to now?" she asks.

"Home," I say. Only, I don't specify that *home* is still Juana's house. "How about you?"

"Same," she says dismally. "Hey, want to get a smoothie? Not hemp, I promise."

She points to the smoothie shop a few doors down from Sun Salutations. The sign has these animated strawberries and bananas diving into a blender. Part of me knows I should say no—that this has already gone further than it should—but I nod. I don't know. JJ's out with Melanie tonight, so what would I be going home to? An awkward dinner with Debbie and Manuel, the two of them casually asking when the hell I'm going to move back home? I've had enough of those already.

Bree leads the way. Her limp is gone, an Ace bandage still tight around her ankle. She orders a peanut butter banana blast, and I get something tropical—her treat. We sit across from each other at a corner table at the otherwise empty Juice Heaven, sucking rather than speaking. Silence grows as thick as our smoothies and I think we're going to give ourselves brain freeze in order to finish quicker, until I push mine away.

"I don't know what to say."

"Oh my God, *right?*" She sighs and laughs and ruffles her

hair. I want to go back to awkwardly slurping mango but then Bree rolls back her shoulders, extending her hand. "Pretend you don't know me—hi, I'm Bree!"

"What are you doing?" I ask, horrified. "No way."

Her smile wobbles. "Okay, fine. No way."

We're quiet again.

Brain freeze is imminent.

"Vic used to take me hiking," she blurts out. Almost like she's been wanting to say it for days, working up the guts to spit it out. "Which is totally wild because I'd never set foot on a mountain trail in my whole life before I met him. But it was amazing. All that fresh air and pretty views. We would climb to the top, and he'd play Soundgarden on a portable speaker. We both loved nineties rock."

"I know," I say stiffly. "From that night in your car, I mean. You were listening to Pearl Jam. Dad loved all that crappy nineties grunge."

"Crappy?" Bree fakes a gasp.

"No offense."

"Clearly." She smiles briefly, then winces as the baby seems to karate kick her insides.

"You okay?"

"Mostly. It's starting to feel like a tight squeeze in there."

I don't know how to respond, so I stir my smoothie, pulling out the straw and dropping mango puree onto my tongue.

"Evie?" She pauses, and her face darkens. "Did you know about me?"

I tense my jaw. "Not until after."

She nods, eyes lowering. "I'm really sorry."

"Was he really going to move in with you?"

Her eyes snap back up. "You knew about that? Did Rita tell you?"

"No, I kind of figured it out on my own."

She nods, chewing on the inside of her cheek. "I think it's important for you to know that it wasn't an easy decision. Like, every time he and Rita talked about getting a divorce, they kept putting it off."

"But, why?" I ask.

"Because of you," she says softly. "They were waiting for you to be out of the house—off at college."

My heart thuds. "*Me?*"

"To be honest, I think that was your mom's idea, trying to protect you. But, then—" She pauses, resting her hand on her belly-shelf. "This happened. I was superstitious about my first trimester. There have been a lot of miscarriages in my family. When we found out the baby's gender, though, it's like everything clicked into place. And then . . . Vic proposed."

"He *what?*" I shriek. My eyes dart up to the cashier, but she's glued to her phone. I lower my voice. "You and my dad were eng*aged?*"

She bites her lip. "Not technically. He didn't give me a ring or anything. We agreed that he'd move in. He was going to. But, then—"

Tears cut Bree's words short, but I'm too busy spinning.

ENGAGED. The word strangles my skin. He wanted to marry her. This peppy, cheerleading, accountant-in-training would have been my stepmom? Not only that, a stepmom who was *five* when I was born. It's disgusting and wrong, and all I keep thinking is that I should leave. I should leave. I should leave.

"I should leave."

"No, don't. I'm sorry, I wish I hadn't said anything. How mad are you? On a scale of one to ten?"

"A thousand?"

She frowns, fidgeting with her straw. "Vic thought it might be tough. He said your mom would be furious."

"Maybe that's why he didn't tell her," I say curtly. "She had no clue. *I* had to tell her."

"Wait—" Bree frowns. "How did *you* know?"

"It doesn't matter," I say. "Thanks to you, I'm the one who got to deliver that truth bomb. It went over so well, she kicked me out."

"She *what?*" Bree's face goes pale. "Are you still—I mean, do you need a place to stay?"

"No. God, no. I'm staying at my friend's."

"Okay, good." She pauses, exhaling with relief. There's still a little bit in her smoothie, so she tips the cup, swallowing the dregs. When she's finished, she offers a lopsided smile. "If it makes you feel any better, I don't get along with my parents either."

"Nope, doesn't help."

"Okay."

But I can't stamp out my curiosity. "You mentioned that the other day. What happened?"

Her face darkens. "They're very religious. I'm not supposed to have sex before marriage, let alone—" Her eyes dip down to where her waist used to be. "We fought a lot when they found out. The fact that I'm not married but Vic is." She pauses, wincing. "*Was*. I keep doing that."

So do I, I don't tell her.

"They live in Albuquerque," she goes on. "A frigging hour away, and I haven't seen them in almost six months."

I tug on my lip, staring down at the table. I mean, it's weird to think we both have that in common—being shunned by our own mothers. Maybe Bree and I aren't in the same boat, but it's kind of starting to feel like we're in the same sea.

"Think you're going to make up with your mom?" she asks.

I blink and look back at her. "Think *you* will?"

Kind of bleakly, we both shrug. Eventually Bree starts babbling again. Nothing heavy. It almost feels like a first date, the way she reels off information. Her love of the desert, her obsession with skiing. The collection of bumble bee trinkets in her jewelry box. Her favorite movie is *To Kill a Mockingbird*, but she prefers the book. She's superstitious and hates technology.

"I mean, obviously I have an iPhone," she adds. "But I don't like feeling dependent on it. Have you ever seen those pictures where the photographer digitally removed people's cell phones and everyone looks so sad and lonely? I'm sad and lonely enough as it is without letting a phone get me down."

I mean, she's got a point.

"Actually—" She cocks her head. "I do regret not taking more pictures of Vic and me. I basically don't have any. The only tangible things I've got of his are a couple of old T-shirts and this personalized pocket protector."

"You have that?" My voice falters.

Dad's pocket protector. I almost smile, remembering when I picked it out. How I went out of my way to get a nice one. This sleek, rectangular model, monogrammed and made of hand-stitched black leather. It was the best gift I ever gave him. I can remember that day so clearly. The look on his face, the way he laughed when he opened it. My lips twitch, thinking about it.

"I keep it in my nightstand," Bree says softly. "But . . . do you want it back? I don't have to keep it. Hey, it's okay."

It's not till her hand goes on top of mine that I realize I'm crying. Bree leans in, eyes full of concern, breath warm and peanuty. I wipe my cheeks, quick and angry as I suck the rest of my tears back down inside of me. I stand up.

"I should go."

Bree smiles reluctantly. It's a little harder for her to unwedge herself from the chair and table, but she eventually does. It's twilight when we walk out of Juice Heaven, the parking lot close to empty.

"I really want to thank you for coming to class tonight. It

was a million times better than the first one where Ziggy had to use a CPR dummy as my birth partner."

"What'll you do when you have the *actual* baby?"

Her face sags. "I don't know. Maybe my mom will have a come-to-Jesus moment."

"Wouldn't it have to be more of a walk-away-from-Jesus moment?"

She laughs. "I guess so. Don't worry though—I won't ask you."

"You fucking better not."

"But you'll still do the class? I'll see you back here next Tuesday?"

The hope in her voice almost sends my cockroach heart skittering into the shadows. I pause, tilting my head up toward the first few evening stars. It's hard to admit that any of this is happening—that I don't despise everything about this girl, that I'm kind of enjoying taking pictures of her, talking to her. That whatever this is might be the only thing keeping me going.

"Yeah. I'll see you then," I say.

Bree opens her mouth but I quickly turn, heading over to my car. She probably wanted to thank me, and it's easier if she doesn't. Easier if I don't have to think about how much this means to her.

CHAPTER 24

I don't know if it's because I miss her or because I'm running out of underwear, but I sneak into my house the next morning before heading to NMPI. Mom's not there, obviously. From what I've deduced from my perch at Juana's window, she's taken up jogging lately. Two or three miles before she heads to work. New clothes, toned muscles—zero interest in reconciling.

It takes me a second to work up the nerve, thumbing the door key before jamming it in the lock. I'm almost surprised when it fits and the door creaks open. Hairs on my arms bristle.

"Mom?" I call out, just to be sure.

Lips mews in response, dancing figure eights between my ankles. I pick her up and rub the top of her head with my chin. Mom never wanted a cat, so I can only imagine how unloved this poor beast must be feeling lately. I reposition her like a football in my arms as I walk.

It's still the same house I stomped out of two weeks ago, but something's different. Not just the swept floors and whiff of detergent. There's been actual, physical change. No more binoculars displayed on the bookshelf. Fewer books in general actually, and the coffee table has been repositioned. But when I realize Dad's favorite beige recliner is completely *gone*, that's when I drop the damn cat onto the floor.

Now it's a race. What else can I find that's missing? What else has she *done*? It makes me dizzy. Hollowed out. I hurry down the hall so fast, I trip over a stack of flat cardboard boxes, stumbling to catch myself. I bend down, scrambling to restack them, and then it hits me: These are *moving* boxes. As in, is Mom moving? And she didn't even tell me? My heart plummets. Faster, harder, hotter with each thought. The binoculars, the books, the recliner.

She is obliterating him. She wants a new life, devoid of her dead husband's memory.

And what about me?

Am I next?

Destined to be

dumped in a box

and tossed out?

Not even important enough to be consulted on what stays or goes.

I rush to the kitchen for water and gulp down a full glass before noticing the dining table's been moved across the room, closer to the window. Morning light streams onto the knotted pine surface, spotlighting a bowl of shiny green apples. I always hated the bitterness of the green ones, but I guess that doesn't matter anymore.

I hand-wash my glass and return it to the cupboard, deflated as I walk down the hall again. My feet scrape against the cold, brick tiles, stopping short, startled by the gaps on the wall. One by one, I realize which pictures are missing. The wedding portraits, Dad's childhood snapshots. Only a few of my old school photos and ballet recitals remain. I've honestly never been so happy to see my curves and toothy grin. I'm still here. She hasn't discarded me yet.

The door to my room is shut, and I almost don't open it for fear that she's replaced my bed with a treadmill or a crafts table. But she hasn't. Nothing's changed. In fact, everything's exactly the same, complete with sheets tangled on my bed and dirty clothes strewn across the floor.

Even though I have a suitcase at JJs, I grab a few extra things—a sports bra, some different tops and underwear—and head back down the stairs, freezing when I hear the front door fly open and then slam shut. My spine goes so straight, I think it might break.

"No, no, no. It's no problem at all," I hear Mom say.

Nobody responds. She must be on the phone.

Suddenly I'm terrified she'll see me. That I'll give her a heart attack too, and then I'll be orphaned. I'm so desperate to hide, I inadvertently slam back against the wall, rattling what's left of our photo display.

"Hold on a sec, Sharon." Mom's Croc-covered feet clomp closer.

Fuck. I'm fucked.

My only option is Dad's office, so I slip inside, breathless as the door clicks shut behind me. I press my ear to the crack.

"Hello?" Mom calls. "Lips? Was that you?" She groans. "No, no, it's nothing," she says back into the phone. "I thought maybe it was Evie . . . I know, I shouldn't get my hopes up . . . You're right . . . We both do."

Footsteps clomp into the bathroom, and I hear the medicine cabinet creek open. Riffle, riffle, riffle.

"Got it." Something like maracas rattle, and I realize it's got to be pills. "I'm telling you, this will make your hay fever vanish. Yeah, I . . ."

She keeps talking, but her voice becomes fainter, followed by a heavy *thud* as the front door slams. Her voice disappears. Now that she's gone, I almost wish she'd seen me. There's an apology in the back of my throat; I can feel it when I swallow.

I shouldn't get my hopes up. That's what she said. Almost like she misses me too.

I let out a sigh, finally registering where I am. The musty smell of books. Dad's office hasn't been touched since he died, and the air is stale, a layer of sneezy New Mexico dust covering the meticulously organized remnants. There's still an orange peel, dried and forgotten on his desk. I walk closer, fingers trailing along stacks of ornithology textbooks and newspapers. Binoculars and crappy clay sculptures from my fifth-grade pottery class. There's a framed picture of me, back when I was ten. Another one of him and Mom, from before they were married.

My fingers hover over the brass knob of his desk drawer. Slowly, I pull it open. A lump rises in my throat at the stacks of pens, stamps, paperclips. The second drawer is full of legal pads and index cards and—blood drains from my face when underneath some envelopes, I find a photograph.

Bree and Dad.

The two of them grin wildly for a selfie. He's holding the camera out, Bree melting into his chest. They're on top of a mountain somewhere. Like, where the fuck did my dad find time to go hiking with his mistress? Where was I? Where was Mom?

Mom. I cringe at the thought, because now I know we were at home together. Making do without him. Not getting along, arguing for argument's sake. Mom, who cared so much about me that she wanted him to wait till I left for college. She gave up everything for me. Sacrificed her freedom for my security, and all I did was fight with her.

All Dad did was whatever he wanted.

Despite an urge to rip it up, I stuff the photo into my back pocket. I want to be furious. I want to stomp out of this room and slam the door so hard, the whole house breaks. But, like always, I can't help clinging to sun-spattered memories. The spare reading glasses I used to play dress-up with. A fly ball caught at an Albuquerque Isotopes game one spring. My newborn photo, back when Dad was straight out of college. Barely twenty-one. Four years older than I am now, having to put his dreams on hold to support a family.

Memory lane starts to burn a hole in my chest, so I pull the door shut, tiptoeing quietly back through the house. I take one last look, wondering if I'll ever be allowed back in or if Mom is planning to sell it and move to I-don't-even-know-where.

Across the room, Lips yawns, falling asleep on a rug where my father's chair used to be.

———

NMPI recalibrates my mood instantly. There's still a Mom-size hole in my heart, but something comes over me when I'm inside this classroom. A feeling of purpose. Like I'm *good* at something.

Declan's not here yet, but I take my usual seat, rolling my eyes at the latest Ed and Ada argument, waving at Violet who's in the middle of a livestream with her millions of followers. Beth walks in offering Hatch green chile muffins because food photography is going to be her final project. The cornbread is warm and golden and fluffy, and I wish my own mom had baked it. No, that's not what I wish. I wish I hadn't lied to her and pushed her away.

"Penny for your thoughts?"

I look over at Suze and realize I've been frowning. Glaring

at this arguably perfect muffin. "I'm fine. Just fighting with my mom."

"Oh, sugar. I'm sorry." She squeezes my shoulder and lets out a long breath. "The fallout of a loss like yours can show itself in some very messy ways."

"Clearly." I scoff. "I guess I wasn't expecting her to jump to the next stage of grief and leave me to rot."

Suze chuckles, squeezing my shoulder even harder. "Honey, the so-called stages of grief are absolute bunk. Grief is grief. It's chaotic and messy, and it's no wonder you can't keep up with her. I'm willing to bet she feels like she can't keep up with you either. Whatever she's done to put that frown on your face, try to cut her some slack. Or whatever *you* did to upset *her*—I bet she's tryin' to cut you some too. You'll find the same page eventually."

I chew on my lip, wondering if she's right. Whatever kind of "life experience" Suze has, I doubt it's as bananas as the situation I'm currently in. Or, I don't know. Maybe everyone's life is fucked up.

"Morning, gang!" Georgy walks past in a floral kimono, and everyone snaps to attention. "I am in absolute *love* with the work you've all been producing lately. Only another couple of weeks till the gala. Everyone in good shape?"

Nods and thumbs-ups cascade around the room. My self-portraits are coming along well. I'm getting better at focus and framing and adjusting the ISO for darkness. And, true to her word, Juana has made an excellent model, posing in bedroom windows, lurking in the shadows. Not to brag or whatever, but I think I've taken some really good pictures. Like, maybe there's a chance I could have a talent for photography, even outside of this workshop.

"This week, we're going to move this party into the editing studio. Because I've had you lovelies shooting RAW all this time, your image files are uncompressed and unedited. So, let us go forth and dig into that behind-the-scenes tweaking that's going to wow your audience."

Everyone cheers. Literally. It's like—

"It's like watching the last scene in a football movie," Declan whispers. "VICTORY!"

I notice him beside me and smile. "Look at you, always sneaking onto my sofa."

"Hey," he says, smiling back.

"Hey," I whisper.

His cheeks go pink. Mine too, probably. Violet clears her throat all emphatically as she walks past our couch, raising an approving eyebrow. My cheeks go from pink to cayenne-red.

"You two coming?" she asks. "Or should I put a sock on the door on my way out?"

"Violet!" I groan. "Ew!"

"Oh, stop it," Suze chuckles. "You're embarrassing them."

Declan laughs and drags my mortified body into this bright, immaculate room filled with enormous computers and a large-format digital printer that probably cost more than my car. Georgy gives an Adobe Lightroom crash course, teaching us how to correct white balance, the various techniques for adjusting sharpness and noise. It's way too much information to cram into an hour, but she promises to meet with each of us one-on-one.

I insert my SD card, and thumbnails dot the screen like mosaic. Bree, as far as the eye can see. I'm not using these pictures for the gala, but I select one anyway—a wide-angle shot from childbirth class. She's lined up against the wall next to all the other pregnant moms. Ziggy made them squat for sixty seconds in a "mock contraction" that looked more like boot camp than baby class. If I tweak it, the moisture on her brow will glisten, maybe even sparkle. Another one shows Bree looking deep in concentration as she envisions serenity (one of Ziggy's many mantras). It's a decent photograph, but if I raise the temperature to warm up the colors, blur the background, and adjust the brightness of Bree's face, it could really pop. I try a few adjustments, and already I'm smiling. Cropping out Ziggy's wild, green hair, ramping up the saturation.

It feels good having control over something.

"Nice!" Georgy brings a swivel chair closer to me and sits down. "This is looking great. The way you've lit her face really makes the image pop."

"You think?"

"Definitely," she says, then hesitates. "The past couple of

weeks you've been presenting the film stills of your friend. Are you thinking of switching gears?"

"No," I say quickly. "These are . . . I don't know."

Her eyes soften. "I know people were a bit uncomfortable before, but you've broken the fourth wall. You're really getting intimate with your subject. It shows."

Intimate. Such a cringeworthy word. But I look back at the photo and she's right; it really is more intimate—*gag*.

"These images are every bit as compelling and dynamic as the film stills. You should choose whichever images you feel passionate about—that's what your audience will connect with."

She offers a few more pointers, then skitters over to a wildly impatient Beth on the other side of the room. I blink back at my screen and feel my head throb, pulsing to the tune of "Eeny, Meeny, Miny, Moe." Bree, film stills. Bree, film stills.

I glance over at Declan, hard at work beside me. I let myself watch him, taking a break from my own nonsense. He's adorably biting his lower lip in concentration, tweaking the contrast on an image of Jiji in the bath.

"Dude." I fake cringe. "Your gramps let you photograph him *au naturel*?"

Declan snorts and pulls up another image. "Is it any less weird if I tell you he wanted to show off his bubble beard?"

"Impressive goatee," I say. "But still weird."

I look back at my screen and sigh. Tweak, crop, brighten.

I try not to think about Declan's soft lips at the pancake breakfast. The way my heart raced when they pressed against mine. Heat starts to drift up my neck, prickling my cheeks, making it impossible to concentrate.

"Hey, so . . . what are you up to this weekend?" I ask.

Declan swivels his chair to face me, grinning way too big. "Are we talking a 'friend hang' or like a real date?"

I'm telling you, my heart—it is a fucking glitter bomb right now.

"Who said anything about a date?" I raise an eyebrow. "I was merely trying to find out if Jiji will be commando in your next photo shoot."

"Oh, *really*?" He sort of faux ominously raises one eyebrow and then drops it down in order to lift up the other. It's like a two-eyebrow stadium wave.

I can't stop myself from snorting.

"That's better," he says and rolls his eyebrows again. "You sure you don't want to hang out with these eyebrows? Saturday night? Hmmm?"

I bite back a smile. "Actually . . . there is a thing. This weekend."

"Sounds riveting."

I laugh, trying not to notice his pecs under an I Messed with Texas T-shirt or the minty sweetness of his breath. This boy. I'm telling you.

"Juana's parents are throwing a party for the twentieth

anniversary of their furniture store." I pause, letting my cardigan fall off my shoulders, not minding the curve of my upper arms. "You could come . . . if you're not too busy playing uta-garuta with your grandparents."

"I dunno." He grins. "I'm getting pretty amazing at uta-garuta. Tournament-ready."

"Fine. Suit yourself."

I make this big show of swiveling back to face my computer, but Declan grabs the armrest, spinning me closer. He's got the biggest grin on his face. "First of all, I can't believe you remembered the name of the card game Baba is teaching me. And secondly, yes. That's a yes."

His eyes flick over and around the room, and when he looks back at me, he tugs my lower lip gently with his. Georgy clears her throat from over by the printer, and Declan and I turn beet red, swiveling back to face our computers.

My insides bounce all the way up to my heart and hug it tight.

CHAPTER 25

Juana is scowling, pacing, mutilating a string cheese when I find her at the dumpster behind Casa Buena. Maybe dumpsters sound like a weird place to take a work break, but it's awesome. Back here—amongst the empty take-out containers and broken lamps—is basically our clubhouse. Like, if we were running from the law and needed a rendezvous point, it'd be here.

Actually, the look on JJ's face right now? I'm kinda wondering if she *is* on the run.

"Hey, are you okay?"

She notices me, and her face sort of tweaks, a Disney smile replacing her frown. "I'm fine! You're late. Ready to play?"

She hands me a slingshot, and we assume our usual positions, fifteen feet away from the dumpster, near some boxes full of Casa Buena's broken unsellables and the dinged-up abnormalities. As usual, I'm here to play smash—this game we invented forever ago, catapulting broken housewares into the dumpster for points—but I let my slingshot fall to my side as I bite my lip.

"Did something happen?"

"No, I'm just ready to play," she says gruffly. "I've been waiting for you for half my break, and I'm ready to play. So let's play already."

"Okay, there is definitely something going on with you."

She ignores me, grabbing a chipped Navajo nutcracker and lining it up with the dumpster. It ricochets off the metal bin with a *clang!* and I add ten points to her score of—I don't know, four hundred thousand.

"Okay, but you seem kind of upset. Are you sure there isn't anything—"

"There isn't!" she shouts. Which makes us both jolt.

We stare awkwardly at the dumpster.

"Did something happen with Melanie?" I ask after a minute.

All my gentleness is met with a glare. "Oh, right. Because of course it has to be about Mel. I know you hate her."

"What?!" I gasp. *Buuuuut* . . . "Okay, I don't *hate* her. I hate what she did to you last year. You were heartbroken when she cheated on you. I don't want to see you get hurt again."

"That was a mistake. It's different this time."

"You say that, but—"

"Look, it's fine," she snaps. "Nevermind. Let's drop it, okay?"

"Juana, what is going on with you?" I try to touch her arm but she pulls back. "Are you mad at me? Did *I* do something?"

"No—" She huffs, keeping the words trapped inside her. "This is a really hard conversation to have with you. You're so upset about your dad—*obviously*—but I know what you think of your mom for sticking around after he cheated. I don't want you to look at *me* like that." She pauses. "God, I swore I wouldn't dump my bullshit on you. You're dealing with enough."

"Wait, are you serious?" I abandon my slingshot and squeeze Juana tight. Harder than usual, to punish my muscles. "Your bullshit is equally important as my bullshit. I had no idea you were afraid to talk to me about Melanie. I don't want her to hurt you, but I would never think less of you for giving her another chance. You have a ginormous, understanding heart. That's what I love about you." I pull back with a sheepish grin. "I, on the other hand, am a horrible human being. I'm a friendship-equality zapper. A friendship leech, if you will."

"And, I will." She snorts. "No, you're not. You're just busy. And depressed, and a borderline stalker and—"

"Okay-okay-okay. Point taken. That's no excuse though. Come on, tell me what happened with Mel, and I swear I won't judge."

For a second, she squints at me. Like, double checking I'm going to be cool. "Okay. So, I invited her to the Casa Buena party this Saturday, and she said she'd think about it."

I raise an eyebrow. "She'd *think* about it? Como que *what*?"

"I know, right?"

"What's she got going on in her life that's so great—that's *better* than a fancy party with her hot-ass girlfriend?"

Juana smiles with relief, and I feel that look all the way down to my pedicure. Trust. My parents didn't have it, but I do with JJ. And it is everything.

"You know what?" I say. "All it means is she's being aloof, trying to see where things stand. You said yourself it was different this time. I bet she wants to make sure you're ready."

"You think?"

"I do. And if you like her as much as I think you do, why don't you make a grand gesture?" I reach for my slingshot, chucking a dented picture frame at the dumpster. "Like, show up at her door with flowers or something. Like, prompose that shit. She'll either say yes or you'll know for sure she's not the one."

Juana bites her lip. She's already smiling, wheels turning, mentally selecting her outfit, the bouquet, the perfect song off SUPERNATURALLY SMOOCHY. "Yeah, I'll do it. Good idea."

"And don't keep any more secrets from me," I order, handing her a saltshaker. "I mean it."

We turn back to the game, focusing on our aim for a few more rounds. I completely overshoot a beaded Christmas ornament, and it lands with a *tink!* on the next roof. Juana laughs at me and, honestly, good as it feels to have averted a fight with her, something starts to weigh down on me. An inexplicable rattle in my heart. Only, it isn't inexplicable. We're playing this silly game, and all I can think about is how the whole thing originated and the fact that this is our first time playing since Dad died. The image of him handing Juana and me our first slingshots is burned on my brain. Fourth grade: he led us on a hike up the Sangre de Cristo Mountains and gave us two dinky, wooden slingshots. He said, *Hit anything without a pulse*. We shot rocks at boulders and dead yuccas for an hour. On the way home, he said we could keep the slingshots if we promised never to hurt anyone. In hindsight, it sounds disturbingly like a gateway to a life of crime . . . but it never felt that way. To us, it was awesome. Sometimes, my dad was awesome.

Our hands start to ache after a while, so we sit down on an old railroad tie and crack a couple sodas.

"Talked to your mom lately?" JJ asks.

I glance sideways at her, then roll my eyes. "You saw me yesterday morning, didn't you?"

"Saw you what?" She shrugs innocently. "Sneak into your own house? Nope."

"Inspector fucking Poirot," I grumble. "Yes, I went in. I needed underwear."

"Mm-hmm." She rolls her tongue along her teeth. "What'd you do when she came back in? Hide under the bed?"

I wince. "In Dad's office."

"Oof. That sucks. But she didn't find you?"

"No, she was looking for allergy medicine."

"So, what do you think?" she asks softly. "Was the house different? My dad said he saw the Goodwill truck outside a couple days ago."

"She got rid of his recliner, JJ. His fucking rec*liner.*"

"Wow." Juana pauses, scrunching her nose. "But . . . isn't that kind of a good thing? Maybe it means she's moving on?"

"Of course it's a good thing," I say, but my lower lip quivers. "I wish it hadn't taken kicking me out of the house for her to find happiness. It's like she's getting her life together *because* I'm gone."

"I really don't think that's it."

Rather than cry, I let out a long, slow exhale. "She looks good, huh? Jogging in the mornings. Getting rid of Dad's stuff."

"Sucks about the chair," Juana says. "But it sounds healthy, right?"

"Yeah, I guess."

"Also, like. No offense. But pot-kettle. You're moving on without her just as much as she's moving on without you." She pokes my arm. "This whole bass-ackwards thing you've got going on with *Mommy Two, Electric Boogaloo?*"

"Mommy Tw—are you talking about Bree?" I gasp. "Come on, that's not fair."

"Just sayin' . . ." She trails off, clearly not having any of it. "Listen, I know I backed you up last week, and we both said spending more time with Bree could be therapeutic, but I also kind of figured you would have gotten it out of your system in about five minutes and realized you need therapy with an actual therapist, not a twenty-year-old slut."

"She's not a slut," I bark. "Dad had as much to do with their affair as Bree did. And I don't want to hear you—of *all people*—spouting bullshit stereotypes like that."

She nods. "You're right. I'm sorry."

"Yeah, well, maybe all this stuff with Bree doesn't make sense to you, but it might be the only thing getting me through this. It feels *right*. I'm sorry she's not a fucking licensed therapist, Your Highness."

Juana bugs her eyes out like, *Soh-rryyyy.*

I roll my eyes right back at her. "She's not horrible, you know. She's pretty smart. And kind of funny. And I know it's weird that I'm doing these classes, but she doesn't have anyone else. Besides you, neither do I."

Juana doesn't answer at first. We both stare at the dumpster—aka our clubhouse, aka our rendezvous point. She rests her head on my shoulder, and I put my chin on the top of her smooth hair. We both sigh.

"Sorry I called her a slut," Juana says.

"I know you are, bitch."

We both snort with laughter and take a couple of chipped Buddha candles from the box between us. JJ scores ten points, then looks at me. "You're wrong, y'know. You *do* have your mom. So what if you're in a fight. She still loves you, and you still love her. You're gonna make up eventually."

I bite my lip, throat sore from holding in tears. Maybe I don't say it, but, damn, I really hope she's right.

CHAPTER 26

"This isn't bad," I say, taste-testing a kernel of Bree's home-made tamari-and-green-chile-glazed popcorn. It's spicy and salty and buttery. Pretty good, actually. I offer her my tube of Nashville Hot Chicken limited-edition Pringles, and she pops a stack of four in her mouth.

"They're good too. But you had to buy them on eBay?" She cringes. "No thanks. Popcorn's way easier to binge on."

"Well, if you're gonna be like *that*," I say, Gollum-ing my chips back from her.

I devour an eight-stack and rest the tube on the coffee table amid S'well bottles and yoga magazines. The other pregos in the waiting area shoot us disdainful looks, as if they're too good for food cravings. They for sure think they're too good for Bree—single and twenty-two; adulterous and thirty-five weeks pregnant. I mean, yeah, she sounds like a hot mess. But, I mean, if *I* can get used to her? So could they. Except they choose not to.

"How's the photo class coming?"

"I dunno. Fine." I shrug and glance down at the camera in my lap. "There's this gala thing in a couple weeks so everyone's freaking out, trying to make sure their images are all *fah-bulus*. Lots of big egos in the art world."

"A gala?" Bree's eyes pop in mock awe. She laughs, throwing a kernel of popcorn at me. "Am I going to be famous?"

"Oh." My ears begin to burn.

Bree catches on and frowns. "You're not using the pictures of me."

"It seemed weird?" I grimace. "Being that we're . . ."

"No, totally," she says. Every trace of disappointment vanishes from her face as she smiles. "You can if you want, but I get why you wouldn't. I'm not exactly something to be proud of."

"That's not—"

"So, what *are* you going to show?" she asks brightly. "Self-portraits? You're so pretty. Vic used to show me pictures of you—I know how photogenic you are."

Vic. The way she tosses his name around so easily. No matter how many times I've heard her say it now, it still stings. But I clear my throat, try to stay on track. "He showed you pictures of me?"

"Are you kidding?" she laughs. "He didn't say you were into photography, though. He was always kind of worried about you. Like, what you were going to do after high school. He said you didn't really have your eye on anything and he worried you wouldn't apply to college."

"He *said* that?" I gasp. And I'm reeling—furious, ashamed, insulted. Called out. It's true, I've never known what I wanted to do with my life. Until now, maybe. "Yeah, photography is new. I never thought about trying to pursue it as a career, though."

"Oh, you should." Bree nods thoughtfully. "I mean, you haven't really shown me any of your pictures, but the way you look when you're taking 'em? Effortless and determined at the same time. I don't know. Photography gives you sparkle. That's what our cheer coach used to tell us: 'do what gives you sparkle.' I always liked that idea."

I try not to laugh because I can tell she's serious. "What gives you sparkle?" I ask. "Accounting?"

We both cringe, then laugh.

"Jeez, not when you say it like *that*!" She laughs for another breath until suddenly her lips droop, eyes quickly glistening. Her fingers curve along her belly. "This baby. He's basically the biggest sparkle I could ever imagine."

I hesitate. "If you really feel that way, then what about what's-their-names—Charles and Diana?"

"Clay and Dierdre." She rolls her eyes—at me or them, I can't be sure.

"All I mean is, if the baby gives you 'sparkle' or whatever, maybe adoption isn't, y'know ... "

I trail off, and Bree grabs her belly even tighter, head flopping against the sofa back as she exhales. "I know. I've been putting them off. Straight to voice mail, like five times a day. And texts. So many texts. Dierdre even sent a care package. It was full of all these prenatal lotions and scrubs and even a butt balm. Can you believe that? Like, a total stranger knows that I have hemorrhoids and is sending me butt balm in the mail."

"Okay, first of all, I *so* did not need to hear about your hemorrhoids. But also, if you're not into it, don't you think you should tell them? Didn't you sign a contract?"

She shakes her head. "This is Santa Fe. They're super laid-back. The whole thing was off Craigslist. At first they didn't mind 'feeling it out' or whatever, but they're getting pushier." She swirls her fingers over her belly, hypnotizing me with her crystal ball. "I really thought I could go through with it," she goes on. "But I love him so much already. Having this baby feels *right*."

I nod because—I don't know—I kinda get it.

Ziggy comes ballroom dancing (solo) into the waiting room, and Bree and I jolt.

"Good evening, mommies and partners!"

Pretty much everyone is immune to Ziggy's eccentricities by now, so we all say hello, and the pregos start the laborious process of rising from the low couches and Moroccan poufs. It's a sight. Really. At eight-ish months, nobody's got much mobility.

"As you all know, tonight is a very special class," Ziggy continues, one palm on her heart. "Before we get into some role-playing, I'm excited to see everyone's birth bundles!"

Oh, right. The birth bundles.

Last class, Ziggy asked all the moms to bring in a little pouch filled with a symbol of strength for the mom, another one for the partner, and something to represent the baby. Talk about crunchy. Ridiculous as it sounds, I'm a little curious about Bree's. She's been rolling her eyes at Ziggy as much as I have, but I get the feeling she's kind of spiritual.

Once everyone's settled, Ziggy clears her throat. "So? Who's first, mamas?"

I glance at Bree, but her cheeks go rosy as she shakes her head. There's a lot of nervous, no-*you*-go-first energy, which is a little depressing. Like, aren't people supposed to get over that shit after high school? Apparently not. Eventually, the bleach-blondest woman steps up to the plate—the one whose husband was checking out Bree that first day.

"Okay!" she says, voice pinched and giddy as she pulls a gold Versace clutch out of her boho bag.

And, I mean, *that's* her bundle—a frigging majillion-dollar purse. Bree knocks my elbow, and we both snicker subtly, struggling to focus on Delilah (maybe Delia, I don't care) and the tube of Chanel lipstick she's currently pulling out of the bag as her Mom Strength item. It's in a shade called "Determinée." Because of course it is. Her Strength of the Father item is a brand-new Rolex for Mr. Wandering Eye. And the baby-energy thing? It's a five-thousand-dollar bond for the kid's trust fund. So, yeah. Wow.

"That's really . . . generous." Ziggy's smile twitches.

I literally have to bite my cheek not to laugh.

Once again, nobody volunteers for the hot seat, so Ziggy points at Bree. "Your turn, hon."

It's surprising how nervous she gets. Bree—an ex-cheerleader—afraid to show a few random trinkets to a bunch of puffy middle-aged moms.

"Okay. God, I don't know why I'm so nervous!" She giggles and pulls a bundle of fabric from her handbag. A scarf.

Not just *a* scarf, *the* scarf—the one he gave us both. It's a gut punch, and I'm tempted to run, scream, cry . . . but this isn't about me. I watch her unwind it a little ways and the first thing to fall out is a necklace. It's ugly, though. Chunky wooden beads on a leather string. It's not my taste and, honestly, it doesn't really look like hers either, but she runs her thumb gently along the beads as she speaks.

"My mom gave me this necklace on my tenth birthday, after a trip to Barbados. I thought it was kind of hideous, but Mom put it around my neck and said, 'I knew you'd make this necklace beautiful.' She said it made me look strong. Like I could conquer the world. I guess I chose it because, when I go into labor, I want to feel like I'm strong. And like my mom is there with me, even though she won't be."

It's sweet. And so honest. Enough to make everyone soften, eyes glistening. Ziggy nods as if Bob Marley himself is performing inside her head.

"For the baby, I brought these." Bree holds up a bundle of miniature Maurice Sendak books called the Nutshell Library, and my eyes begin to sting. "Vic gave these books to me when we found out I was pregnant. He told me they were his favorite thing to read to his daughter, when she was little. I know my son will always treasure this gift from his dad."

She smiles down at the books, careful not to look at me.

Ziggy hesitates. "Do you have something for him—the energies of the father?"

Bree takes a shaky breath, and the whole room aches. I'm still on the verge of tears, but now I'm sweating too, terrified of what I'll have to endure. What *Vic memory* she's going to flaunt in my face. But when she pulls out Dad's pocket protector, I actually smile. It's almost funny, that this ridiculous monogrammed birthday gift has all of a sudden become everything.

"This was super important to Vic," she says, thumbing the stitch-work. "His daughter gave it to him. Sounds silly but, like, maybe the organizational powers of the pocket protector will help me through my labor?" She pauses to laugh. "Sorry, that sounded a lot more normal in my head!"

I blink, biting down hard on my lower lip.

"No, Bree. That was lovely." Ziggy offers a warm, appreciative smile. "Thank you for sharing."

The assignment moves left around the circle after that, to another pregnant mom with another bundle of keepsakes, and instead of putting the pocket protector back into her bag, Bree hands it to me.

"You should have it back," Bree whispers.

"But—" I force a swallow. "It's your dad-energy thing."

Her lip quivers, but she manages an eye roll. "Come on, we both know this is silly. Besides, I think Vic would want you to have it."

She doesn't think this is silly. Bree thinks all this birth bundle stuff is completely legit. But I let myself take the pocket protector anyway. It's lighter than I remember and scuffed around the edges. Treasured. I fold it snugly between my hands, careful not to cry as I exhale.

"Are you sure?" I whisper.

"I'm sure."

"Then . . . thanks."

CHAPTER 27

Debbie Lujan's knuckles pound rapidly against Juana's bedroom door. And no, she doesn't wait for the all-clear before poking her over-spritzed, French-twisted head into the room. She's all eyeliner and a skinny, black cocktail dress for the Casa Buena anniversary party. Which is tonight—as in, *still hours away*. But I swear to God, she looks like the survival of our species relies solely on her recipe for stuffed mushrooms.

"Did you polish the silver ice buckets like I asked you to?"

"Yes, Sergeant," Juana drawls.

"Well, I can't find them." She huffs and pushes the door all the way open, high heels clacking against the hardwood floor as she gives the room a suspicious once-over. "Where are your clothes?"

Juana lifts her head off the pillow where we're both zoned out, playing *Animal Crossing* in our PJs. "There're clothes everywhere, Mom. Dirty ones, clean ones, black ones, pink ones. Take your pick."

Debbie's mascaraed eyes narrow. "Don't sass me, mija. My patience is about *this big* right now." She pinches her thumb and forefinger together. Which seems generous—I'm not even sure she looks *that* patient. "Where are your party clothes? And yours too, Evie. I've got better things to do than worry about how the two of you look. Manny already spilled nacho cheese on his Ralph Lauren shirt."

"Sure thing, Debbie." I smile politely, knowing she must be *constantly* wondering when the fuck I'm going to move back home. "We'll be ready in five minutes."

She mouths *thank you* to me, then stomps back out of the room, slamming the door shut behind her. I grab my plum-colored dress with ruching up the sides and start wiggling out of my pajamas. It isn't actually my dress. Violet lent it to me because: a) I still don't exactly have my entire wardrobe to choose from, and b) nothing I own is fancy enough for a cocktail party anyway. Violet was happy to let me storm her closet in exchange for inviting her and Georgy to the party. I think the Santa Fe tourist scene was starting to bore her followers.

It's a beautiful dress though, and it even looks halfway decent on me.

Juana stands beside me in a flowy, black cocktail dress and holds her camera up for a quick selfie. I smile, but I can't get my mind off the fact that it's the same dress she wore to Dad's funeral. A day spent numb and desperate. Cried at and pitied by dad's work colleagues. Awkwardly small-talking the dentist. Back then I didn't know Bree existed. Two months later and it's like we might almost be friends.

Time is weird.

We do our makeup in the bathroom mirror, elbows dueling for space. I want to know how last night's promposal thing went with Melanie, but I hold my tongue. The fact that JJ hasn't mentioned it doesn't bode well, and I don't want to get blamed for suggesting she make a grand gesture.

"How do I look?" Juana twirls when she's done. "Like the prim and charming daughter of respected local business owners?"

"Hundred percent." I grin and roll back my shoulders. "What about me? Does this shade of purple complement my broken home life?"

"Oh, totally. You're a knockout."

We spend the next two hours running around as fiesta-frenzied as Debbie. The playlist needs to be set up with additional speakers on the lawn, the mood lighting lit, the seating set, the—blah blah blah. Juana's house is always grand and impeccable, but now it looks like the ballroom at the Marriott where we had our homecoming dance last year. Except fancier. At homecoming there were platters of fried chicken and buckets of soda. Here, the servers are wearing bow ties, and the toothpicks have pearls on one end.

Guests start to trickle in at the stroke of six, and Juana and I hide in the corner for as long as humanly possible, knowing that boring conversations with strangers are inevitable. I'm two bites into a miniature brie-and-chorizo quiche when she bumps my shoulder.

"Your boy's here," she whispers, eyebrows wiggling.

"He's not 'my boy,'" I groan back. "You make him sound like a puppy."

But I glance over at him anyway. He sees me, and his face brightens, not unlike a puppy's.

"That's my cue to get the fuck out of here." Juana squeals and kisses me on the cheek, trapping herself in conversation with her annoying manager so I can have some one-on-one time with Declan. I mean, *that* is true friendship.

"You clean up nice," I say as he walks up.

Declan tugs on the lapel of a skinny black suit and smiles. "Found it in my closet from last time I visited, when Baba and Jiji took me to the opera. Apparently, I've grown a little."

We both look down at Declan's pants that come up above his ankles, revealing teal socks with tacos on them.

"Is it okay if I say you look beautiful?" he asks, his voice low and close to my ear.

Don't blush. Don't blush.

Okay, fine, blush.

"Um . . . yeah," I tell him. "Thanks. And so do you—very beautiful."

He laughs and grabs a skewered shrimp as it whizzes past us, swallowing it in a single bite. We stand close, fingers not quite brushing, salsa music thumping in time with my heart. It's nice, but my brain's already starting to pick at the rough, end-of-summer scab. All I've thought about all summer is how it's inevitably going to end. We still haven't actually talked about it, though. Before, it didn't seem necessary, but now he's only inches away, his eyes glinting on me, darting down to my lips, and suddenly I'm bursting to know if I'll ever see him again or if I really *am* destined for heartbreak.

"Declan, I—"

"Evie, thank God!" Debbie comes racing over, speaking through clenched teeth and a wide smile. "Elaine Jimenez is on her fourth Pinot Grigio, and it's barely 7 p. m—where's Juana?"

I raise an eyebrow at Declan, who looks even more over-whelmed than I do. "Um, she was here a minute ago. Want me to look for her, or—"

"No, no." She shakes her head, eyes flitting briefly to Declan. "Where are your friends? I was hoping the famous one might take some photos for the website."

"I'm sure they'll be here soon."

"Well, text her! It's already seven!"

Debbie glides off in a panic, and we both laugh.

"Whoa," Declan says.

"This party means a lot to her." I hold up my camera. "Say cheese."

He smiles adorably.

I study my camera settings for a minute, too chickenshit to

get the nerve back up and ask him when he's leaving. "I better take some party photos. Don't want Mrs. Lujan busting a vein."

Declan nods, and I start to surf the crowd with my view-finder. There are a lot of who's-who types at this party—city council members, a famous fantasy novelist. *Click.* Guy dribbling caviar onto his tie, a B-list actress. *Click.* My heart melts when I spot Juana because—squee!—she's with Melanie. Their fingers are intertwined, grins coy. Mel's got love in her eyes, and I'm glad they're trying to work it out. Maybe she cheated, but at least she regrets it; that's got to count for something. I hope things really do work out for them this time.

I give them a little privacy, zooming in on the front door as it swings open. It's such a shock when I see my mom on the other side that I almost drop the camera. Declan follows my gaze, and we press our backs against the wall, watching her peel off a white, linen blazer and hand it to one of the staff. At first, she stands there, wringing her hands and getting her bearings. It's impossible not to notice a difference. The way her skin seems to glow. I'd say she looks happy, but when she spots me, her body stiffens like cold honey.

"Does she look mad?" I whisper.

"I've literally never seen her before," Declan says. "But, no. I mean, she looks nervous."

"Do I look nervous?" I ask.

He cocks his head and squints.

I lift the camera strap off my neck and rest it on the table beside me. I swear to God, my heart rate quadruples. It's weird to be twenty feet away from the woman who raised me, feeling like we're strangers, knowing the awful things I said and did to her. At the same time though, it's like I can feel hope rising up through my chest, expanding my ribs.

Mom nestles her purse under her arm and takes a few tentative steps.

"Hi, Evie." She smiles awkwardly at Declan. "Hello."

I've missed her voice.

"Hi, Mrs. Parker, I'm Declan. And I'm leaving."

He catches my eye and flashes a tight smile before heading over to Georgy and Violet, who have just walked in. I look back at Mom and bite my lip. Now that we're up close, I can see even more differences. Her skin looks less puffy, eyes clear and bright.

"Is that a new dress?" she asks.

"Kind of. I borrowed it from a friend."

"It's pretty." Her voice falters. "You look so pretty, sweetie."

"So do you."

A lull takes over. I toss around a few different sentences in my head, but it occurs to me how *even more* fucked this situation has become since I last saw her. Like, she could conceivably forgive me for lying about Dad's suitcase—it was a rookie move, though my intentions were good. But the Bree stuff? It felt remotely normal when I wasn't looking Mom in the eye. Now I am though, and I honestly think I might hurl.

"I have to pee," I blurt, tripping back. "Want anything, on my way back?"

"I'll take a club soda," she says.

For a second, I'm stunned. Because, club soda? But I don't want to make a big deal out of it, so I nod. "I'll be right back."

I dash around the corner and lock myself in the guest bathroom, staring at this purple dress that isn't me, the life I never thought I'd end up living. With every breath I take, the knot in my stomach adds onto itself till it's pressing hard against my ribs.

So, Mom. Remember Bree?
I was stalking her for a while,
and now I'm her birth coach.

God, I really, seriously might puke. I pat cold water along my cheeks and walk into a spritz of calming, hinoki aromatherapy mist. It smells like pine trees and life goals and almost makes me think there *is* a planet on which my mom won't disown me for befriending the enemy.

My lips purse at my reflection. *Come on, Evie. You got this.*

I grab two club sodas from the bar and head back toward Mom, freezing in my tracks when I see her. Nearly dropping our cups when I realize she's looking at the playback screen on Luke's Nikon because, I can't fucking believe I left my camera on the table for anyone to see. My mind flicks through each image, starting with the most recent. The politician, caviar-stain guy, fantasy novelist. A few other party pics come to mind, but that's not why Mom's jaw is currently halfway to the Indian Ocean. Right now, amid a whirlwind of shrimp cocktails and bizcochitos, my mother has found Bree Hewitt.

Holy. Shit.

The whole room shrinks to the size of a pixel as I realize how frigging cataclysmic this is about to get. Before I've come up with any kind of excuse, I lunge forward, dropping the club sodas on the coffee table and snatching my camera out of Mom's hands.

Bree, hugging her bump.

Practicing guttural breaths.

Blue eyes sparkling into the camera.

My heart sinks and throbs. "Mom, what are you doing? This is *my* camera. You can't just go looking through my things without asking."

"I, I didn't know," she says, face flushed. "I wanted to see what you've been working on, and then I . . . I . . ."

She stumbles back, disoriented. I dig my fingers hard into my palms, afraid that I've done it again. That I've fucking broken her, all over again.

"Mom, I can explain," I say, even though I can't. Not in a way she'll understand. I try to swallow, but my mouth feels webbed. Chalky from too many spinach empanadas.

"I don't understand." She looks at the camera, blank and blinking. "Are the two of you friends now? Did Dad introduce you to her *before*?"

"No! No, of course not."

"Then *what*?" she whisper-shouts. "Explain it."

"I'm so sorry, Mom."

"I said, *explain*."

"There you are!" Georgy comes padding over, all smiles and sangria. "Fun party. Is this your mom? Hi, I'm Georgina, but everybody calls me Geor—"

"I'm sorry, but I really don't care what everybody calls you," Mom snaps. "I am in the middle of a private conversation with my daughter."

"*Mom*," I moan. Heat prickles my eyes as I flash Georgy a helpless frown. "She found the pictures—the ones of Bree."

"*Oh*." Georgy's eyes go bigger than the crepes being served. "Mrs. Parker, don't be upset with Evie. She's progressed so much as a photographer this summer. Those pictures show a lot of promise."

"Excuse me?" Mom snarls. "You're *encouraging* this? When I asked my brother-in-law to help Evie find her footing and he suggested your class, *this* is what you had in mind?!"

"No! Of course not, I mean, not at all," Georgy stammers, and I've never seen her so flustered. "Evie's been working on another project too. This was somethi—"

"For weeks I've been berating myself," Mom shrieks. "Desperate to get my act together so you wouldn't be so goddamned ashamed of me. And for what? Look at these pictures and tell me which one of us should be ashamed now, Evie?"

Tears fill my eyes. I can't speak.

"How could you do this?" she chokes. "It's one thing for you to lie about Daddy moving out, but now *this*? Do you hate me that much?"

"Of course not," I whimper.

Mom's eyes start to glisten too. She shakes her head. "I can't stand to look at you right now. I'm sorry, but I think I'd better leave."

"I didn't do it to make you mad—Mom, wait!" I cry, but she's already gone, storming through the crowd.

I wipe my eyes and run after her, but the front door slams in my face, sucker punching my soul. One of the caterer guys pops up in front of me with a smile and a taquito, and I instantly burst into tears.

"I'll call your mom," Georgy offers, rushing to my side. "I feel like this is partly my fault."

"It's not," I sob.

Declan and Juana and Violet make their way to me too, and the group of them usher me down a deserted hallway where I won't ruin Debbie's soiree.

"Sweetie, what happened?" Violet asks, offering a stack of yellow CASA BUENA: QUE VIVA 20 AÑOS! cocktail napkins to soak up my tears.

"She found the pictures of Bree."

"Oh, shit." Juana squeezes my shoulder.

They hand me cocktail napkin after cocktail napkin, giving

me hugs, telling me everything will be alright. It won't, though. Can't be. In my pocket, I feel my phone buzz. Then again. And again. Bree's name pops up on the screen, and I want to scream at how ridiculously awful her timing is.

"I can't deal with her right now." I push the phone against Juana's chest.

She takes it from me, scrolling quickly through the messages. Her eyes bulge. "Shit, Ev. I think you better call her."

"What?" I pause. "Why?"

"She says it's the baby."

"But—" I snatch the phone, a sinister throb to my heart. "She's not in labor though, right? She's only thirty-six weeks."

Juana shrugs. Georgy and Violet exchange a worried glance. I dial the number and start to gnaw on my nails as I listen to it ring.

"She's not picking up."

"Call her again," Georgy orders.

I do, and this time she answers. "Bree? Are you okay?"

No response.

"BREE? Are you there?"

"Evie," she says. Her voice is faint, forced. "I'm bleeding."

I gasp and cover my mouth. "You're *what*? Like, how much?"

"I don't know, not a lot. But—" she gasps. "Some."

"Tell me what happened."

"I called Clay and Dierdre. I told them I changed my mind. I decided I can't go through with the adoption, and they were furious. I've never heard someone so ma—*aaaagh*—d!" She pauses, and I can practically hear her grit her teeth.

I put my hand over the phone. "Declan, start a timer."

He nods, fishing his phone from his pocket.

"I swear, I've never heard people yell like that. They said they've already paid for so much stuff. They bought a stroller and a car seat. They even decorated the baby's room. She sent all these pictures to prove it. Chevron wallpaper and a mobile over the crib. It looks so pretty."

"That's not your fault," I tell her. "You never promised them anything, Bree. You're allowed to change your mind."

"Yeah, but I let them pay for an extra sonogram a couple weeks ago. Is that horrible?"

"No, it's not. We can pay them back. That's not what's important now."

"Okay," she whimpers. "I don't know what to think, y'know? It was so relentless, all the yelling. It took forever to get them off the phone, and then I had to turn off my ringer. Thank God I never gave them my address. I mean, they said I *had* to give them the baby." She pauses, her voice low and terrified. "Do you think they ca—*aaaaagh!*"

I motion to Declan, and he stops timing, flashing me the screen. Five minutes. Contractions are one of the things Ziggy started explaining to us in the last class. I am *so* not an expert, but I'm pretty sure five minutes is about the time you're supposed to go to the hospital. Fuck.

"It got me so scared," Bree says, once the contraction has passed. "I was freaking out. I can't *believe* I was going to give those people my baby."

"I know, I know. Try to stay calm."

"I don't think I can," she chokes. "This kind of stress can't be good for the baby's development, right? Plus, I've been feeling kind of off for the past few days. Just, like, really really tired all the time. And crampy. I decided to treat myself to some ice cream, and I went to lie down. But then, I swear to God, I felt like I was peeing in my pants. I was like, *what*? But it wasn't pee. I think my water broke. But there's blood too, and—*aaaaagh*."

Georgy must be able to hear Bree screaming from three feet away, because she takes her phone out of her clutch. "What's her address? I'm calling 911."

I whisper it to her, then raise my voice. "Bree, I'm on my way."

All she does is groan. She's become a cavewoman on the other end of my phone.

"Do you hear me, Bree? I'm coming for you. Everything is going to be okay."

CHAPTER 28

The ambulance is already there when we pull into Bree's apartment complex. I think Georgy ran two red lights on the way, but who cares—I was grateful for the ride and way too freaked out to drive. She and Juana and Violet and Declan follow me up the stairs, taking them two at a time despite the fact that we're in heels (well, not Declan). The front door is open, and I can hear voices coming from the bedroom. My body suddenly takes on this medicine-ball weight. I don't think I can move, but then Georgy nudges my back.

"Go in," she whispers. "She needs you."

I step inside, almost surprised to realize that this is my first time inside Bree's apartment. It's nothing like I pictured. Cozy white furniture and hanging plants. Ocean mist walls covered in framed antique maps and sketches of birds. I can't help wondering if Dad got her into wildlife or if that was another thing that brought them together. Like, maybe they really were soul mates. At the end of the hallway, a couple of giant EMT guys in matching blue uniforms bustle purposefully around Bree's tiny bedroom. She's lying there on a stretcher, knuckles white around the metal rails.

"Bree, are you okay?" I ask, rushing over, crouching on my knees beside her.

She nods stiffly, her face moist with sweat, eyes wide and panicked.

I look around the room, and it's just as she described on the phone. A pint of chocolate ice cream is tipped over on the floor, melted and oozing into the carpet. And her bed—God, her white sheets. They're damp and splotched with red.

"Is she in labor?" I ask the blond EMT.

"'Scuse me?" He blinks. "Who are you?"

"She's in labor, right?" I say again. "The contractions were five minutes apart earlier."

Bree grunts and grabs my hand. "Evie, come with me? Please?"

That wasn't part of the deal, but—crap. I press my lips together and nod. "Of course."

"You're just a kid," the blond guy snaps.

"I'm her birth coach," I bark back. "I demand to ride in the ambulance."

I can thank Ziggy for my ballsy tone. *Show them who's in charge. Don't take no for an answer.* That was mostly in relation to medical interventions—things like busy doctors suggesting a C-section to save on time—but we did a lot of role-playing in class, and I bet she'd be proud of the way I'm standing here, shoulders squared and jaw tight.

"I said, *I'm. Coming.*"

His eyebrows soar up to his hairline, but he's too busy to argue, strapping her to the stretcher and getting her hooked up to fluids and oxygen and stuff.

"It's fine." The other EMT smiles. "I'll need you to keep her calm."

I nod and then turn to my friends, hovering in the hallway.

"What can we do?" Georgy asks.

"Meet us at the hospital?" I pause, looking around the room for some kind of prepacked duffel, which I don't see. "Wait, stay and grab some clean clothes. Pajamas, slippers, cough drops, snacks—whatever." I notice her birth bundle on the nightstand. "Toss me that."

JJ obeys, and then the four of them scatter.

Bree screams when the guys lift the stretcher and rush her down the hallway. She looks as pale and exhausted as a wet sponge. When we get to the ambulance, the EMTs start barking at each other, using all this doctorly terminology that I can't understand. All I know is that they're scaring Bree, and they're scaring me.

"Low, guttural breaths," I tell her, imitating one. Maybe it's the most embarrassing thing ever, groaning like a sick donkey, but right now I don't care about anything but getting Bree through this. "Try not to scream, it'll make you dizzy."

The surly EMT raises an eyebrow—like, *How do YOU know any of this shit?*—and leads Bree and me into the back of the ambulance while the other guy hops into the cab. The siren blares, and we take off down Old Taos Highway. I feel like I'm on a TV show. Buttons and wires and metal tanks. A strap loops around Bree's belly, monitoring the baby's heartbeat. I don't want to ask right in front of her if the baby's going to be okay, but that's all I keep thinking about.

Bree moans and squeezes my hand, but I don't let on that it hurts. I keep breathing. We both keep breathing. Beeps echo all around the small, sterile cabin. Lights blink. Sirens whir.

"Evie?"

She keeps saying my name, over and over again.

"I'm here. Everything's going to be fine."

Every few minutes she groans like an animatronic gorilla. I'm trying to keep track of the time but I can't. Was that three minutes? Two?

"Evie?" she says again. "Will you call my mom?"

My eyes bulge, but she's already reeling off the number, quick and breathless and ending in a scream. Frantically, I type it in. I mean, how badly do I *not* want to call this woman? I am toxic with moms lately, but I know I can't say no. I press the call button and wince, turning to face the ambulance doors. Privacy is kind of impossible in this tiny, tin box, but I don't want Bree to overhear our conversation. The phone rings and rings and rings and finally goes to voice mail. She might think I'm spam, though, so I press redial, and this time a woman picks up on the second ring.

"Yes?" says a cold, cello voice.

"*Aaarrgh!*" Bree screams from behind me. Two minutes after the last one. Her contractions are getting closer together. This baby is ready.

"Uh . . . Mrs. Hewitt?"

"Who is this?"

Short answer? "I'm a friend of Bree's. She's in labor. Like, now. We're on our way to the hospital and . . . and I really think she wants you there."

There's a pause, and I picture Mrs. Hewitt standing in the kitchen, pouring herself a cup of tea, kettle forgotten as water spills over a delicate china cup.

"Mrs. Hewitt?" I whisper again.

She clears her throat. "I'm sorry, but we've been through all this. Sabrina knows how her father and I feel."

At first, I just blink. Like, that's it? I clear my throat, still trying to whisper. "But she's your *daughter.*"

"I have to go," she says quickly. "Tell her . . . tell her good luck."

The line goes dead, and something helpless smothers my insides. Mom is mad at me, but she would come to my rescue. Despite my unfathomable betrayal, she would be there for me if I needed her . . . right?

I turn back to Bree—aka Sabrina, aka a girl who chose love

over family and now has neither. I let her squeeze my hand as another contraction hits her like a Mack truck. We both exhale, trying to breathe through the pain. Because, yeah, my hand *must* be broken at this point.

"Did you talk to her?" Bree asks.

I stare into her terrified blue eyes. She's cursing, moaning—guttural and raw. Her skin looks pale under the cold fluorescent lights, and I think the truth might destroy her.

"We're here," the EMT says, saving me.

The ambulance screeches to a halt outside the emergency room entrance, and we rush from the back cabin like celebrities fleeing the paparazzi.

The next few things happen at lightning speed and in slow motion, all at once. Bree is transferred to a wheelchair. The old EMTs vanish, and a nurse rushes her inside. My high heels *click-clack* against the shiny linoleum floor to keep up. Bree begs for an epidural; the nurses whisper quietly behind clipboards.

"Can't you give her the drugs?" I ask—shout almost, in the middle of triage.

"Alright, calm down." A white-haired nurse with dead-rodent breath pushes me aside to take vitals, winding a blood pressure sleeve around Bree's bicep. "When did your contractions start?"

Bree groans.

"A few hours ago," I say. "Right, Bree?"

"And what about this swelling?" She frowns, poking Bree's bloated ankles.

It's kind of rude, but, I mean, they are huge. Were her ankles the size of grapefruits last time I saw her?

"I don't know," Bree howls, eyes jammed shut. One hand's still attached to mine, the other squeezing a thick elastic band that's tied too tight around her belly.

The nurse huffs. "You've got to stop moving the fetal heart rate monitor, honey." She rolls her eyes at me. "That's the only thing keeping track of the baby's heart rate, understand? You've got to keep her calm."

"Bree—" I say, then freeze.

Because, like, what is "calm" when there is a *human being* trying to crawl out of your abdomen? But then I remember the birth bundle shoved into my handbag. I reach in and pull out her ugly wooden necklace, pressing the beads into her palm to distract her. It actually works. Her fist forms around them, mouth curling into an O as she goes for the more traditional Lamaze breathing. I pucker my mouth and do it along with her.

"Everything's going to be okay." I let out a slow breath and inhale again. "You're doing great."

A smaller, plumper nurse walks over and smiles at Bree. It's not a warm smile. More like, *Oh, you're here.* She attaches an IV to Bree's wrist. "So, the baby's going to make an entrance tonight, huh?"

"I'm not due for a month!" Bree cries.

"Did you know you have preeclampsia?" she asks, still calm, still *oh, hey* in her tone. "Looks like your doctor is on vacation, and we don't see it anywhere in your records."

"Preeclampsia?" I gasp. It's a familiar word. Ziggy mentioned it—something about high blood pressure, risk of complications, early labor. Doctors don't always detect it, and maybe Bree's didn't either. "Is she going to be okay?"

"And who are *you*, exactly?" She looks me up and down, then smiles curtly at Bree. "Your little sister's going to have to sit this one out."

Bree claws at my arm, head shaking frantically. "Please don't go."

I glare at the nurse. "I'm not her sister."

"Husbands only," the woman chirps.

"There is no husband!" I scream, and the nurse freezes. Another nurse and an orderly stop to look at me too, and it's like they all finally see me as an actual human being for the first time. "The father is dead, okay? My father *died*, and I'm all she has. Please," I beg, tears in my eyes. "You need to let me stay."

The nurse's jaw pulses for a second, steel in her eyes. Finally, she nods. She calls for the orderly to push the wheelchair through heavy double doors and into a delivery room. My hand doesn't disconnect from Bree's for a single second.

CHAPTER 29

For the next five hours, I watch Bree writhe around in the most excruciating pain imaginable, and when the doctor decides she's fully dilated, that's when shit gets *really* disgusting.

Bree pukes.

Then pushes.

Then pukes.

Then pushes.

I'm telling you, teen abstinence programs should force us to watch this shit.

Scarred. For. Life.

"Push, Bree, push!" the doctor says, sitting on a swivel stool at the bottom of the delivery bed. "Atta girl."

I feed her more water through a plastic straw and press a cold washcloth against her forehead. "You got this, Bree. You're doing great. You're so strong. The baby's nearly out."

Surgical lights flood Bree's vagina like a Broadway show.

Machines beep. The nurses and I grip her legs to keep them in a tucked, labor-friendly position. She's got on a hospital gown, but it's pushed up to her waist, and I can see her insides moving as the baby inches down her like a parasite. Her face contorts. That means another contraction is coming, another chance to push. I push with her, blowing cool air onto her forehead.

The exertion of pushing makes her nauseous again, and a nurse wipes away the tiny puddle of vomit. More water. Cold compress to the forehead.

"I can't do it!" Bree screams. She shakes her head, throwing the wooden necklace across the room. It clanks against the window and drops to the floor. "I *can't do it*."

"You're almost done, mommy." The doctor reaches for Bree's hand—the one that's not currently breaking every bone in mine. "You're crowning, mommy. Feel the baby's head."

Bree lets the doctor guide her hand down in between her legs, and then Bree lets out the most joyous kind of yearning cry I've ever heard. The next time she pushes, her eyes connect with mine. She bears down without making a sound.

"You're doing great," I tell her, over and over again. Because she fucking is.

As much as I don't want to look south of the border, my gaze slips, and there it is—a little head, all slimy and wet. One more push and the whole baby is out and being placed on Bree's heaving chest.

And then, that's it. Bree's crying, but in a different way. She's holding her baby, kissing the top of its gunky, white head. For the first time in hours, she's let go of my hand, and I stumble back, replaced by nurses, pushed into the shadows. Bree is lost in her baby's eyes. Kissing his tiny fingers.

His cry is thin, and it rattles like glass in a thunderstorm. Almost immediately, the nurse takes his little body off her in order to swaddle him.

Another nurse pulls me aside. "We're taking the baby to the NICU. He's pretty small and having some trouble breathing. Bree needs to rest. Why don't you get her things together and meet her in her hospital room in a little while?"

"Is he going to be okay?" I whisper.

She smiles, but it's borderline grim. Borderline not at *all* reassuring.

Bree's eyelids become heavy as a new nurse changes her IV bags. The baby disappears in a plastic-covered cot. The nurse pushes me out into the hallway, and I guess that's it. I'm done.

CHAPTER 30

The waiting room is over-air-conditioned and oatmeal-colored, and it sends chills up my spine, remembering Friday, May twelfth. All those hours spent silently sitting beside Mom. Hands clasped, praying for Dad to make it. This isn't the exact same waiting room—not even the same wing of the hospital—but that doesn't matter. No waiting room will ever be the same for me again.

Juana spots me and stands up, rushing over. The sight of my friends, exhausted and disheveled under the harsh glow of fluorescents, almost makes me cry with joy.

"Babe!" JJ wraps her arms tight around me, rocking me back and forth. "Holy shit, that took forever. Is Bree okay? Is the baby, y'know, a baby?"

"Yeah, he's a baby." I yawn. "I mean, she did it. She was amazing."

"Oh, thank God," Violet whoops.

"Amazing," I say again. "Not like anything I ever saw. Ever seen? Ever—"

My brain is mush, words coming out with the clarity of a meat grinder. Georgy must be able to tell, because she leads me over to the seating area and lowers me down. She points to a plate on the coffee table full of tartlets and fruit and cookies from the party. "Hungry?"

I shake my head, and Declan takes hold of my hand. I almost wince, but he doesn't squeeze it like Bree did, just balances it in his. Enough to know he's there.

A large, boisterous family files in beside us. The men are chewing on cigars; the women are in colorful saris, cradling flowers and teddy bears. Pink teddy bears, pink blankets—for their new niece or granddaughter.

I look back at my friends, retracing each moment, not wanting to scare them or gross them out with too many details. Even the PG version turns Juana's face green.

"They had to take the baby to intensive care," I say finally, and I sound like I know what I'm talking about, even if I don't. "He was so small—a whole month early."

"What did he weigh?" Georgy asks.

"They might have said four pounds?" I say hazily. "I'm not sure. He looked tiny, though. I've never seen a baby that small before. Hey, did you bring the stuff like I asked?"

Declan grabs the duffel bag from behind his chair and hands it to me. "We weren't really sure what to get, so we got everything."

"And I can run out for anything else she needs," Georgy adds. "Trashy magazines, candy. Whatever."

"Thank you," I say, hugging her.

She squeezes back. "Oh, sweetie. I can't imagine what you must be going through And, I feel so bad for what happened earlier—with your mother."

My mother. God, it's been hours since I thought about our fight. The look on her face when she realized I've been taking pictures of Bree. More than just the pictures—what the hell will she do when she finds out I helped bring Bree's baby into the world?

That'll be fun.

Before I can bury myself alive in those thoughts, I take the floral duffel bag from Declan and walk slowly toward the maternity wing. I want to be there when Bree wakes up, even though she let go of my hand. Even if my work here is done. I follow the signs down a stark, quiet, 2 a.m. hallway. All I can hear are vital-sign beeps and humming fluorescents. The door's ajar, and I poke my head through it. Bree's room is big, but she's sharing it with another couple. They're fast asleep and blissful in a too-small hospital bed across the room. I quietly pull the curtain around Bree's bed, encapsulating us in hideous beige fabric.

Her eyes flutter open. "Evie?" she says, voice hoarse.

"Hey." I smile, and before I toss her hospital bag on a chair, I unzip it, feeling around for the honey throat lozenges. "Here. Ziggy said they'd come in handy."

She accepts one gratefully and sits up a little taller, wincing as she props herself up on a thin hospital pillow. Sheets and pillows—that's what I should have had them add to the bag. Oh well.

"How're you feeling?"

"Like ass," she croaks, curling toward me. "Sore everywhere. I'm going to miss my shift today too. Do you think Ziggy will be mad?"

"Furious," I deadpan. "I'll call her in the morning."

"Thanks." Bree coughs, and then her eyes bulge. "Nobody said it was going to feel like this."

"Like what?" I can't help asking. "What does it feel like?"

"My throat hurts. My head is spinning. My insides ache. It feels like there's a ten-pound dumbbell pulling my stomach out through my assho—"

"Okay, okay, stop!" I slap my palms against my ears and gag. "I changed my mind."

"Have you seen the baby?" she asks, beaming. "He's so beautiful. And his little nose. I can't imagine anyone more perfect."

"I only saw him for a second," I say quickly. And it hits me that I didn't really try too hard to get a good look. Like, before, when she was pregnant, it was all sort of abstract. Now he's real. And honestly, I'm not sure if I'm mentally prepared to meet this thing that is biologically connected to me.

"Well, he's beautiful," she says again. "Like Superman."

"He can fly? Already?"

"No!" She laughs, then winces. "His hair—you wouldn't believe how much he's got."

"Wow, your very own Sasquatch."

She smiles briefly, sucking on the lozenge. It gets quiet between us. Bree's chest rises and falls beneath her blue hospital gown. After a while, I wonder if she's fallen back asleep.

"Evie?" she whispers.

"Yeah?"

"I don't know how to thank you."

I shake my head.

"No, I mean it." Her voice is hoarse and soft but still determined. "I don't know how I got so lucky, having you come into my life."

My heart falls into my lap. "Um, Bree? I should probably admit something to you."

"What is it?"

"Okay, so. It wasn't entirely luck." I look toward the door, half hoping a doctor will barge in and stop this truth from spilling out of me. "I was kind of, like . . . following you? Around town. For a while. Before we *met* met."

I squeeze my eyes nearly shut, waiting for the shock-horror to dawn on her. For her to look at me, shell-shocked and violated, the way Mom did, and then kick me out for good. But Bree actually laughs—well, one-quarter laughs, three-quarters grimaces at the pain in her gut.

"I kind of guessed," she says mildly. "When you showed up

the night that I sprained my ankle? I mean, I totally assumed you and Declan were making out, but it's not like the Sun Salutations parking lot is some notorious hookup spot. I kind of wondered if you ended up there to keep tabs on me. And when I saw your car outside the café—I mean, nobody goes to lunch at 10 a.m. I had my suspicions."

"But so . . . you're not mad?"

She smiles. "Are you kidding? I mean, maybe if you'd *never* come talk to me. But you did."

"I did."

"And look where it got us!" Her eyeballs bulge around the room and out toward Mars. "I really meant it when I said I'm lucky."

"It's fine."

"It's *way* more than fine. I know it was selfish to ask you to take the class with me. I didn't want to be alone with all those perfect married people, but I didn't think it through. You said you didn't want to be involved in the labor and delivery, and then I begged you anyway. I was really, really scared. But I didn't quite realize I was asking you to go into labor with me."

"I did *not* go into labor," I say, forcing a laugh. "I think you broke my *hand*, but you're the one who popped an entire baby out. You did everything, Bree. It was . . . kind of incredible."

"Thanks." Her voice goes raspier, more exhausted.

"I should let you get some sleep," I say.

"Will you come back?"

"Oh . . ."

When I don't elaborate, Bree's face falls. "You don't have to," she says. "I get it."

"No—" I pause. "I mean, I will. If you want me to, I will."

Her eyes flutter shut again. Before she falls asleep, she whispers, "I'd really like that."

CHAPTER 31

Juana drives my zombie body home as the sun rises over the mountains. She puts the car in park, but we stay comatose in our seats. We've been up for a bazillion hours. We are toast.

"You okay?"

I shrug my shoulders, aching, rolling them back till I hear a well-deserved pop along my spine. "I hurt everywhere. I need hand surgery. I want to amputate my feet and take a bath for a hundred years."

"I can't condone voluntary amputation," Juana says. "You know I'm jealous of your perfect little toes. But the bath I can help with. My mom has these bath salts that will change your freaking life. Come on."

We step out of the car, and immediately my heart wrenches. Mom is across the street, pulling a white cardigan over her scrubs as she heads to her car. When she spots us in Juana's driveway, her Crocs skid to a stop.

"I better talk to her," I murmur. "See you inside?"

"Take your time." Juana smiles supportively and backs away.

I clear my tender throat and walk uncertainly, somewhat painfully over the dusty, pebbled road. The way she's looking at me, it's obvious she's shocked. Me, dirty in last night's dress and bare feet. Breath stale, mascara caked beneath my eyes.

"Evie, what happened—are you okay?"

"Nothing, I'm fine." I pause to cross my arms, gathering shards of fractured thoughts. "We were at the hospital—and no, I'm not hurt. I was there with Bree. She had the baby last night."

Mom gasps, clapping a hand over her mouth.

I should shut up, but I'm nervous and rambling. Stomach churning, spitting out facts while the horror on Mom's face spreads like stress-cracked glass. "He was born a month early. I guess she had preeclampsia? So, yeah. The baby wasn't getting enough blood and oxygen. He's tiny—only about four and a half pounds."

"And *you* were there? With *her*?"

"Please don't hate me," I beg. "I don't know how to explain it other than I've been getting to know her. At first, it was because I hated her so much. I had to find out who this person that destroyed my family was."

"And?"

"And—" I huff, running tired fingers through my tangled hair. "She isn't the only one who destroyed us. Dad's the one who went after her. I mean, he was horrible to you, Mom. You worked so hard to hide it from me—which I appreciate—but, because of that, I had *no* idea. Obviously, Bree's not innocent, but I didn't realize I was allowed to blame him too. And not just for leaving, but for the shit he put you through. You said so yourself—you spent my whole life taking care of me. And I get why you needed to let loose or whatever. It was your turn. You're allowed to have a messy, chaotic grief party."

"Is that what we're calling it?" She snickers, but her eyes are wet, ready to spill. "Well, my grief party may not be over, but I'm trying to evolve through it. Lots of spring cleaning. Purging some of Dad's old stuff."

My jaw tightens at the memory of our disrupted walls. The staggering lack of Dad's recliner. "I wish you'd at least asked me first."

"Sweetie, there's still plenty of Daddy's stuff around. But I needed to do this for me. I needed to make the house *mine* again. Start a new chapter, you know? It was actually my therapist's idea. I've joined a bereavement support group." She smirks. "Which sounds awful, but it's not. I've met some great people. They offer one for kids too, whenever you're ready."

I sigh and pinch my nose, looking at the ground. Because . . .

What if

they tell me

I've been

grieving

wrong?

Mom huffs at my trademark indecision. "Well, you need *some*thing, Evie. I'd hoped that would be the photography class. But Jesus, I never would have suggested it if I'd known you were going to end up running around town with Bree. Lying to me about Daddy—I'm honestly furious that you went behind my back like that."

My lower lip quivers. "I did it to protect you. I thought I was protecting both of us."

"I know." She sighs, and her frown lines deepen. "I know. That's what Dr. Ireland said—that you were in shock and processing your grief. It hurt, and you shouldn't have done it, but I get it. My God, though." She pauses, eyes widening. "I can't wait to tell Dr. Ireland you delivered Vic's mistress's baby. She's going to have a field day."

"I know you're disappointed in me."

"Oh, honey, I'm not." She lets out another massive exhale. "I love you, and I'm here for you. But if Bree is going to be a part of your life, I think it's best if I have absolutely no part of it. That girl is *not* welcome in our house."

"God, Mom. It's not like I was going to invite her over." I cross my arms but try to let my huff turn neutral. Just a breath. "So, like, am *I* at least welcome in our house?"

"Of course," she says. And for the first time in weeks, she pulls me into a hug, her elbows forming a protective cage around me. "I wanted you to come back weeks ago. It's been torture watching you through the window, getting text updates from Debbie."

"So *that's* why Debbie's always up in my grill."

"She's an excellent informant." Mom snickers, pulling away.

"Which reminds me, she mentioned something about a photography exhibition at NMPI?"

"It's this Friday. Do you want to come?"

"I don't know, Evie." She pauses. "Are there pictures of *her*?"

Heat rises up my belly, splashing against my cheeks.

"Never mind," Mom says quickly. She lets out a flustered groan. "I shouldn't have asked. I'm happy that you're expressing yourself creatively, and that has nothing to do with me. I'm not going to get in the way of you showing your best work."

Hearing her say that means everything.

But ... I shake my head, buoyed by a sudden calm. Yes, I have spent the summer taking pictures of Bree. Hiding them, hiding behind them. But I also started out trying to protect Mom, and I still want to do that.

"I've worked on a lot of different projects at NMPI," I say, standing a little taller. "That stuff, with her, that was more for me than anything else. I'm not going to show those pictures, Mom. I swear."

"Oh, thank God." Relief sweeps across her face. "Only if you're sure. Either way, I would really like to be there."

She looks down at her watch and swears under her breath. "Ev, I've got to go. I'm late for a meeting. But I'll see you tonight? You'll move back home, and we'll have dinner? I've been trying to get back into cooking lately. No more frozen nuggets."

"Thank God." I smile. "Sounds good."

"Come on, one more hug." She crushes me again, moaning in motherly delight. "Ooh, I missed you."

She hops into her car, and I start to walk back across the street—only to get my things, to tell Juana I'm finally moving back home.

"Honey?"

I look over my shoulder. Mom's at the bottom of the driveway, leaning out the car window. "I wanted to ask you—" She hesitates, her face pinched and pale. "Gosh, this is hard. Um . . . if it's alright. I was wondering. Would you be okay with me bringing a date? To your photography showcase?"

"Oh." My jaw collapses, and Mom turns scarlet.

"I know it's soon," she stammers. "And I shouldn't be asking you *not* to show pictures of Bree and then turning right around and suggesting that *I* be allowed to bring someone new into the picture. I didn't mean—"

"No, it's fine," I say, almost giggling at her nerves. "You can bring someone."

"Oh, good. Okay. Thank you." Relief swells in her exhale.

I exhale too. I mean—no joke?—this is a giant mountain of change. Losing a dad, gaining a Bree, regaining a mom, and now a—a what? Stepdad?! But she's clearly nervous as hell, gripping the steering wheel for dear life, and all I really know is that I want to be home again. Want the both of us to find a new way to be normal.

So, I smile. "I'll see you tonight, Mom."

"I can't wait, honey."

CHAPTER 32

The gala barrels upon us like an elephant stampede. All week, we fight over the large color printers and mat cutters. Editing and tweaking and printing; measuring and hanging and rehanging. I'm so immersed that I don't make it back to the hospital, even though I told Bree I would. Maybe I'm too busy, or maybe I'm keeping my distance on purpose. Wanting to focus on what Mom and I have, now that we're finally back on track. Bree does text a lot of pictures, though. Her whole smartphones-are-bad thing clearly went out the window. The baby's still in intensive care, but she says he's making progress. In the pictures, he's got these aimless, mini chocolate chip eyes and zero eyebrows. When he cries, you can make out each rib beneath. And he does indeed have exquisite hair.

Oh, and his name. He's got one of those too.

Parker Hewitt.

Parker

Hewitt

Has a nice ring to it, huh?

"For the millionth time, yes. It is a glorious name, bound for greatness." Juana fluffs my hair, gliding a warm, copper gloss across my lips. "But will you stop showing me pictures already? You're stalling."

She's right. I am. I put the phone in the back pocket of my new favorite jeans, smoothing out the cropped cami Juana helped me pick out. I follow her inside this enormous converted barn, knees seizing as I realize how many frigging people are in here. Hundreds of them. Milling, gawking, praising, critiquing.

"I can't," I moan. "Everything's printed so big. And check out that guy over there—is he scowling at my self-portrait? Am I scowlable?"

Juana squints, following my horror. "Who, that guy? That's not a scowl. That is a deep introspective gaze. You, Evie Parker, have created a mind-splosion for his right brain." She links her arm through mine, dragging me farther into the room. "Besides, stop stressing about your photos and let's talk about this barn. I texted a picture to Melanie, and she thinks it looks like a magical speakeasy netherworld. Isn't she so poetic?"

"Like the next Elizabeth Acevedo," I deadpan, and she swats me.

"Seriously though, this is putting Mom's Casa Buena party to shame. Look at her over there, drooling over the sconces and the sangria fountain."

She's not wrong, about drooling Debbie or the general fabulousness. NMPI rented out this ginormous horse ranch a few miles outside of town in Pojoaque, and the way our images command every inch of wall space feels like the MoMA—where, no, I've obviously never been. Friends and family and the Santa Fe art crowd wander around in denim and expensive jewelry, sipping signature cocktails and nibbling pâté. It's all very *everything*, but the thought of them criticizing my work makes me want to vomit as far as the Jemez Mountains.

"Ooh, chocolate-covered strawberries!"

Juana hands me one, and I roll the stem around between my fingers, too nervous to eat.

"There you guys are." Declan appears beside me in black jeans and a brand-new Love Santa Fe T-shirt with a Zia symbol for the O. "I had to get away from Jiji. You print three enormous photographs of a guy and suddenly he thinks he's Bieber." He high-fives Juana and then leans toward me. We are in uncharted territory, but not so uncharted that I don't let him take my hand.

"I need cheese," Juana says quickly. "Takers? Y'know what, never mind. I see Violet. Bye!"

Declan looks at me and smiles. My cheeks flush.

"So," he says.

"So," I say.

"Lookie, lookie!" says Suze, charging toward us with her fourth husband in tow. Mr. Suze, aka Brooks, looks like a tomato in a cowboy hat. Round and red-faced and sucking back a Bloody Mary. They stop in front of us, and Brooks points an accusing finger at Declan.

"Saw your work over there, son. Pretty talented. Pretty *darn* talented."

Declan reaches out to shake Brooks's hand. "Thanks, man. You must be proud of Suze. She's done awesome work this summer."

"You kiddin'? Suze is the best little photographer in here. I've got some contacts in the art world. I'm going to get this little gal of mine into museums."

It would be sweet. If he didn't keep calling her *little*. But Suze doesn't seem to mind.

"And which one are you?"

"Evie Parker," I tell him. "The portraits over there."

He nods, impressed. "Those aren't half bad either."

"Thanks?" I shoot Declan a quizzical smirk. "I never thought I'd like being in front of the camera, but I had the best time putting them together."

"Darlin', I'm going to miss you!" Suze says, giggling either at me, or at Brooks tickling her back.

"You too, Suze."

She takes my hands, and her face grows somber. "This has been one of the best summers of my life, but I know it's been one of the hardest for you. I want you to know how proud I am of you—not just your photography, but the way I've seen you grow in the past few months. It's been a blessing to watch. You're an incredible girl, Evie. I really do wish you all the best. And please come visit us in San Antonio. Any ol' time."

They walk away, and I turn to Declan. "Wow. I'm actually going to miss her. Is that weird?"

"Oddly, I think I am too." He takes my hand again, weaving his fingers through mine. There's a smile on his face, but his hazel eyes are heavy, wrapped up in storm clouds. "Evie, do you think we could talk for a minute?"

I swallow. "Okay."

He barely has one syllable out when I notice his eyes dart behind me. "I think I see your mom."

"Crap. I should probably go talk to her."

"No worries." He releases my hand. "We can talk later."

I take a deep breath, inching through three hundred people toward Mom and her *date*. When I'm close enough, I realize it's the guy from Fourth of July pancakes. The one who made her laugh so hard.

"Wow, honey. What a turnout!"

She gives me a quick hug and a nervous smile. Maybe because we're still on rocky ground, occupying the same house like paper dolls, fragile and delicate. Or—I dunno— maybe she's nervous about Pancakes Guy.

"Um . . . Evie, I'd like to introduce you to someone. This is Paul. Paul, this is my daughter, Evelyn."

Things I notice about Paul: he is bald and buttoned-up. But

he has kind eyes and nice teeth, which I know are important things to my mom. So, I let him shake my hand and try not to dwell on his dorkiness.

"Evie, it's great to meet you. Rita's told me so much about you."

"Nice to meet you too," I say. "Thanks for coming."

"Are you kidding? I've always wanted an invite to one of these NMPI events." He chuckles, tugging the lapels of his suit jacket. "Thanks to you, I've hit the big time."

Mom laughs. And I mean *luh-affs*. It's cute, though. And it's not lost on me what this guy signifies—the fact that my mom is really moving on. But if I'm willing to befriend Bree, I've got to be open to the Pauls of my future too.

"Happy to help," I tell him. And smile.

"Sweetie, your photographs are great," Mom says as she rubs my arm. "I mean, *really* beautiful. Look at the crisp mountain edges in the background there. How did you do that?"

"It's mostly about aperture. And a little Photoshop."

"Stunning," Paul adds. "Absolutely *haunt*ing use of light."

I blush. Ten points to Paul. Plus, he's referring to my favorite of the three images—a self-portrait behind the Chevron station, car exhaust creating heaven in the darkness—so I might even bump Paul's point status up to fifteen. The tension between us begins to thin out as we discuss my work. My self-confidence swells, basking in their adjectives, the patter of impressed whispers as strangers stop to look. I made the right choice, showing these portraits. Not to brag or whatever, but I'm good at this. Okay, that was totally bragging.

Paul wanders off for a soda, and Mom raises her eyebrows. "So—what do you think?"

"He seems nice. I'm happy for you."

"Thanks." She grins. "We only met a few weeks ago, at the support group. He lost his spouse too. I don't know if it's going to be serious, but spending time with him has been really comforting."

"I'm glad you're doing it. The group thing, I mean."

"Me too." She smiles, linking her arm through mine. "And, honey, your photos really are breathtaking. You should send some copies to Uncle Luke. I think he'd be excited to see what you've accomplished this summer."

"Sure," I say, even though Luke will probably want his camera back, and I don't really want to remind him.

Mom hugs me, and the goodness of it still surprises me. How much I missed feeling close to her. We untangle, and she nods toward Juana and Declan, not-so-covertly watching us from the dessert table. She waves them over.

"He's cute," Mom whispers. "Is he your *boy*friend?"

"Mom!" I gasp. "We're not—he's not—he's just . . ."

"My God, look at you!" She laughs, cupping my scalding-hot cheeks. "I'm happy for you, sweetie."

"Mamacita Rita!" Juana runs up, reaching her arms around the two of us. "You look smokin' hot. And was that a new beau I saw you with? Qué guapo!"

Declan clears his throat and extends his hand. "Hello, Mrs. Parker. I'm Declan Maeda. We met at the Lujans', but—"

"Oh, and I was so rude to everyone!" Mom cringes. "My apologies, Declan. And please, don't call me Mrs. Parker. It's Rita, or Ms. Davis."

My jaw implodes.

"Nice to meet you, Ms. Davis." His fingers brush against mine, and I hijack his pinky, squeezing it tight. He grins, eyes struggling to break from mine. "Your daughter has worked really hard this summer. Art school, beware."

Art school. Huh.

"I am proud of her." Mom beams. "The proudest."

Forks clink against glasses and everyone's eyes gravitate toward Georgy as she saunters up to the podium in something sparkly and elegant that Coco Chanel probably rose from the grave to create for her. Paul rejoins us, along with Baba and Jiji, who have never looked more thrilled or proud or adorable. Pretty soon, the entire Art of Storytelling group has somehow gravitated together.

Sten straightens the bow tie on Peter's seersucker suit, then leans over to me. "Everyone loves your work, Evie."

"Yours too, Sten."

We hug and coo and compliment each other some more. Violet walks up with an earbud in position, her phone angled at her face as she makes these exaggerated, animated expressions. She turns her livestream toward the crowd and leans close for a hug.

"Evie, I'm going to miss the shit out of you," she whispers.

"You too," I whisper back. "I can't believe I know a famous person now."

"Are you kidding? *I* know a famous person!" She angles her phone at the two of us, pointing dramatically at my face. "This is the girl who took those gorgeous film stills! This is Evie fricking Parker, y'all! And she is one. To. Watch!"

I blush like my life depends on it and put my hand over the screen. It's too much, but I'm grinning, jaw burning with glee as the two of us turn our focus onto Georgy at the podium.

"Good evening, everyone," Georgy says, her silky voice perfuming the crowd. "I'm not one for speeches, but I would like to say a few words. My students have shown impeccable skill, creativity, and perception this summer. They've challenged themselves and pushed boundaries to seek truth in their own lives."

My legs stiffen. She means all of us, but I am totally patient zero, whether or not my boundary pushing is currently on display.

"When we started out this summer, everyone was here for a different reason. For some of you, it was as a hobby, to push-start a career, or maybe as a little marriage counseling!"

If it were me, I'd be mortified, but Ada and Ed seem to think it's hilarious being called out on their bickering. Beth and her husband sort of nod knowingly too.

"And whether or not you meant to, I think you all ended up finding yourselves a little bit this summer. You have inspired

me—which isn't something NMPI mentioned in the contract!"
Everyone laughs, and Georgy pulls a note card out of her
pocket. "I know ending with quotes is so 'college graduation,'
but as I said, I'm not one for speeches. As my hero Kurt Vonne-
gut said, 'I urge you to please notice when you are happy, and
to exclaim or murmur or think at some point, *If this isn't nice, I
don't know what is.*'" She looks back up at each of us and smiles.
"Well, gang, if this isn't nice, I don't know what is. Thanks for a
great summer."

"That was lovely," I hear Beth tell her husband.

And, yeah. It really was.

Everyone claps for Georgy as she struts off the stage,
replaced by another teacher praising another class. All ten of
us—plus our overeager parents and grandparents and husbands, wives, children, friends, dogs—encircle her to say
thanks. I lace my fingers through Declan's, tugging him toward
the barn doors. The two of us wander out into the breezy summer evening, and I can see gray wisps of rain off in the distance. The temperature has dropped with the setting sun, and
most of the guests are starting to tug at their shawls and jack-
ets. Summer will be over before we know it.

"Nice speech, huh?" I say, dropping Declan's hand
awkwardly.

"I'm no expert," he says. "But yeah."

I rub a few piñon needles between my fingers, releasing
nutty, candied sap into the air. "So . . . hey."

"So, hey." His fingers sweep across those perfect, Marvel-hero bangs.

I take a deep breath, but then chicken out, clamping my lips into a smile.

"What's the plan here?" Declan asks coyly. "Keep me at arm's length all summer, then break my heart right before I hop a plane back to Brooklyn?"

"*Your* heart?" I gasp. "You have one of those too?"

He chuckles. I mean, it was a joke, but it also kinda wasn't? To be honest, I hadn't really thought much about his heart.

Only mine.

Only me.

My shoulders fall. "I'm a confused human, Declan. You must know that by now. And this hasn't exactly been the easiest summer for me."

"The absolute un-easiest ever," he says softly. He kicks the dirt with the curved, white toe of his Adidas. "And I'm sorry if I pushed this on you. I tried not to, seriously. I know you wanted a buddy system. But, like, you're *you*. Beautiful. And smart and funny and exciting. And I couldn't leave town without you knowing it."

Breath stumbles out of me. I'm amazed, almost. That he so effortlessly knows my strengths when I could write essays on my flaws. But maybe it's beyond the point of a boy paying me compliments under a tree. Those strengths are mine, and I'm ready to own them.

"Well, thanks. I guess you're pretty great too." God, my cheeks could be used as flares right now. "I'm sorry I waited too long. I fucked the whole thing up. Now it's too late, and I—"

Mid-ramble, Declan leans in. His lips touch mine, one hand curving around the back of my neck. My eyes drift shut, and I melt into him. If only time would stop and I could feel this way forever—up on my tiptoes, lips parted, arms around his shoulders. Because I'm completely gone, in love with this dizzy feeling.

A flash of light cracks in the distance, and Declan and I both pull away. There's lightning coming over Truchas Peak. Another bolt strikes, beautiful and crackling and staining my vision.

I look back at Declan. He's grinning, all kinds of bashful and heartfelt. I smile too and clear my throat, but no words come out. Because I'm happy, but I'm also a little bit adrift. Feeling my heart in all its glory, wondering if it will shatter when he's gone.

"I wish we had longer," I whisper.

"Me too."

"So . . . stay?"

He squints down at me. "I know what this is about. You want me to keep photographing Jiji in the bathtub."

I laugh. "Totally. Or, I was thinking, more like creating content for the Holistic Zone?" I raise an eyebrow. "Dot org? The traffic on that site must be like *whaaaaat*?"

"Ha ha." He scowls playfully. "You know I'll be back though, Evie. NYU has a fall break coming up in October. Uta-garuta's not going to play itself."

"I'm envisioning a very bizarre double-date night."

"But it could work?" His voice falters. "Me, coming back?"

I hesitate. Soon it'll be senior year. I'll be juggling Mom, and Bree, and the baby. Hopefully applying to art schools—maybe even NYU. But you know what? Rather than make life more complicated and torturous, I go bold and go in for a kiss, stopping only when the sky finally opens up and big, juicy raindrops soak into every inch of us. Everyone else runs into the barn for cover, but we need this rain so badly, I don't want to scare it away. I tilt my face up to the sky, accepting each bead of water into the core of my being. This rain is everything.

My hands run the slippery length of my cheeks as I smile up at Declan.

"Are you planning to wait it out?" he asks, dripping wet and grinning at me.

"I will if you will," I say, and kiss him again.

CHAPTER 33

When I stop by the hospital in the morning, I have to register and get a badge before being allowed into the NICU ward. The hallway is quiet, each room full of wheezing tubes and special lights and little bassinets covered in protective plastic. I can't help thinking about Snow White. How they put her in a clear, glass coffin and the dwarves sat around watching her sleep. All these parents watching their babies struggle to breathe and sleep and exist. I get to room 301, and there's Bree, standing in the center, hovering over a little plastic crib with Parker inside it.

"Hey, you," I say quietly, hanging back a few feet, afraid to breathe. Afraid I have germs, even though I washed my hands up to my elbows and used hand sanitizer and pulled my hair into a bun before coming into the room.

She looks over her shoulder, a smile spreading across her face. "Hey! How did it go last night?"

"It went great. There was some really beautiful photography. And—" I hesitate, still flushed at the thought. "Georgy? My teacher? She offered to write me a college recommendation. I emailed the school guidance counselor to find out what requirements I'll need to fill this year to apply to liberal arts colleges."

"Evie, that's fantastic!" she whisper-shouts, still too loud for this tiny, quiet room. "You deserve it."

"And I think I'll use the pictures of you. For my admissions portfolio."

She blushes, tongue-tied and looking back down at the baby. "Hey, come a little closer. You can barely see him from over there."

My heart lurches, legs heavy. I'm terrified of how I'll react when I see him. Yes, because he is a four-pound alien covered in tubes, but . . . he is my father's baby.

"Want to say hi to your big sis?" she asks him.

Sis.

The word gives me momentum, pushing me the rest of the way until I'm standing right over him. Parker, my baby brother. All limbs, no fat. With his tiny, sunken chest. Bright lights warm him, bouncing off his colorless, gray eyes. I don't tell Bree that he looks like a peeled zucchini. Instead, I whisper, "He's beautiful."

Because he's that too. A human being I never thought I wanted and now suddenly can't imagine life without.

"Thanks." Bree smiles. "I think he's pretty great too."

Parker clutches Bree's pinky with the world's teeniest fingers. I'm not sure what to do, so I graze his Band-Aid-size forehead with my thumb. His skin is soft and fuzzy. I've never seen anything so tiny. So fragile.

I have a brother.

Parker has a sister.

I am someone's *sis*.

The word nestles into my heart, getting comfortable. Did my dad wish for this? That one day, Bree and I would connect? That I would have a sibling, and he would have a second child— later in life, when he was ready?

"Hiya, Parker." Bree hesitates. "What do you think? About the name."

"It's good."

"I had such a hard time deciding. Vic and I never got to have that conversation. Parker seemed kind of versatile. He can be a football player, a poet, a scientist. He looks like a Parker, don't you think? So strong and earnest."

"Strong" is not how I would describe a gourd-sized human, but I nod.

She starts talking about the medical side of things, how many strides Parker is making, what medications he's on, but all I can do is stare at him. Smaller than the dolls I played with as a kid. The length of a bowling pin. Without meaning to, I reach for Parker's other hand, and right away he grips my finger. Bree and I both giggle. And, all of a sudden, I'm like what's-his-name. The Grinch. My heart has grown three sizes.

"You're right," I say. "He is a strong little dude."

Four pounds is small, but it isn't nothing. Especially the way Parker keeps squeezing my pinky. I can feel his skin around mine, cool and light and delicate. His chest pumps up, down, up again. A NICU nurse walks in, and I yank my finger away reflexively. The guy's not even in here to talk to us, but now I'm a foot away, and I don't have the guts to step forward again.

Not yet, anyway.

"Hey, so, I have something for you."

Bree raises an eyebrow at me before returning her loving gaze to Parker.

"I almost brought Dad's pocket protector." I chuckle awkwardly, reaching into my back pocket. "I figure I'll loan that to Parker when he's older. But, for now . . ." My cheeks flush, fingers shaking as I pull out the photograph of Bree and my dad, the one I found in his office. "You said you didn't have any photos. I thought Parker might like to see one of his parents together. Maybe we could tape it? To the side? Unless that's too germy, in which case . . ."

I trail off when I realize Bree is crying. "Oh, Evie, thank you!"

She stares at the picture, covering her mouth with one hand. Bree loved my dad. That much is clear. I won't pretend it doesn't hurt. I might never accept how badly my father scarred me—how he destroyed Mom and left Bree's reputation in scraps. But he's gone now.

I'm still here. Bree is here. Parker's here too, all four pounds of him.

I stay with them a little longer, watching Parker breathe, telling Bree about the gala. And when I say goodbye, I kiss my fingers, then touch them to the bottom of Parker's tiny, curved foot.

After I leave, I whisper his name over and over again. Giving it space, letting it stretch and strengthen.

Parker

Parker

Parker

Parker

Parker

I call him my brother till the word stops sounding foreign on my tongue. Until, finally, it sounds like home.

ACKNOWLEDGMENTS

First of all, revising a book in 2020 was rough, and I couldn't have faced any of it without my family. Thank you to my husband, Andy, for all the love and laughter, tears, hugs, hope, optimism (some pessimism), and blocks of uninterrupted time. To my beautiful, creative, funny, resilient babies, Trixie and Harvey. Thank you for (mostly) giving me time and space to write, for believing in me, and for being my weighted blankets at the end of many long, difficult days. To my parents and my sister, India, thank you for being my weird and lovable family. I don't know where I would be without your support, ideas, recipes, cartoons, jokes, and love.

And to every single person on the planet: 2020 was a horrible, awful, stressful, scary year, and continues to devastate us. My sincere condolences and commiseration to all, as well as immeasurable gratitude to the health-care professionals and essential workers.

TBH, 2021 has been off to a rocky start as well, full of violence and hate. So much still needs to be done—and undone—in this country. All my admiration and thanks to the leaders and activists who are fighting for justice and change, and helping to open our eyes. I promise to never stop learning or facing the truth and always stay fired up.

A huge thank-you to my editors at Bloomsbury Children's, Claire Stetzer and Mary Kate Castellani. You both had such sharp, insightful notes that gave me so many aha moments. Thank you for believing in Evie's story, championing my writing, and putting up with the fifty emails it took to narrow down a title! More Bloomsbury love to Allison Moore, Erica Barmash, Faye Bi, Phoebe Dyer, Lily Yengle, Diane Aronson, Beth Eller, and Danielle Ceccolini, as well as cover artist David Lanaspa—this book wouldn't look as good as it does, with so few mistakes, or reach as many people as it will without all of you.

As always, endless thanks to my boxing-coach-of-an-agent, Lauren Galit. How did I get so lucky? You are there for me always—with feedback, banter, reality checks, and encouragement. I couldn't have done it without you and Caitlen Rubino-Bradway. Seriously. There aren't enough funny socks in the world to show my appreciation.

Which brings me to early readers! Erin Price, my agent-sibling, thank you for offering to be a beta reader during the pandemic. Your wise, nuanced perspective gave me the push I needed. I can't wait to repay the favor. Thank you also to my dear friend Lisa Zawacki for sharing your hard-earned wisdom concerning NICU babies—all my love to you and yours. And to Veronica Vega at Salt & Sage Books, thank you for your careful read and spot-on observations.

Because photography is a big part of this book, and very close to my heart, I have many talented teachers and artists to thank. In particular, Steve Northup, for sparking my interest in the history of photography and showing me how to make a pinhole camera. And Jenny Gage, my college mentor and friend, thank you for taking me under your wing and challenging me to find my style.

To *all* my incredible friends, but especially the authors I've gotten to know in the past two years: Shana Youngdahl, Eva V. Gibson, Shannon Takaoka, Jennifer Moffett, Rocky Callen, Kyrie McCauley, Nora Shalaway Carpenter, Liz Lawson, Dante Medema, Steven Salvatore, and Brigid Kemmerer. The advice, giggles, signal boosts, good vibes, and pity parties have been lifesaving. One day, we'll meet!

Humongous, socially distanced hugs to you, Reader! It means the world to me that you chose my book—which in no small part depends on the support and encouragement of BookTok, bloggers, blurbers, bookstagrammers, librarians, educators, and indie booksellers. Seriously, the bookish community is incredible. Thank you.